Murder at the Boardinghouse

FOR MOMMY
IN LOVING MEMORY
Yvette Barbaste Guéçamburu
(1950-2004)

Murder at the Boardinghouse

a novel

by

Elizabette Guécamburu

CENTER FOR BASQUE STUDIES
UNIVERSITY OF NEVADA, RENO
2023

This book was published with generous financial support from the Basque Government.

Center for Basque Studies
University of Nevada, Reno
1664 North Virginia St,
Reno, Nevada 89557 usa
http://basque.unr.edu

Cover Design by Alissa Gates Booth

Library of Congress Cataloging-in-Publication Data

Names: Guéçamburu, Elizabette, author.
Title: Murder at the boardinghouse : a novel / by Elizabette Guéçamburu.
Description: Reno : Center for Basque Studies, 2023. | Series: Basque
  originals ; 30 | Summary: In a 1940's Basque boardinghouse,
  fourteen-year-old Anna investigates a murder that happens right under
  her curious nose.
Identifiers: LCCN 2023019913 | ISBN 9781949805802 (paperback)
Subjects: CYAC: Murder--Fiction. | Boardinghouses--Fiction. | Basque
  Americans--Fiction. | Mystery and detective stories. |
  Nevada--History--20th century--Fiction. | LCGFT: Detective and mystery
  fiction. | Novels.
Classification: LCC PZ7.1.G79675 Mu 2023 | DDC [Fic]--dc23
LC record available at https://lccn.loc.gov/2023019913

Printed in the United States of America

PROLOGUE

"*Ostia*! It's cold."

Shivering in his wool-lined denim jacket, Pierre Elissetche briefly lifted his hands from the wheel of his work truck to cup them around his moustache. He exhaled into his callused fingers. The heavy fog had settled over the valley like a blanket. A wet, cold blanket. The chill seeped into his bones. Pierre would take an icy mountain day back in the Basque Country over this Central Valley fog any day of the week. He rubbed his nose. It was colder than (his sheepdog) Pintto's snout after he had been running in the snow.

He couldn't wait to get home.

Pierre glanced over at the passenger seat to see the box wrapped in red and green tissue paper—topped with a bright white bow in the shape of a snowflake. Inside the box was a small dollhouse that he had purchased for his daughter in Stockton the day before. His wife, Maite, had sent him to the biggest department store on Main Street—he wasn't allowed to leave town without that dollhouse.

Anna was going to love it.

In the truck's bed behind him, he could hear the other supplies he had bought for his sheepherders rattling around. Crates of canned beans. Coffee. Campbell's Soup. Del Monte canned peaches. Baskets of eggs and salt-cured bacon. Bread. Chorizo. And red wine.

Lots of red wine.

Pierre turned right onto another lonely country road, heading west to the fertile pastures by Patterson—where his sheep were wintering for the upcoming lambing season. He had made this trip many times before, so he was lulled by the familiarity of it. He was also slightly numb from the hangover he had from the parade of highballs he had consumed the night before at the Pyrenees Hotel in Stockton.

1

What a dinner. The sweetbreads were the best he had ever had.

He would never tell Maite that, though.

Because then he'd have to sleep outside with Pintto. And as great and warm as that border collie was, the hairy xakurra had fleas.

The further out of town he drove, the thicker the fog became. He could barely see the expanse of alfalfa and wheat that lined the road on each side. The short green grasses faded into white nothingness. Next time, he should make his business partner, Joanes Larralde, make the supply run. He was tired of this. The idea would make Maite happy. Pierre could almost hear his wife agree, "Good. Let Larralde do it, for once. That man is lazy. I work harder before noon than that man does all day."

Pierre yawned and started humming to himself. In about an hour, the fog would fade as he got closer to the western side of the valley. The apricot orchards of Patterson would replace some of the farmland, and a few dairies would spot the landscape. And he'd be close to their winter home. In the summer, they would pack up and herd the sheep to the Sierras.

He sang the American Christmas song he had heard in the department store in Stockton. It was cheerful and catchy—even though he didn't much care for American music. After all, it was always too loud and full of words sung too quickly for him to understand.

Why did Americans have to talk so damn fast?

Pierre tapped on the wheel.

"*Geeegle bells, geegle bells . . . geegle all zee weeey!*"

"*La, la, la, la, la, la, la, la, la, la, la, la, la, laaaaa!*"

So distracted by his song, Pierre didn't hear the train whistle that was partially muffled by the thick, foggy morning. He continued down the road, unaware that at the intersection ahead, a freight train was thundering to meet him.

Pierre drummed a few more beats on the wheel of his Dodge truck, and out of the corner of his eye, he saw a dark shadow moving through the whiteness.

Then, another whistle sounded. This time, it was just yards in front of him. The terror was immediate—he slammed on the brakes.

But the brakes failed.

Pierre pushed them again and again, but nothing happened. The train was barreling down on him. The yards narrowed to feet.

He closed his eyes and behind his lids an image flashed of little Anna. Her dark hair a halo around her rosy-cheeked, smiling face.

The last thing Pierre heard was the screech of steel and the roar of the train engine.

And then he knew nothing at all.

PART ONE

CHAPTER ONE

Four Years Later

Gardnerville, Nevada
Friday, November 19, 1943

"I'm home, *Ama*!" Anna Elissetche burst into the boardinghouse kitchen breathing heavily, a canvas bookbag slung over her slender shoulder. Her shoulder-length black hair was falling out of her ponytail. With a pat for Pintto, the slumbering black and white sheepdog by the back door, Anna stepped to greet her mother, Maite Elissetche, with a kiss to each cheek.

Peeling carrots with rough, reddened fingers, Maite cast a glance at the clock in the corner, "You should have been here nearly an hour ago. Where have you been? School gets out at three o'clock."

Trying to avoid her mother's gaze as those spectacled blue eyes bored into hers, Anna held her bookbag close to her side, "I—had a meeting after school."

Maite sighed and looked away, adding a peeled carrot to the pile blooming on the wooden table in front of her, "Right. And I bet that meeting was at the county library and someone forced you to borrow all those books I see weighing down on your shoulder."

Anna felt pink heat rush to her pale face, "Well, I needed to get more books because I don't want to run out over . . . Thanksgiving . . ." Anna's voice trailed off as she saw her mother, who was only five feet tall (which included the platform loafers she always wore) still manage to look down her nose at her fourteen-year-old daughter.

"You have enough books."

5

"But—"

"*Haurra!*" Child!

Anna knew better than to keep protesting.

Done with the carrots, Maite bustled to the big pot of simmering white beans on the stove to give them a stir with the large wooden spoon that was at least a third of her height. "We won't have much of a Thanksgiving if you are late to get the turkeys. Fred at the butcher shop might have sold them to someone else by now. I should have asked Benat to go get them, instead!" With a clank of the spoon on the dish next to the giant iron stove, Maite let the threat settle into the air. Anna loved to drive the hotel truck on errands. Even though she was too young to drive according to the State of Nevada, her mother had taught her to drive a couple years prior, saying, *A woman needs to learn to drive so she is not dependent upon a man to drive her places.*

"Don't worry, Ama, I'll go right now. You don't need to bother Benat, he's probably busy." Benat Cedarry was the owner of the boardinghouse—and Maite's employer. Benat's wife, Louise, used to run the kitchen. But, when arthritis forced Louise to retire three years ago, the Cedarrys offered the job to Maite. The position came with a small apartment attached to the kitchen for Maite to live in with her daughter. Maite, a young widow, quickly accepted the job and moved with her daughter to Gardnerville. It was a respectable living—a stable living. Exactly what Maite needed most at that time. After all, Anna and her mother had struggled after Pierre died. It was so sudden— and so tragic. Thankfully, the Basque community always looked after its own.

Anna enjoyed life at the boardinghouse, although it was a lot of work. Feeding a bunch of hungry boarders every single day was a never-ending process—like trying to get rid of Pintto's fleas. As soon as she'd clean Pintto, the silly dog would run to the first patch of dirt he could find and roll around in it.

Feeding Basque boarders, many of them sheepherders, felt the same way.

(They smelled the same way, too.)

Anna dashed across the kitchen to the open door that led to their private apartment. Passing through the small sitting area, she entered her bedroom, which was separated from the sitting room by an accordion door. Her bedroom nook was sandwiched between their private bathroom and the outer wall of the boarding-house. It was just large enough for a small bed, a nightstand with a lamp, and an old photo of Anna and her father at the sheep camp cuddling in thick coats. The photo was teetering near the edge of the nightstand. Anna paused to carefully slide it back to its rightful place. Then, she wiped a bit of dust from the top of the frame.

At the foot of her bed was a dark green trunk with worn brass edges that Anna used to store her clothes. Opening her tan canvas bookbag, she pulled out the three books inside. *Death on the Nile* by Agatha Christie, *The Murder of Roger Ackroyd* by

Agatha Christie, and a random Nancy Drew novel that the librarian had made her borrow because it was more "age-appropriate" than her first two selections which, according to Mrs. McGillicuddy, were "alarming and dreadful."

Whatever she meant by that.

Tucking the books under her bed, Anna decided she had no time to worry about Mrs. McGillicuddy because she had to drive to pick up Thanksgiving turkeys.

Anna climbed into the cab of the tan Plymouth parked behind the boarding-house. "The Sierra Hotel" was painted in neat black letters on the side of the door that Anna closed behind her. She reached beneath the seat for the pillow she knew would be hiding there. Her mother's platform shoes didn't help her see over the dashboard, but the cushion sure did. Settling it under her bottom and smoothing her blue shin-length skirt around her, Anna drove out onto the highway.

The late November sun was low in the sky, haloing the nearby craggy, brown mountaintops that lined the highway to the west. Anna could see a little snow on the summit, but it was the dried grasses and sagebrush that mostly littered this side of the Sierras. Dusk was approaching, and the thought made Anna push a little harder on the gas pedal with her black and white saddle shoe. If she didn't get those turkeys before the butcher closed for the day, Maite would turn Anna's library books into toilet paper for the boarders to wipe their *ipurdiak*.

And that would be the perfect excuse for Mrs. McGillicuddy to revoke her library card. The woman had been longing to do it ever since Anna borrowed *Dracula*, renewed it four times, and returned it smelling like garlic soup.

She could NOT afford to upset the woman any further. With that depressing thought, Anna turned a little too roughly onto the side street by the butcher. The truck gave a strange lurch when she slowed in front of the shop—nearly making her hit the iron mailbox in the front. She had better calm down. Or she wouldn't just lose her reading privileges. She'd also be walking everywhere from now until 1960.

She hopped out of the truck and dashed into the shop, the bell on the door loudly announcing her arrival. Sausages, hams, and cured meats of all kinds hung from the ceiling like savory icicles. Fred Richter emerged from the back room, a meat-splattered white apron tied around his middle. He was tall with a shock of red hair and bushy sideburns threaded with grey. "Ahh, hello there, Miss Anna. You caught me just in time. I was getting ready to close."

Smelling the array of bratwursts hanging above her head, Anna sighed with relief and approached the glass-fronted counter, "Thank goodness. Ama would have never let me live it down if I missed you."

Fred chuckled and, with beefy hands, reached for a box beneath the counter. Then he said, "I'm afraid that I only have one turkey for her. The Air Force base in

Reno requisitioned most of the turkeys in the area, so we've got to make do with only half the supply. But, to make up for it, I've added four rabbits?"

Anna pushed her hands into the pockets of her pink cardigan and bit her lip, "Can you make it five rabbits? Joanes Larralde is a pig and can eat a whole rabbit by himself."

The butcher leaned forward and confided, "So can I."

Examining his tall frame, Anna tilted her head thoughtfully, "Yes. I can believe that."

A bark of laughter erupted from the man, "Now you sound like my wife."

Anna smiled and her olive-green eyes spotted the barrel of apples in the corner, "Are those apples for sale?"

Fred glanced over and nodded, "They are from the trees behind our house. You can have a few if you want."

"Thanks!" Anna decided she'd try to bake an apple pie to show her mother that she knew how to use an oven.

Adding another rabbit to the box from the pile behind the counter, Fred dropped some apples into a brown paper bag and tucked it into the corner of the crate. Then, he hefted the box and made his way to the door, "I'll put it in your truck. I assume you drove here—even though I doubt you can reach the pedals."

Anna protested as she followed him out the door, "Hey, I am taller than my mother."

"Not by much."

Anna parked the Plymouth behind the boardinghouse and tucked the pillow back under the seat. She saw the handsome hotel bartender, Antton Garai, smoking a cigarette by the kitchen door. Pintto, tail wagging, was looking up at him adoringly. Anna felt a blush trail across her face. Antton was the most handsome man she knew. About medium height, he had silky dark hair, piercing hazel eyes, and a shadow of stubble on his face—no matter how closely he shaved.

"*Neska polita!*" Antton called out with a smile as he crushed his cigarette with the heel of his boot and approached the truck. "You look very grown-up in that truck. You should start a taxi service—then you could buy your own books, not just borrow them."

Anna's blush deepened. "Ama told you that I was late again?"

"*Bai.* But don't worry. No reason for you to hurry home, anyway. Old Victor just slept in the bar all day farting *La Marseillaise*. You didn't miss much." Antton glanced back at the large crate in the back of the truck, "Want me to carry that inside?"

Anna nodded and climbed out of the truck, smoothing her shoulder-length black hair behind her ears. Antton lifted the heavy crate from the truck with a grunt, "*Diós*, this is a lot of meat."

Anna scurried ahead to open the kitchen door for him, "Well, there's never enough meat to satisfy Joanes."

Antton paused, a grimace passing over his handsome features. He gave her a cryptic look before muttering under his breath as he passed her into the kitchen, "There's never enough of anything for that *bastardoa*."

Maite looked up from the stove, her eyeglasses fogged by the steam rising from the soup pot. It smelled like Anna's favorite *porrusalda*—leek potato soup. "*Mil esker*, Antton. Can you put that in the cold box in the pantry?"

Antton heaved the crate into the pantry off the kitchen and Anna turned to her mother to break the bad news, "Ama, Fred only had one turkey. The government took the rest for the soldiers at the base in Reno. He gave us five *lapinak* to make up the difference."

Maite began to grumble, "Just five?"

"It was just going to be four, but I got Fred to give us another one. And some apples."

"It's all the fault of these damn Germans," Maite muttered to herself as she wiped her hands on her apron.

"Which Germans?" Anna raised an eyebrow, "The Nazis or Mr. Richter?"

"I don't know. Both. *All* of them," Maite's voice grew firm.

"Anyway, guess what? I'm going to make an apple pie for Thanksgiving."

Maite feigned shock, "You know how to cook?"

"I've seen you burn enough potatoes over the years, I think I can figure it out," Anna teased.

Maite lifted her spoon and pointed it at her daughter, "I do NOT burn potatoes. That would be a crime."

Antton held up his hands in a peaceful gesture as he returned to the kitchen, "Anna—listen to your mother. She doesn't burn anything."

Maite nodded in satisfaction.

"You're just buttering her up so that she'll always save the best lamb chops for you," Anna crossed her arms over her chest.

"I'm not a stupid man," Antton admitted as he snatched a piece of bread from the basket in the corner. The movement was lightning quick—a reason he was such a great accordion player. Antton's fingers could fly over the ivory keys, making the instrument sing. No matter how many lessons she took from him, Anna knew she'd never be that good.

"You are not stupid," Maite allowed. Then, she added with a chuckle, "And you are not ugly, either!"

Antton came over and gave the woman a big, sloppy kiss on each cheek, "See, this is why you are my favorite woman of all, Maite Elissetche!"

"You only say that because you are hungry. Now go take the trash out and dump it in the back," Maite shooed the handsome bartender from the kitchen.

Hanging her pink cardigan on the coatrack in their small sitting room nearby, Anna came back to wash her pale hands at the kitchen sink to help her mother with the rest of the dinner. She heard Teresa Harguindeguy, the waitress who also helped Ama in the kitchen, setting out the heavy plates, silverware, and glasses for the boarders and the few local guests who ate in the dining room each night. The Cedarrys' niece, Teresa was sent to America three years ago after her mother, Benat's youngest sister, died at the hospital in Bayonne. Shy and quiet, Teresa made the long trip alone—at only sixteen. She lived with Benat and Louise at their house a few blocks from the boardinghouse.

A few minutes later, Antton returned to the kitchen. "I think there's something wrong with the truck. There's a puddle underneath. Oil or fluid. Not sure. It wasn't there before, though."

Maite turned to narrow her eyes at Anna, "*Haurra*, what did you do to the truck?"

"Nothing, I swear!" Anna could never admit that she nearly crashed into the butcher shop's mailbox. She'd never get to drive again. But really, she didn't do anything wrong. Not this time.

"*Ez zaitut sinesten*," Maite shook her head.

"You don't believe me?" Anna's voice rose.

Always the peacemaker, Antton used the skills that made him such a good bartender, "Let's calm down, ladies. These things happen with trucks all the time. No need to think it's anyone's fault."

"Fine. I'll have Gregorio Sarratea look at it next time I see him. He'll probably come to play *mus* with the men on Sunday," Maite let the matter rest, for which Anna was very glad. She gave Antton a grateful, adoring look. She just couldn't help herself.

Antton Garai was the most perfect man.

CHAPTER TWO

On Sunday afternoon, in the lazy lull between lunch and dinner service, Anna pecked at her accordion in the corner of the dining room. A group of men were gathered at the table nearest the kitchen. They were wearing their cleanest shirts and pants while they drank wine and coffee that was heavily laced with brandy. Their ruddy cheeks were flushed with laughter, drink, and the large meal they had eaten earlier. The men swapped stories about the deer they had killed (the antlers getting bigger with every telling). They played hand after hand of *mus*—each taking a turn at grabbing a new wine bottle from the bar so they could refill each other's wine glasses. This allowed the men to appear modest about how much wine they had actually consumed.

So, yes, it was a typical Sunday afternoon at The Sierra Hotel.

Maite made Anna practice her accordion during these hours—the half-drunk men an easy audience for a girl who liked to read more than she liked to play a *pasodoble*. Lucky for Anna that poor Victor Arrossa had ear drums filled with decades of dust from Nevada windstorms. He thought her playing was exquisite—and he tipped her a penny every week if she played a waltz.

Little did he know that it was "Twinkle, Twinkle, Little Star."

With a shout and a winning hand of three queens and an ace, Joanes Larralde threw his cards down on the table and rose. Satisfaction made his cheeks puff out—which drew attention to his oily, bald head. He was her father's old business partner. After the death of Pierre, Larralde had purchased his late partner's share from Maite—who wanted no part of a sheep business. In the summer, Joanes kept the sheep up in the mountains. This time of year, he stayed at the boardinghouse when he brought his large flock to the nearby pastures of the Carson Valley.

Larralde scooped up his winnings from the table, giving half the coins to Benat Cedarry, his *mus* partner for the afternoon. As Joanes walked away, Benat called out, holding up an aged finger, "Wait! I'm missing ten cents, Larralde." A dry tone entered the older man's voice, "I'm sure you didn't mean to short me. You'd never do such a thing."

"Of course not!" Joanes was indignant, but a flush had deepened on his cheeks that wasn't caused by the brandy.

To escape the knowing stares of the other men, Joanes walked over and gave Anna a quarter. "For you, *mademoiselle*."

Anna accepted the coin and thanked him—but, inside, she was surprised. In all the years she had known him (which had been most of her life), he had never voluntarily parted with one penny. Benat Cedarry must have really embarrassed him.

Good.

No one likes a cheat.

As Larralde walked out of the room in the direction of the stairs, Benat gave Anna a wink.

The other men stood up to leave, some to head to their homes nearby, and some to head to their rooms upstairs. Anna stood from her chair in the corner just as Maite emerged from the kitchen and rested her hand on the shoulder of a man who was wearing a denim shirt and puffing on a short cigarillo, "Oh, Gregorio! Can you check out the hotel truck? I think something is wrong with it. I can bring it to your shop this week if something needs to be done?"

Stubbing his cigarillo in the nearest ashtray, Gregorio Sarratea nodded, "I can look at it right now. There's still a little light left outside. Emelia won't be expecting me home quite yet."

"Thank you!" Maite followed the younger man through the kitchen to where the truck was parked out back.

Sensing the afternoon was over, Anna left the dining room and returned to their small apartment next to the kitchen. Setting her accordion in the corner of their sitting room, Anna gave a stretch and decided that she might have time to read another chapter of *Death on the Nile* before her mother returned.

Someone was about to die in that Egyptian desert, and she couldn't wait to find out who.

The chapter turned to two. Then three. The minutes stretching into an hour while the sun set in the western sky. Anna was half squinting in the dimming light before she realized that she should turn on the lamp at her bedside. Rubbing her eyes, she reached to turn on the lamp and then settled back on her bed—her green and white crocheted pillow cozy behind her shoulders. She yawned.

Tucking a scrap of used notepaper in her book to mark her place, she rose from bed and opened the accordion door to their sitting room. She saw that the light was on in Maite's room across the apartment from hers.

"Ama?"

A pause. And then, "*Bai*?"

"What are you doing?" Anna asked, coming to the doorway of her mother's room—which was slightly larger than her own. Maite's room was large enough for a small escritoire in the far corner—over which her mother was now hunched, pen in hand.

Maite looked back over her shoulder at her daughter, "I just remembered that I forgot to answer a few letters last week." She clucked her tongue, "*Diós*, I must be getting old. My memory isn't what it once was." She laughed, "Don't get old, *coucou*. You'll end up with grey hair like me."

Anna tilted her head to the side, "But, you don't have grey hair, Ama."

"And you know why! When you are old like me, you must also have a daughter that will help you dye it."

"So, is that the secret, then?" Anna laughed.

Turning back to her letters, Maite waved Anna away, "Go and start warming up the leftover pot of soup for dinner. Tell Teresa we're just going to have a simple menu tonight. Pork chops, canned green beans, and boiled potatoes with *perrexila* and butter. I'll be there to help in a little while."

When Anna entered the kitchen, she saw that Teresa had already put the soup on the stove to warm and was peeling garlic. She gave her Maite's message, and the quiet young woman nodded with a smile, "*Patatak zurituko ditut.*"

"Okay. I'll help you peel potatoes after I go set out the dishes and silverware." Anna pushed open the swinging door to the dining room to see Domingo Echeveste, one of the boarders, enter with Catalina Rodriquez—the young woman that came to clean the hotel in the mornings. Starting as a sheepherder, Domingo had worked his way up to become the camp-tender, or foreman, for Joanes Larralde. He helped to manage the sheepherders and deliver supplies. Serious, and a hard worker, Domingo lived at the boardinghouse for much of the year. He began spending time with Catalina soon after she started working at the hotel last fall.

She lived nearby with an elderly woman whom she helped care for. Several years older than Anna, she was friendly—with caramel colored skin and a wide smile.

"*Hola*, Anna!" Catalina waved and quickly moved to help Anna set out some place settings on the long, wooden tables.

"*Gracias*, Catalina. *Cómo estás*?" Anna answered while Catalina proceeded to tell her about the delicious tamales that they had for lunch yesterday at her cousin's house up in Reno.

As the young woman moved around the table setting plates, Anna thought she noticed a tiny swelling at Catalina's waist. Her yellow shirt dress was a little snugger than she remembered. She, all of a sudden, remembered hearing Catalina vomit in the guest toilet by the dining room last week. She had said it was the flu, but . . .

Wait . . .

Anna felt her mouth drop open. She caught Domingo's knowing eye.

Domingo smiled and rubbed a hand on Catalina's back, causing her to pause her detailed recount of their day with her family.

"I think our secret is out," Domingo tilted his head to Anna.

A happy blush stole over Catalina's round cheeks, and she whispered, "You can't tell anyone yet. We'll do that soon. We plan to marry in the next couple of months."

Anna loved when she had a secret. It didn't happen often, because when you lived in a boardinghouse, everyone knew everything about everyone. Even things you didn't want to know.

This was a secret of large, and growing, proportions.

The last time Anna was this excited was when she managed to guess the killer in *Murder on the Orient Express*. But this was better because first, no one got stabbed twelve times and second, Maite didn't even know yet.

"Can I come to the wedding?"

Catalina stepped forward to hug the younger girl, "*Seguro que sí.*"

His wavy black hair brushing the top of his brown collared shirt, Domingo added with a low chuckle, "If you manage to keep the secret, without telling the entire boardinghouse, you can even be a bridesmaid."

Catalina cried in delight, "*Buena idea.* She looks beautiful in pink."

This was getting better and better. Anna clapped her hands, "I've never been in a wedding before!"

"Well, there is a first time for everything," Domingo remarked. He turned to the bar, and grabbed his fiancée's hand, "Come on, Catalina, let's get a drink before dinner."

"*Hasta luego!*" The beaming young woman gave Anna's arm an affectionate squeeze before she followed Domingo to the other room.

CHAPTER THREE

Opening the oven door slowly, Anna was nervous. She had followed the recipe from the newspaper to the very letter, but that didn't mean that she hadn't managed to mess this up.

There was a collective ooh of appreciation from the women in the kitchen as Anna pulled her two apple pies from the oven. Anna sighed in relief. They looked like something people would actually eat. Not just pretend to eat while being polite.

"Look at that!" Maite clucked her tongue and smiled as she checked the rabbit stew simmering on the stove, "It smells like a real American pie."

Louise Cedarry, the boardinghouse owner's wife, leaned forward to examine the steaming pies. "They are so pretty! The edges are golden brown and look just perfect." The older woman beamed at Anna, her light eyes twinkling in approval. Her short, curly, grey hair haloed her round face, and she wore a dark green dress with sleeves to her elbow. A cheerful floral scarf was tied around her neck. She clapped her hands, "I can't wait to try it later."

"*Qué bonito*, Anna," Catalina admired, as she folded a stack of red checkered napkins into little fans. Earlier, she had pressed all the table linens using Maite's iron in their sitting room.

Teresa, her light brown hair pulled back into a bun, slid a tray of cubed potatoes and carrots into the place the apple pies had vacated. The young woman had sprinkled parsley and thyme over the top of the root vegetables which were glistening with melted butter. A white apron tied over her light blue dress, Teresa gave the pies a long sniff and then gave Anna an approving smile, "*Goxoa*."

Maite moved from checking the rabbit stew to stir the pot of pea soup that was warming on the corner of the large iron stove. With a satisfied tap of the wooden spoon, Maite took a sip of wine.

15

Louise quickly reached to lift her own small wine glass, "A toast! To all the women of The Sierra Hotel! *Txin-txin!*"

"*Txin-txin!*"

"*Salud!*"

Maite clinked her glass with Louise. She turned to her daughter, "*Haurra*, take the deviled eggs and salami plate that Louise brought to the bar for the men. They are drinking too much. I don't want them to get *mozkorra* before lunch is ready. This turkey needs another hour. *Diós*, this is why Bascos don't eat *indioilarra*. It takes too long to cook."

"And it's dry," Anna added.

Maite looked briefly affronted, "My turkey is *not* dry."

Anna picked up the glass platter of deviled eggs from the corner of the kitchen, "*Ama, all* turkey is dry. This is a fact. It's why Americans put that fruit sauce all over it. That way they can pretend to like turkey."

Louise slapped her chubby hand on the table and laughed, "Those silly Americans. They don't know anything about good food."

Folding the last napkin, Catalina nodded in agreement, "*La señora dice la verdad. La comida americana es . . . mediocre.*" She trailed off as her face scrunched up in distaste.

"*Bai, bai,*" Teresa chuckled, picked up the platter of salami and crackers, and followed Anna to the bar.

As the door swung behind her, Anna called out, "Don't worry, Ama, if anyone can make a nice turkey, it's you."

Walking away, Anna heard her mother ask Louise, "*Diós*, was that a compliment?"

After offering deviled eggs to the small gathering of men at the bar, Anna approached Victor Arrossa and Matthieu Dallut-Bec at the table by the front window which faced the Nevada highway. The middle-aged Frenchman's bulbous nose was red and drippy from a head cold. Matthieu had a benign look on his long, olive face, so he clearly couldn't smell the flatulence wafting from the elderly Victor sitting next to him. Sipping happily on his Picon, Victor took an egg and greeted Anna with a toothless grin, "*Neska ttipia!*" Little girl, he called her.

Next to him, Matthieu politely accepted an egg, "*Merci beaucoup, mademoiselle.*" The Frenchman was an artisan from San Francisco hired to build the altar at the new Catholic church in Carson City. He had been boarding at The Sierra Hotel for the past two weeks but was expected to finish his project sometime in the new year. Bespectacled and serious, Dallut-Bec kept to himself, so Anna didn't know much about him. He was always pleasant and polite, though. He left a coin for Catalina after she cleaned his room, so he was classier than Joanes Larralde (although, it didn't take much to be classier than Joanes).

At the thought of the sheepman, Anna glanced over to see Larralde take three salami slices from Teresa and stuff them into his mustached mouth. He was standing by the bar talking to Benat Cedarry and Domingo Echeveste. With his thinning grey hair covered by a black *boneta*, Benat was telling the men a story—his sun-spotted hands gesturing with enthusiasm. Domingo was chuckling at whatever the boardinghouse owner said, while Larralde took a swig of his drink and nibbled at the lemon rind inside. At the other end of the bar, the Goytia brothers, Fermin and Manuel, stood talking to Ernesto Rodriguez—Catalina's twin brother. A handyman at the casino in Carson City, Louise had insisted that Catalina invite him for lunch. Ernesto brought a case of *cerveza* with him—something which had quickly endeared him to the Goytia brothers, who had managed to already drink more than their fair share (if the loud slamming of their dice cups on the bar top was any indication). Fermin and Manuel were sheepherders for Santiago Achaval— the largest sheep owner in the Carson Valley. As their employer despised Joanes Larralde (after he tried to poach their winter pastures), it was not surprising that the Goytia brothers stayed as far away from Larralde as the well-worn bar would allow.

Never poach a pasture from a Basque sheepman. Never. For he will carry that grudge until St. Peter comes to drag him from this Earth.

And maybe even longer.

Antton was making three more Picons. The short glasses were lined up on the dark wood in front of him, the liquid shining like amber as he stirred the drinks with a skinny silver spoon. A radio by the front wall in the corner was on low, Glenn Miller and his orchestra murmuring about "That Old Black Magic."

The wide red front door of the hotel creaked open, a burst of cool air rushing inside as a sandy-haired man in his mid-twenties stepped in with a cane. Wearing a tidy navy-blue blazer and a crisp white shirt, Mitchell Lauden limped into the bar. Seeing Anna, he smiled warmly, "Hullo, Miss Anna. Happy Thanksgiving!"

"Happy Thanksgiving! It's nice to see you. Have you come for lunch?" Anna offered the young lawyer a deviled egg. A frequent guest, Mitchell Lauden had a small office near the library and stopped in for lunch or dinner a few times a week. He had survived polio as a young boy and used an ivory-topped cane made of sturdy ebony.

"I'm afraid not. Just stopping in for a drink before I head to Mother and Father's. Her cook, Francine, has cooked a feast with all the trimmings and Mother will be offended if I don't eat every bite on my plate and compliment the meal as if she had cooked it herself." He paused, "Although, your mother's meal is sure to be better." His tone was wistful.

Mitchell stepped closer to the bar and greeted Benat with a handshake, "Good day to you, Mr. Cedarry."

"Happy to see you! How is your mama? And the senator? I haven't seen them since the dinner they had here last year for those five local boys before they left to fight in England."

"They are well, thank you. Father is up for re-election next year. But he's considering a run for lieutenant governor, if all goes well." Shifting his weight on his cane, he continued, "Speaking of those local boys . . . Did you hear about Timmy Armstrong? That tall, red-headed boy from the dinner? He got shot down by a Messerschmitt at the beginning of the month. His parents are devastated. Father went to see them last week."

The older man grew solemn, "I had not heard. What a terrible thing."

After Benat quickly translated, Domingo frowned in sadness, as well. He picked up his fresh Picon, and replied in Basque, "We should salute him now. Get him a drink, Antton."

From behind the bar, Antton was adding cherries to the top of a short tumbler of garnet-colored liquid, "You want your usual? Manhattan?"

Mitchell gave Antton a smile and reached for the glass, "I love it here. You never forget my favorite drink. Thank you, Antton. Or, should I say, *meal-esh-care*?" With a subconscious glance that made him look quite handsome, he added, "Did I say that right?"

"Close enough," Antton allowed with a tilt of his dark head.

Benat lifted his glass, "To Timmy Armstrong."

Domingo raised his glass up high in his left hand, while making the Sign of the Cross with his right.

"Did someone die?" Victor said loudly—noticing the change of mood. A glob of egg was still in the corner of his mouth.

"*Bai*, Victor. An American soldier," Benat answered in nearly a yell to make sure the old man heard him.

"*Aleman putak*," Victor grumbled in reply.

Anna pretended not to hear that comment, but it was hard not to since he said it loud enough to hear all the way in Reno.

Mitchell pulled out a chair at the bar and sat down, sipping his drink. Anna left the remaining deviled eggs on the bar and prepared to head back to the kitchen when the radio switched to an advertisement for Ovaltine. A bright holiday jingle played, "*This Christmas, serve your kiddies the best hot cocoa around . . . It's a jolly time for Ovaltine!*"

Anna suddenly remembered, "Oh, Mr. Lauden, we are having a Christmas dinner dance on Sunday, December 19th. Ama will be making oxtail stew and Mrs. Sagouspe has agreed to play accordion afterward. We've convinced Antton to play, too! You should come. Maybe bring a special lady friend?" Anna said this brightly, hoping that he would come. "The pretty woman you brought to dinner a few weeks ago was lovely."

"Yes, Bridget Farquhar. Her father is a donor to my father's campaign. Big rancher out in Spanish Springs." He paused and considered, "Yes, maybe I will bring her. She would enjoy it. Thank you for the invitation."

Suddenly fancying herself the official secret-keeper and matchmaker of everyone at The Sierra Hotel, Anna vowed to make Antton play a special romantic waltz at the Christmas dinner.

Maybe Catalina and Domingo could announce their engagement?

It would be the kind of night for something special to happen.

CHAPTER FOUR

Just over two weeks later, Maite set two large steaming bowls of *mozkorsalda* on a wooden tray—covering them with ceramic lids. "*Haurra*, you make sure they eat every bite of this. I put extra garlic to fight the *gripa*. Tell the *gizonak* that if they are not better tomorrow, I am taking them to the *medikua* in Carson City. I will not have anyone die in this hotel."

Anna put two napkins and two aspirins on the tray, as well. In the days since Thanksgiving, Matthieu Dallut-Bec's head cold had moved to his chest and Victor Arrossa had become ill, as well. The poor men were in quite a state. The Sierra Hotel sounded like a tuberculosis ward. The pungent garlic soup was her mother's favorite remedy for just about anything.

As Anna picked up the tray, her mother repeated, "Tell them they must eat all the *salda*. All of it."

Anna slowly carried the soup to the front of the hotel—climbing the staircase with careful steps. The afternoon sun was nearly to the mountains. The stairs opened to a sitting room with two rectangular windows that faced the highway and the front of the hotel. The sitting area had an old, worn, dusty rose sofa and three matching cushioned reading chairs that were castoffs from an estate sale in Genoa. Anna's bed and nightstand had come from the same sale.

Across the room was a door to a storage room that housed unused bunkhouse furniture and built-in shelves for the boardinghouse linens. To the left was a long hallway with four doors on each side. At the end of the hallway was a small, windowed door that opened to a narrow exterior staircase outside of the hotel. It gave the boarders a way to get in and out of the hotel without having to go through the main front door. Victor's and Mr. Dallut-Bec's rooms were the first rooms in the hallway, so it was quick work for Anna to drop off the soup and pass along her mother's messages. Poor Victor's eyes were rheumy and sad when she left—Anna felt his discomfort and promised to check on him later. At least Mr. Dallut-Bec had appeared somewhat improved, but his congested nose was still the size of a potato.

Descending the staircase to the hotel foyer facing the bar, Anna saw Antton wiping drink glasses. Soon the boarders, and some of the locals, would stop in for a drink. Antton had the radio playing in the background and he was humming along with Bing Crosby. Near the bottom of the stairs, Anna heard the metallic thud of the letterbox on the wall outside the front door and spied a middle-aged woman wearing a long grey skirt and a grey jacket climb back onto a post office bicycle to continue delivering mail.

Anna grabbed the letters from the brass box and began to sort them. Domingo had a letter from a property office in Minden; the Goytia brothers had a blue air mail envelope with a stamp from Spain; and her mother had a letter from her father's first boss in Yuba City, a letter from an insurance office, and a mail-order catalog of men's clothing and shoes. Tomas Hardoy, the boarder that had been away on a job in Elko, had a letter from his sister in Bakersfield.

And, at the bottom of the stack, there were two letters from Patricia Cedarry written on stationary from Holy Names in Oakland—one letter was for Anna and one letter was addressed to Antton Garai. Patricia, Benat and Louise's only daughter, had left for the women's college after she graduated from high school a few years ago. Bright and curious, Patricia had been a top student in her class. The Cedarrys had been aghast at their daughter's wish to go off to college. Good Basque girls did not leave home. They did not live away from their parents.

Their disapproval was so intense that Benat had nearly threatened to lock Patricia in her bedroom to prevent her from leaving. From their response, one would think Patricia asked to join a naked circus—not attend a women's college run by Catholic nuns. Only with the intervention of her high school principal did the Cedarrys begin to change their mind. Holy Names had offered her a scholarship, and after she graduated, she'd have a good, respectable job as a teacher. For the rest of her working life.

Walking to the bar, Anna called out, "The mail is here. We have letters from Patricia."

Wiping off a bottle of Canadian whiskey with a damp rag, Antton turned with a charming smile, "*Bai*? I never get mail from anyone. I hope I remember how to read."

Setting his letter on the bar top, Anna arched an eyebrow, "You get mail from Patricia all the time." Sighing, she added, "You do remember to write back, don't you? It's important to write to the girl you are courting. Otherwise, she'll think you are lazy and rude."

"Well, I wouldn't want that," Antton said with mock solemnity.

Anna heaved another long-suffering sigh, "Do you want me to include a message from you in my reply, again?"

"Would you?" He brightened, "*Mil esker*. It's much easier that way. My handwriting is terrible."

"It's because you never write to anyone."

"I write all the time!" Antton protested.

"Writing a list for the hotel supply order does not count. It's just you writing 'Whiskey' and 'Picon' and 'Red Wine' on a piece of paper. Every week. Over and over again."

He shrugged, "Sometimes we need gin, too."

Anna laughed and set the letters for Domingo, Tomas, and the Goytia brothers on the bar, "Will you give these letters to the *gizonak*? I need to go study before helping Ama with supper—I have an arithmetic exam this week before Christmas vacation."

"*Bai*. Tomas is supposed to return from Elko today. Good luck on your exam, *neska*."

In the middle of the kitchen, her mother was stuffing garlic into the array of lamb shanks lined up on the butcher block table. Teresa was pouring two large cans of crushed tomatoes into the pot of vegetable soup that was beginning to bubble on the stove. "Ama, I got the mail. Where do you want me to put your letters?"

"In my bedroom is fine. *Mil esker*," Maite used the back of her hand to push her glasses further up her nose, "Did you do your schoolwork, *haurra*?"

"I'm going to do it now. I have an exam on Thursday before the Christmas holiday." Anna snatched a piece of bread from the basket in the corner and nosed around the kitchen until she found the butter. Spreading a layer on the bread, she continued, "By the way, I think you're going to have to take Victor to the doctor tomorrow. He looks like a sick calf with shaky legs and lots of *flema*."

Maite clucked her tongue in concern, "*Gizajoa* Victor." Poor Victor. "I'll borrow Benat's car to take him to Carson City after breakfast. Gregorio Sarratea said he will get the truck fixed tomorrow or the next day."

Settling in the cozy bedroom, Anna sprawled across her bed, legs swinging behind her—an arithmetic textbook, a notepad, and Patricia's letter arrayed in front of her. She started with the letter. She saw Patricia's tidy, cursive script covering the page:

Dear Anna,

Greetings from Oakland! I apologize for taking so long to write, but we had examinations and research papers due last month. Time has gotten away from me, truly! The girls in the dormitory plan study sessions to coincide with episodes of Your Hit Parade. So, is it any wonder we get nothing done?

How are you? How is your Ama? How is Antton? I write to that silly, handsome man, and does he ever write back? No, he does not. If it weren't for you, I'd think that Antton moved to New York City to work at the Rainbow Room! (Heaven knows the wages would be better than Aita can afford to pay him.)

Please tell him hello, anyway. And don't forget your promise that you will beat any girls that come sniffing his way with Aita's old Basque paddle.

I'm counting on you.

By the way, I won't be coming home for Christmas this year. Ama's cousin Genevieve has invited me to stay with her family in San Francisco for the holiday. She has little ones, so it should be fun. I will miss all of you, of course. Very much.

Is the hotel Christmas party happening again this year? I love Maite's oxtail stew. No one makes it quite like your mother. (Don't tell my Ama I said that.)

Hugs & muxuak,

Patti

Promising herself that she'd compose a long, detailed reply later, Anna neatly tucked the letter back into the Holy Names envelope and set it aside.

Arithmetic beckoned.

A puddle of drool had spread over her textbook when Anna lurched awake at the sound of a man yelling. She had fallen asleep in the middle of the section on quadratics. Darkness had fallen outside her small window, and she felt her stomach rumble.

Deep voices raised in anger drifted through the walls of their small apartment. Anna rolled off the bed, smoothed her dress, and hoped her hair didn't look like the rat's nest they found in Victor Arrossa's room last winter. Cautiously approaching the door to the kitchen, Anna peaked her head inside to find the yelling was even louder in the kitchen. The doorway to the dining room was swung open, and there was Teresa, gawking at the male spectacle in front of her.

With the letter he had received that day clutched in his fist, young Tomas Hardoy stood over Joanes Larralde—who was sitting at the dining table nearest to the kitchen with a roasted lamb shank in his hand.

"*Gizon zozoa*," Hardoy hissed at the older man, "You promised that you were going to pay this hospital bill. It was your fault that I got hurt! It was your sheep that

I was shearing. I was in the hospital for five days. All because you don't know how to manage your business." The younger man paused and took a deep breath. His face was quickly becoming almost as red as the bandana tied around his neck. Hardoy continued, "The hospital sent the bill to my sister. In Bakersfield. The hospital said you gave them her address."

Calmly taking a bite of lamb, Larralde took his time replying. "I have enough of my own bills. You expect me to keep track of yours? I'm not your *ama*." Larralde's dismissive tone was not helping. Not at all.

Hardoy's face turned purple. Anna halfway expected his whole head to explode. Tomas Hardoy had a big temper—it's why he traveled from place to place for work. He had difficulty getting along with others. Maite said it was because of his dark red hair and the fact that he was short (she said short men had bigger tempers than tall ones), but Anna wasn't so sure.

Hardoy's voice was low as he called him a liar, "*Gezurkaria!*"

After a long sip of red wine, Larralde looked up at him with pity, "It's not my fault you were clumsy. This is the kind of thing that happens when you're in business for yourself. Now, if you worked for me, that would be a different thing."

The other dinner guests were watching the scene like it was a play in a theatre. Having heard the commotion, Antton had abandoned his post at the bar and approached the men. He held up his hands in a placating motion, "*Gizonak*, let's not ruin Maite's delicious dinner with this crazy *zozokeria*." He put a calming hand on Hardoy's shoulder and squeezed it, "Please, Tomas. You are scaring the Americans. We don't want them to take their business to the saloon in Minden. Their food is terrible."

Barely restraining the impulse to push Antton away, Hardoy took a shaky step backward and looked around the dining room. A dozen people were watching him, including an old lady who was clearly riveted by the excitement (given that her abandoned vegetable soup was dripping off the end of her spoon), so he said nothing more. He angrily smoothed out the sleeves of his denim shirt. Then, he uttered one last thing before stomping away:

"This isn't over, Larralde. You will pay this debt one way or another."

After Hardoy had left, Larralde took a large bite of lamb shank, looking bored by what had just transpired. A bit of parsley clung to his lip, "So charming, Garai. So charming. Maybe you, too, have a future in politics."

Shoulders stiffening, Antton's eyes narrowed, "You'd best shut your mouth, Larralde. It's going to get you killed one day."

"*Ez* . . . I think you have far more to worry about than me."

CHAPTER FIVE

Anna opened one eye. And then the other. Dim, morning light was angling into her small room from the window. She blinked. Ouch. Her eyelids hurt. Reaching up to her face, she noticed that her arm did, as well. Ugh. A cough erupted from her chest, startling her out of the rest of her stupor.

The *gripa* had come for her.

ON THE DAY OF THE CHRISTMAS PARTY. She groaned, which made her chest hurt, too. This was terrible. She had been looking forward to this for weeks. It was going to be so fun. It was one of the few social events of the whole year. During the music after dinner, the Goytia brothers agreed to bartend while Antton played the accordion—sharing the music duties with Mrs. Sagouspe. The tables in the middle of the dining room would be pushed aside to make room for the *jota* and the seven jumps dance, *Zazpi Jauziak*.

But, what about all the work Anna had to do to help Maite with the dinner? They were expecting sixty guests—which was double the number they usually served on Sunday evenings. Anna had also promised to help Teresa with the serving. She had too much to do. She couldn't be sick.

No, no, no.

Pushing herself out of bed, Anna shivered as her bare feet touched the cold wooden floor. She fumbled about for her slippers, then pulled on her red flannel robe and padded from her room to the living room. Eyes half-closed, she stood in the doorway to the kitchen.

"Ama?" she croaked weakly.

Maite was stirring a large pot of soup on the stove. Anna sniffed the air. She couldn't smell the soup at all. But she could tell by the color it was butternut squash.

"Ama?" she croaked again, a little louder this time.

25

Maite glanced over. In an instant, as was the case with mothers everywhere, she knew her daughter was sick. There was no mistaking the pale cheeks, and the glassy, unfocused eyes. She sighed, "*Haurra*, go back to bed. I will call Catalina to come help today. She's planning to come to the party with her brother, anyway. Louise will be here after lunch, too, to help me with the oxtails."

"Are you sure?" Anna rubbed a hand over her olive-green eyes.

"*Bai*. I don't want you and your *gripa* near this food. Go to bed," Maite ordered in her sternest voice—the one she used with drunken sheepherders and little boys who wouldn't eat their vegetables.

"Okay," Anna replied weakly.

"Later, I will make you some *mozkorsalda*. And, if you are feeling better tonight, maybe you can clear the dirty plates or listen to the music for a little while."

"What about the Christmas decorations? I didn't finish putting them up yesterday," Anna recalled the shiny red and green garland only covered half of the dining room. And the Christmas tree in the bar, while it had lights on it (thanks to Antton), she hadn't put the decorations on it yet.

"After you sleep for a few more hours, we will see."

That probably meant no. Anna shuffled sadly back to their small apartment. Without taking off her robe or slippers, Anna crawled back into her small bed and pulled the blankets over her head. With a wheezy cough, she fell into a deep sleep.

Feminine laughter woke Anna from her feverish sleep. Her cheek was stuck to her worn linen pillowcase by either saliva, or snot—she wasn't quite sure which. Or maybe it was both. Metal pots clanking in the kitchen nearby, Louise's voice rose above the din to give a surprisingly good imitation of Bing Crosby's latest hit, "*I'm dreeeeaming of a White Chreeesmaaaas weez every Chreeesmaaas card I write . . .*"

Louise's voice was low, and mostly on-key—at least it sounded that way to Anna's stuffed-up ears. Anna heard Catalina applaud and laugh, "*Bravo!*"

Smiling, despite the way it made the muscles in her cheeks hurt, Anna rolled herself from bed. She pulled her wavy black hair back into a low ponytail. Maite was always trying to tame her daughter's thick, wild hair. Yet, Anna secretly thought it was her best feature. After all, her nose was a little too long and her skin a little too pale. Others had green eyes that sparkled like emeralds, but Anna's just looked like cocktail olives.

Anna shuffled over to the doorway to the kitchen. The cheeks of the women gathered there were pink from the steam of the bubbling pots—and the contents of the highball glasses that were scattered around the room.

Turning around, Catalina's round face looked concerned as she took in Anna's disheveled appearance, "*Pobrecita.*"

From the stove, Louise held up a small pan, "I just made you some *mozkor-salda*. Maite made me put so much garlic in it that we will scare the *gripa* back to where it came from!"

Maite examined her daughter from across the room, "*Haurra*, you need to eat all of it. Or I will have to take you to the *medikua* to get a big shot in your *ipurdia* like Victor." She paused and added dryly, "But I'm sure you won't cry like he did."

Cackling at Maite's last words, Louise poured the steamy soup into a wide-rimmed bowl. With a wave of her hand, Louise beckoned Anna to follow her to the dining room. She set the bowl on the table closest to the kitchen and pulled out the wooden chair, "Sit. Eat. You look sad. Like your dog Pintto when he couldn't find the leg of lamb bone that he buried last week in Maite's garden."

Louise retreated to the kitchen. Dejected and cranky, Anna slumped down on the chair, stirring the hot soup aimlessly. The dining room was nearly empty; just a few of the boarders were lingering about. No hot lunch was being served that day—all efforts in the kitchen being devoted to the dinner preparation.

Sipping a cup of coffee and wearing his signature black *boneta*, Benat Cedarry sat just a few places down the long table, narrow glasses perched on his nose, reading the *Reno Evening Gazette*. Turning to Anna, he smiled indulgently, "You'd better eat that before Louise comes back. Or she will think you don't like her cooking."

Hunching her shoulders forward, with her elbows on the table in a way that would drive her mother crazy, Anna began eating her soup. The garlic was pungent, but the toasted bread in the broth was silky and soothing as she slurped it down.

At the middle table, Joanes Larralde leaned back in his chair, eating a simple meal of bread and cheese, a glass of red wine in front of him. Domingo Echeveste sat to his right, slicing an apple expertly with his pocketknife, before crunching down on it.

Looking up, Anna saw that someone had finished putting up the Christmas garland. The shiny red and green looked festive circling the cream-colored walls. Louise had probably asked Antton to do it. The older woman had forbidden her husband from going up any ladders after an incident involving a squirrel, a cherry tree, and a shovel.

Domingo picked up the wine bottle nearby and topped off Larralde's glass for him, "I have some news. Catalina and I will be getting married soon."

"Congratulations," Larralde offered, sipping his wine. He paused, and mused, "Did you get her pregnant?"

Anna nearly choked on a piece of garlic. Eyes watering, she pretended not to hear the comment. Stirring slightly in his seat, Anna saw Benat grimace in disapproval at Larralde's crassness.

Anger briefly flushing Domingo's face, the sheep foreman ignored the question and replied in an even voice, "I asked her to marry me, and she said yes. I'm a lucky man."

"Well, felicitations, Echeveste." Raising his wine glass, Larralde saluted his employee. "When is the big day?"

"Sometime in the next couple of months. We plan to meet with the priest this week to find a date. She wants to have the luncheon here at the hotel. Something simple and small. You are invited, of course."

With a white rag over his shoulder, Antton strolled into the dining room and grabbed a piece of bread and cheese from the platter on the table near Larralde and Domingo. Starting to turn away, he paused when Larralde said, "Echeveste is getting married! We should have a toast tonight. Save a bottle of champagne at the bar."

Pretending that Larralde hadn't spoken, Antton pivoted to Domingo, his expression pleased, "*Zorionak*! Catalina is a nice girl."

"Thank you, Garai. Yes, she is. I do hope you can come to the wedding," Domingo answered.

"I wouldn't miss it." With a grin, Antton tore off a large bite of bread, "I think I will steal a dance with the bride. To show her what she is missing by not choosing me."

"Hands off," Domingo laughed.

Larralde interrupted with a leer, "Don't worry, I don't think your dear Catalina is the one for him."

Antton flashed an uneasy glance to the hotel owner sitting across the room pretending not to be listening to their conversation. The bartender gritted his teeth, "Joanes, let's not change the subject away from Domingo's happy news. *Bai*?"

"Fine. Well, I'm sure in about seven months there will be even more happy news," Larralde smiled at his own joke.

"Ahem—" From across the room Benat cleared his throat in obvious displeasure and straightened his newspaper with a snap.

Taking that as his cue to leave, Antton gratefully left the dining room. Domingo's strong fingers squeezed the hilt of the pocketknife still in his hand—as he clearly searched for words. Finally, he tucked the knife away and rummaged in the pocket of his shirt, pulling out a folded piece of lined paper.

"I wanted to talk to you about the savings account you set up for me when I started working for you. With 10 percent of my wages going into the account for the past five years, I have nearly $800 saved up." Domingo paused, and gathered himself, "Now that Catalina and I are getting married, I will need to find a place for us to live. She can't keep living with old Mrs. Frunz and I can't keep living here. Earlier this week, the property office in Minden wrote to me. They found us a small house. The owner died recently and the home needs work, but we are young and can do that ourselves. The down payment is $575. So, I will need the money from my account this week."

Larralde reached for another piece of bread and cheese. Taking his time, he sandwiched the cheese inside and took a bite. After a moment, he said, "These things take time."

Dark eyebrows furrowing in confusion, Domingo retorted, "How long will it take? I don't want the house to go to someone else."

"Well, the stock market has been very bad lately. Many companies have been losing money. Investments are losing value," Larralde explained. He couldn't quite meet Domingo's eye.

"What does that even mean?" Alarm had raised the younger man's voice. He straightened in his chair.

"It means that your account is worth less than you think," Larralde answered.

"How much less?" Domingo's face had gone pale.

Larralde paused, searching for words. "It . . . it . . . it is worth about—" Clearly doing some calculating in his head, Larralde finally admitted, "$250." A flush of obstinance had replaced the embarrassment on his face.

"Two hundred fifty dollars!?" Domingo shot up in his chair and leaned forward onto the table in front of his boss, "How is that possible?"

Tilting his head, he allowed, "These things happen sometimes." Then, he grew defensive, a frown pulling at his oily face, "You—you just don't know how business works."

The rest of her soup forgotten, Anna shot a glance down to Benat. The hotel owner had given up all pretense of his newspaper and was openly watching the exchange between the two men.

"I trusted you with my savings," Domingo said the words slowly, as if the realization of what had happened settled over him. "You lost my money." The foreman's tone was flat. Lifeless.

"I will get you $250 by the end of the week," Larralde said quickly.

Domingo said nothing. A faraway look was on his face. Then, he stood up. His gaze straight on his employer, he said, "You stole my money. There was never any savings account at all. You just put the money in your pocket. Like a thief. *Lapurra.*"

"I am not a th—"

"Shut your mouth," Domingo's words cut like a knife.

Larralde pushed back from the table, his temper flaring, "Don't you dare talk to me like that, *bizkaino porkeria*." Dirty man from Bizkaia.

Domingo grabbed Larralde by the front of his shirt. He pulled him forward roughly, knocking over his glass of red wine. He bit out, "Say that one more time."

Abandoning his coffee and newspaper, Benat walked towards the men, "*Gizonak*, not in front of the little girl."

"He called me a thief," Larralde spat.

Benat turned to the sheepman, "I've heard stories that you did this once to another sheepherder in California. I wondered if it was just gossip. After all, in twenty years of owning this hotel, I've heard a lot of stories about a lot of people. But now I believe that story about you was true."

Domingo released Larralde's shirt, and the older man stumbled backward—hitting the table behind him. In a low rage, the camp-tender hissed, "*Kriminal.*"

Undaunted, Larralde dug in, "I am not a criminal. I invested your money as I promised you I would. B—but the investment lost value. It happens."

Benat interrupted with a snort, "As the *amerikanoak* say—Bull. Shit."

Domingo's dark eyes flashed, his hands shook, "You have stolen my future. And my Catalina's future. You will pay for this."

The boardinghouse owner rubbed the back of his neck and considered Larralde with a critical eye, "I will not have trouble in my hotel. Joanes, you have one week to find a new place to live."

Larralde's mouth dropped open, "You are kicking me out of the boarding-house? You believe this man's lies?"

Domingo began to lean forward again, but Benat's arm was surprisingly swift and strong for a man his age. He pushed him back—squeezing his shoulder, "Stop, Echeveste. He will never admit what he has done. Not ever."

Backing away from the men, Larralde's mouth quivered in rage, "I will easily find another place to live. This place is terrible. Dirty. Like a house of *putas*."

As if withdrawing patience from a vat inside his belly, the elderly man rubbed the front of his flannel shirt slowly. He sighed heavily, "Just go to your room now, Larralde. Before I let this man kill you right in the middle of the dining room floor."

CHAPTER SIX

From her warm bed, Anna watched through her window as the snow and fog covered the late afternoon light. She could hear the distant rumble of voices beginning to enter the hotel—cocktail hour and appetizers began at 5:00 pm. Anna coughed and buried her head in the blankets. She was so sad to miss the Christmas party. After the excitement at lunchtime in the dining room, Louise had shuffled her out of the room and Maite forced her back to bed. While she knew it was mainly because she was so ill, Anna realized that the women were probably more afraid she would witness something even more inappropriate for a fourteen-year-old girl. This disappointed her. She could handle more than they thought—obviously. After all, she was already driving, reading novels about murders, and successfully keeping secrets about pregnancies. She didn't want to brag, but she felt prepared for just about anything. And if she weren't, she'd just go to the library and get a book about it.

If Mrs. McGillicuddy protested, she'd just hide the book in her knapsack and return it later without telling her.

Problem solved.

The blanket over her head wasn't doing much to block the sound of the party gathering in the main part of the building. How annoying. Anna flung the bedclothes off her head and stared at the ceiling. She heard footsteps as the boarders changed into their "Sunday best" for the festivities.

Maybe she should read. That usually made her feel better. Scooting up in bed, she reached to flip on the lamp. Opening her nightstand, she pulled out *Death on the Nile* and laid it on her chest. Idly, she flipped the book to the spot she'd marked with a spearmint wrapper. She supposed returning the book smelling like wintergreen was an improvement from garlic soup. At least the fussy librarian wouldn't think she'd been hunting vampires again.

31

"Anna? *Chica?*" Catalina's voice sounded from their apartment, and a gentle knock rattled the accordion door to her tiny room.

"I'm awake!"

Sliding open the door with one hand, Catalina held a steaming mug in the other, "*El remedio de mi abuelita. Miel, canela y mucho, mucho limón.*"

Anna leaned forward to grasp the warm mug in her hands. She sniffed it. Even with her stuffy head, she could still smell the honey, cinnamon, and lemon. The steam tickled her nose. She took a sip. It was like a warm hug that went down her middle. "Gracias, Catalina."

"*De nada.* I hope you feel better soon. We will miss you tonight. Domingo will have no one to dance all the Basque dances with. I am still learning them. My big feet are too clumsy!" Catalina laughed good-naturedly. The young woman smoothed the blanket at the end of Anna's bed by habit, tucking it in the corner. She was wearing a dark blue dress with white polka dots. Her shiny brown hair was caught up in a bun behind one ear. That evening was to be the announcement of their engagement. But the scene in the dining room earlier had cast a dark cloud over the happy day. Anna could see a tightness is Catalina's normally joyful face.

Drinking her *remedio*, Anna ventured, "Are you okay, Catalina? It was a terrible afternoon and I'm so sorry all that happened. It's upsetting, I'm sure."

"*Sí,*" Catalina's eyes filled, but no tears fell. Her voice was steady as she continued, "But, I love Domingo and I also trust in God to provide for us. I have been praying to *La Virgen.*"

"I will pray, too," Anna promised. "Something will work out. It must."

Head shaking to clear away the sadness, Catalina stepped back, "Anyway, you don't have to worry about a thing. Señora Sagouspe brought her daughter to help serve the food, and Louise asked their neighbor to send her niece over. It's some blonde *americana* named Barbara."

"Oh, I know her. She goes to my school. She came once to help here during an anniversary party for some Americans in June. She did well. She didn't drop any plates, so that was a good sign."

"Maite would never forgive her if she dropped oxtail stew on the floor."

Anna laughed, and then coughed. She drank a big gulp of her *remedio* to soothe her throat.

"*Pobrecita,*" Catalina fretted, "Rest. *Tu madre* said she'll check on you later."

And, with that, Catalina returned to the party.

On the Nile riverboat, the murderer was about to be revealed by the famous detective, Hercule Poirot. Anna turned the pages with increasing speed, eager to reach the end.

"*Haurra?*" Maite pulled open the door to gaze at her daughter as she lay abed. Wearing a festive red apron over her dark dress, Maite was steadying a small dinner tray with her arm. There was a bowl of butternut squash soup and a small plate of bread and butter. Setting the tray on the nightstand, Maite laid the back of her palm on her daughter's forehead, "Feels cooler than earlier." She eyed Anna's book and her voice turned teasing, "You must feel better if you are reading one of your books."

"I can feel terrible and still want to read," Anna admitted.

Maite laughed, "*Bai*—Don't I know it!"

"How is the party?"

"It is fine. The girls are serving dessert soon. And then the music will start." Maite pointed to the tray, "Eat your soup. Time for me to start cleaning the kitchen. Those little elves are busy with *Papa Noel* until Christmas next week. So, they can't clean the pots for me."

Anna smiled sadly, "I'm sorry I can't help you, Ama. I feel bad."

Maite waved off her words with a tsk, "There will be plenty of work to do when you are feeling better. I don't want you spreading *gripa* all over the hotel. These men are too weak to handle it."

As Anna sipped more soup, Maite told her that Teresa would bring her a full plate of food after she takes a dinner tray up to Larralde's room, if she's still hungry.

"I think I'm fine with the soup." Anna leaned forward, "Joanes didn't come to the party?"

"*Ez.* It's the smartest thing that man has done in a while. He told Antton to have us send a plate upstairs, instead. It's for the best. No one wants a fight at a Christmas party."

"Joanes deserves to get punched, I think."

"*Haurra*, he probably deserves even more than that. The sooner he leaves this hotel, the better. For everyone."

Her mother left, and Anna finished her soup. The sound of accordion music filtered through the walls. Growing sad to be missing out, Anna picked up her book and continued to read. Her eyelids grew heavy, but she fought sleep until she managed to read the very last page. Satisfied that the mystery had been solved, Anna clicked off her lamp.

The faint music lulled her. She heard the notes of a waltz, the murmurs of goodbyes—and then she heard nothing more. Anna fell asleep, not moving a muscle—until the sound of a scream jolted her from her slumber.

PART TWO

The Sierra Hotel

1st Floor

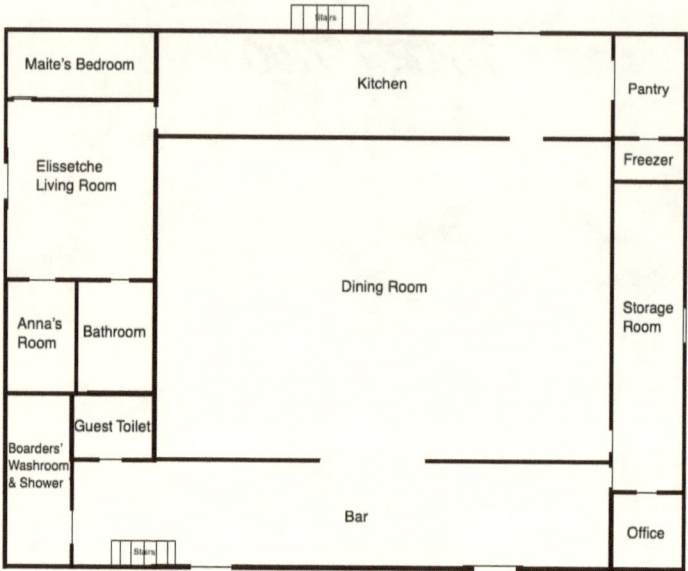

Front Porch

2nd Floor

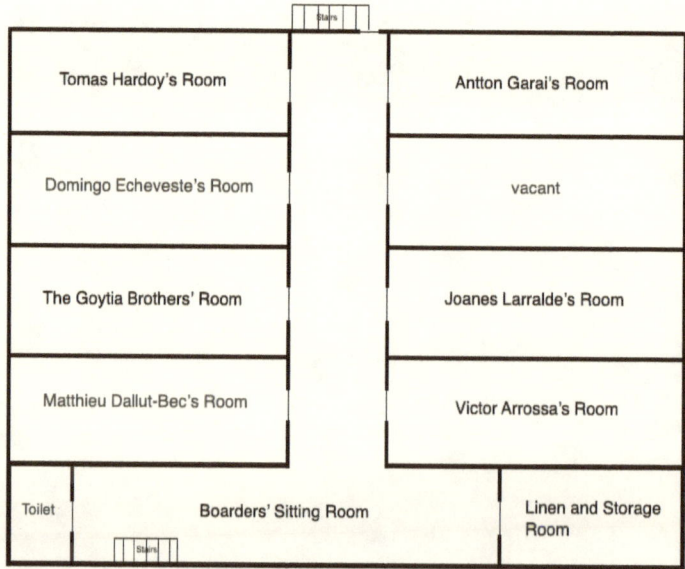

From Anna Elissetche's Secret Murder Journal

(Hidden under her mattress next to all the books she's ~~stolen~~ borrowed from the library.)

Tuesday
December 21, 1943

So much has happened in the last day and a half, that I don't know where to begin. I hope you'll forgive me if my brain is a little scattered. I'm still slightly feverish from the gripa and my right eye has developed a twitch. I'm pretty sure it's because my eyes have been watering for two days, but it could be due to stress since I've been witness to a murder.

<u>I've been witness to a murder!</u>

I underlined it because I still can't believe it. There was a murder in the boardinghouse. Where I live. Can you believe it? I know I most definitely can't.

Okay, so I actually didn't witness it happening. Not directly. But I did see the dead body and all the blood and that's practically the same thing, right?

I should probably back up a little.

Yesterday, I woke up to the sound of Teresa screaming bloody murder. I know that's an expression that Americans use ("screaming bloody murder") but it turns out that it's a thing that actually happens. And it's a horrible sound. No wonder people use that expression. Now I know why people don't say "She screamed bloody murder because she won a pair of nylons playing bingo." Rather, it's because it's got to be something bad. Something so horrific, terrible, and ghastly that every teeny hair on your body stands up and yells, "WHAT IS GOING ON? GET YOUR IPURDIA OUT OF BED!"

Yes, I know I use too many adjectives.

My English teacher Miss Gleason says it's a lazy habit and that I need to stop. But that woman has NEVER BEEN A WITNESS TO A MURDER, so what does she know? She's never had to describe that feeling you get when a scream wakes you up from a dead sleep (excuse the pun) to find AN UN-ALIVE PERSON LAYING

IN A POOL OF THEIR OWN BLOOD. After all, the biggest excitement in Miss Gleason's life was when she got her cat to wear the bonnet she knitted for him without getting her long and pointy face scratched.

So, I jumped out of bed and pulled off the pillow that had stuck to my face by gripa mucus and ran out of my room. Following the sound of Teresa's screams, I dashed through the first floor, and up the stairs to the landing. Ama was a few yards ahead of me. In the hallway of the boarders' rooms, I could see Teresa standing outside of Joanes Larralde's room, a shattered set of dishes at her feet. Bright yellow egg yolk splattered her white apron, and coffee was running across the wood grains of the floors.

Teresa was muttering, "He asked me to bring up breakfast today. He asked me. But . . . But . . ." Her light eyes were wide with shock. Ama pulled Teresa back a few steps while the hallway filled with the other boarders who had been eating breakfast down in the dining room. Everyone was breathing heavily.

Fermin Goytia stepped forward to look inside Joanes's room. "Diós." His brother Manuel did the same and made a hasty Sign of the Cross, a pallor settling over his tan face.

Before I knew what my feet were doing, I stepped forward to look into the room. So horrified by what I saw, I didn't feel Ama's strong hands pull me back from the scene.

But I had seen enough. That image imprinted itself in my brain forever.

Joanes Larralde was laying on the floor near the bed. His blood was all over the floor. I could see that his throat had been cut, and a pocketknife lay on the floor next to him. His skin was grey and lifeless. The room had been ransacked. The lamp by the bed had fallen over. The nightstand was askew. The chair by the small table was flipped over. The dresser drawers were open—Joanes Larralde's clothes were spilling out in a waterfall of stained underwear.

The man was too cheap to buy fresh underwear, apparently. I wish I could say that I didn't have that thought while I stared at the scene of his death, but I did. I nearly said it out loud, too. Which would have embarrassed Ama and caused her to spank me for the first time since 1936. My ipurdia still remembers that day.

Monsieur Dallut-Bec came to his senses first. Maybe it was because his bulbous nose created a larger pathway to his brain. The Frenchman told us all to back away from the door. "Do not touch anything. This must be investigated," he said. "Someone must call the police."

It was in this moment that I realized that Joanes Larralde had been murdered. On purpose. I should have figured it out immediately upon seeing this heinous scene, but my excuse is that I'm 14. The most violent thing I'd ever seen in real life was Benat hunting down a cottontail rabbit on my first Easter Sunday in Nevada. He skinned it, roasted it in white wine, and then tried to convince me that I wasn't eating the Easter Bunny.

"I'll call the police." I tried to say this in the calmest, most grown-up voice I could muster. Not the voice of a person that didn't like the dark. (Which was not me. No, it was not.)

Ama took charge. "Antton, go with her. I'm going to take Teresa to the bar and give her a shot of brandy to calm her down. I think she is going to faint. Gizonak, go downstairs right now so we can wait for the polizia."

I'd like to say that my hand wasn't shaking when I called the operator, but I've decided not to lie in this journal. After I placed the call, Antton squeezed my shoulder, "Are you alright, neska ttipia?" I told him that I was. But I really wasn't—for two reasons.

#1. I had just seen a dead body and Joanes Larralde's dirty underwear.

#2. Antton Garai was squeezing my shoulder in the mostly lovely, caring, amazing, and <u>stupendous</u> way. I thought I was going to die. (Maybe that's a bad analogy to use right now.)

Before we left to join the others in the bar, Antton said, "I think we should call Mitchell Lauden. He's a lawyer, he knows the polizia, and he was here last night for the party. He would want to know."

It was a good suggestion (Antton is handsome <u>and</u> clever). But first I did make Antton tell me whether Mr. Lauden had brought Bridget Farquhar to the party. I really wanted him to marry her and have lots of cherubic, blonde children. The kind I saw on the greeting cards at the drugstore in Carson City.

I was disappointed when Antton told me that Mr. Lauden had come alone. He seemed annoyed by my question. Perhaps because I was suddenly distracted by Mitchell Lauden's romantic life and not the blood that was seeping into the floorboards of the hotel.

Maybe Antton wasn't wrong to be annoyed.

I left a message with Mr. Lauden's secretary after being connected to his office. I kept the details to a minimum. I didn't think his elderly secretary would want to hear about Larralde's waxy, dead skin, or that I now knew that he hadn't bought new underwear since Herbert Hoover was president.

We waited in the bar with the others until the sheriff arrived. Teresa's pale face now had blooms of color on her cheeks. I suspected Ama had given her more than one shot of whiskey. I was tempted to ask for one myself, but I decided I needed to keep my wits about me. Because THERE HAD JUST BEEN A MURDER.

I'm sorry I keep writing this in obnoxious capital letters, but I still need to convince myself that what I saw was real.

About thirty minutes later, Sheriff Hiram Williams arrived. Tall, with carrot-colored hair threaded with grey, and imposing. A well-polished Douglas County Sheriff badge was pinned on his tan canvas shirt, and he walked with a sort of limp. He looked far more tired than a man his age ought to look. I felt bad for him.

His day wasn't going to get much easier. Because THERE HAD BEEN A MURDER AT THE BOARDINGHOUSE.

Okay, I really should stop that.

The middle-aged sheriff's deputy with him looked even older than the sheriff. He was hunched over his notebook, scrawling words with an arthritic hand. I supposed most of the younger men were off to the war. So they weren't available to help the local sheriff's department deal with the break-ins, drunken squabbles, and livestock-thieving that happened in this part of Nevada. (Last spring, my classmate Lester tried to rob the bank for money to buy a box of bottle rockets, but someone recognized him by his paint-splattered boots and reported him to Sheriff Williams. He took the case to Lester's grandfather, who proceeded to kick his grandson's ipurdia from here to Tuesday. For three weeks, he couldn't sit in his desk at school without wincing.)

No wonder Sheriff Williams looked so tired. People really did stupid things. LIKE MURDER PEOPLE IN BOARDINGHOUSES.

Puta, I did it again.

(Please don't tell Ama I said puta.)

Soon after arriving, the sheriff went upstairs to examine the scene. He told all of us to remain in the bar until he returned. Ama passed out another round of brandy because Teresa started looking green again. While the Goytia brothers tried to break the awkwardness with chit-chat, Victor Arrossa appeared to have missed the commotion upstairs altogether—he was blissfully sitting at a round table by the front window extracting dirt from under his fingernails. Since Victor had been retired for ten years, I wasn't quite sure what that dirt actually was.

I was pretty sure I didn't want to know.

Antton busied himself tidying up the bar and polishing liquor bottles, but Domingo and Tomas Hardoy stood around looking incredibly uncomfortable. Shifting from one foot to the other, both men looked ready to bolt from the hotel like spooked mustangs.

Even though it was probably only minutes, it felt like the sheriff had been upstairs for hours. Finally, when he descended the front staircase, his hat was in his hand, and he was spinning it thoughtfully. His deputy was not with him.

"Well, yes, he's been murdered, alright. Can I use the telephone to call the coroner? Deputy Arnold will stay with the body until he arrives." He paused and cast a wide glance around the room, stopping in turn on each man in the room. Except Victor, of course, because the older man was currently sniffing his fingernails like he had something delicious under his cuticles.

"I'm going to need all of you to answer some questions for me."

And that's when I knew that this was all <u>very</u> real.

It's Still Tuesday
December 21, 1943

I'm sorry for cutting my last entry short, but my hand started to cramp, and Ama called me to help her start making dinner for the boarders. Teresa isn't coming to work this week since the hotel will be closed to outside diners. (The sheriff advised the Cedarrys that this would be the wisest course of action until this whole matter is resolved.)

It is a good thing, too, because poor Teresa was quite distraught yesterday. She barely made it through her questioning by the sheriff. Given the language barriers (since the sheriff doesn't speak Basque and most of the folks at The Sierra Hotel only speak enough English to order ham and eggs at the coffee shop or to ask the gas station worker to put ten gallons of gasolina in the tank), I've been helping to translate the sheriff's questions and the witness responses. (More on that later to come!) During Teresa's entire interview, she was shaking, and tears bubbled up in her eyes, making her long face look like a mountain trout. Her uncle, Benat, nearly had to carry her like a sack of patatak to get her into his car and drive her home.

Ama is letting me stay home from school this week, as well, as my cough still sounds like a gerbil might be ejected from my body at any moment. I'm glad for this as it helps me to complete my secret mission . . .

Solving the murder.

Yes, you heard me correctly. I'm going to solve the murder of Joanes Larralde because I'm certain that the sheriff can't do it without me.

So, this morning I went digging in the trunk by my bed and found the purple journal that Louise Cedarry gave me for Christmas last year. I hadn't touched it since she gave it to me because reading books is way more fun than writing inside of an empty one. Besides, what would I have said, anyway? My life really wasn't that interesting.

UNTIL NOW.

This will be the place where I document all my thoughts, notes, and theories. It will be a real detective journal, because as a person who has read every mystery novel at the Douglas County Library, I think I am more qualified than Deputy Arnold (who is clearly not up to the task).

A tricky part of this whole thing will be trying not to annoy Sheriff Williams—yet being friendly and chummy enough that he will tell me the things I need/want/<u>must</u> know. I suspect this may become a problem, but I've decided that I must push on, anyway. He does need me to help with some of the translating for most of his interviews, though, so this is to my benefit.

Ama will be harder to fool, though. And it is essential that she does not know that I am planning on conducting my own investigation. Because if she finds out I'm doing that, she'll keep me so busy peeling garlic and onions, that I won't have time to do anything else. My hands will smell so bad that no one will want to sit next to me in school when classes start again in January. I will be a pariah who has no friends, eats lunch alone, and mumbles about dead bodies.

I must go now. It's 6pm. Time for me to ring the cow bell to let the boarders know that dinner is ready. "Because herding men to dinner is like herding animals." Ama always says that. "Ring a bell, and they will come. Like silly, stinky sheep."

Anyway, later I'll try to add some notes from some of the interviews I helped with yesterday. More interviews will be to come because the sheriff said he'd be returning to the hotel for more questioning in the coming days.

Everyone at The Sierra Hotel the night of the party is a potential suspect. This is basically every Basque person from ten miles around. (Which, according to Benat, is the maximum distance that a donkey has ever walked without taking a poop or biting someone.)

This might be harder than I thought.

CASE NO: 22-43

NAME OF DECEASED: Larralde, Jean

RESIDENCE OF DECEASED: The Sierra Hotel, Hwy 395, Gardnerville

DATE OF DEATH: est 12/19/43, body found 12/20/43.

Persons of Interest — Attendees of Party, 12/19/43

Achaval, Elena
Achaval, Joseba
Achaval, Santiago
Achaval, Xavier
Alpetche, Marie
Alpetche, Martin
Arretche, Gabriel
Arrossa, Victor
Bicary, Jean-Baptiste
Biscaichipy, Pierrot
Cedarry, Bernard
Cedarry, Louise
Culebro, Jose
Dallut-Bec, Matthieu
Echeverria, Pedro
Echeveste, Domingo
Elissetche, Anna
Elissetche, Maite
Espinal, Melxor
Garai, Antton
Garcia, Alejandra
Goytia, Fermin
Goytia, Manuel
Hardoy, Thomas
Harguindeguy, Teresa
Higgs, Barbara
Istillart, Gracie
Istillart, Maitexa
Istillart, Pettan
Lassa, Mixel

Lassa, Rosie
Lauden, Mitchell
Mendiburu, Carmen
Mendiburu, Mariana
Mendiburu, Nicolas
Pascoal, Jean
Paulsson, Janie
Paulsson, Lester
Richter, Fred
Richter, Helen
Rodriguez, Catalina
Rodriguez, Ernesto
Sagouspe, Jenny
Sagouspe, Manes
Sagouspe, Marie
Sarratea, Emelia
Sarratea, Gregorio
Sarratea, Miguel
Sarratea, Roberto
Underwood, Clara
Underwood, Pete
Zubillaga, Carlos
Zubillaga, Ignacio
Zubillaga, Luisita
Zubillaga, Maria
Zubillaga, Pilar

From Anna Elissetche's Secret Murder Journal

(Laying open on top on her chest because she fell asleep with her pen in her hand. She also got ink on her sheets.)

Wednesday
December 22, 1943

Yikes, I fell asleep last night before I could write more in my journal. I'm disappointed in myself, because detectives aren't supposed to sleep on the job unless they are the silly detectives at the beginning of the novel that are too stupid to solve the crime themselves without the experienced outsider coming to town to do it for them.

Anyway, I forgot to document an important piece of information in my last entry. I just woke up, so I wanted to get this down on paper before I go help Ama with breakfast.

So, when the coroner, and his assistant, arrived yesterday around midday, they went upstairs with a small Kodak camera to photograph the scene and to give the sheriff the initial analysis before removing the body. While the others were distracted in the bar, I snuck upstairs (no one pays much attention to a 14-year-old who is short enough to be an 11-year-old).

I sat in the chair closest to the hallway and picked up an old, yellowing issue of *Le Figaro* from the small table in the sitting area. I opened it and pretended to read while I heard the men talking in Larralde's room. I could hear a series of "clicks" as the coroner took photos.

I could tell they had moved into the hallway because their voices got louder.

"What is your estimate for the time of death?"

"It's hard to say, Hiram, but from the way the body looks now, I would put it between 9pm and midnight last night. Give or take. I may have more details on that for you in the next few days as I work on my report."

"Okay, thanks, Elias. Do you need help removing the body?"

"We've got it. The deceased isn't a tall man, so it shouldn't be hard to get him onto the gurney. It's gonna be quite a mess for the hotel to clean up, though. I don't think there's much blood left in this body."

"I'll leave you to it, then. I better go check on my suspects downstairs. I sent Arnold down to stay with them when you arrived. He won't be much resistance if one of them tries to make a run for it."

"You think one of them did it?"

"More likely than not, but we'll see how it goes. There was a Christmas party full of guests last night at the hotel, too, which complicates matters. I'm getting too old for this shit."

"You're younger than me!"

"But you didn't get a bum hip because a drunken husband thought you were the man sleeping with his wife and shot you with a Colt 45."

"*Were* you sleeping with his wife?"

"No!! Are you kidding? Marjorie would shoot me dead if I did that. And she wouldn't just wound me."

"What were you doing there?"

"We got a report that a man was trying to shoot every tall man that he saw."

"It's a thankless job being a sheriff."

"Don't I know it. At least the people you see every day are already dead."

Their conversation trailed off. Heavy footsteps moved in my direction. Then, they stopped. I held the brittle newspaper up to my face like a shield.

"Excuse me? What are you doing up here?"

I pretended that he wasn't talking to me. Even though there was no one else there.

"Hello?" he persisted.

I played it cool and slowly lowered the paper, "Oh, hello. I was just doing a little reading."

His eyes narrowed, "That newspaper looks older than you are."

"It's from France. Which sadly isn't even its own country at the moment." I wasn't hopeful I could lure him into a conversation about world events. He seemed more of a "local news only" kind of fellow.

"You're the cook's daughter, right?"

"Yes, we live here in the boardinghouse in a small apartment off the kitchen."

"Is there a particular reason you're sitting up here lurking?"

"I wouldn't call it lurking," I protested.

The big man crossed his arms over his chest, "It's lurking."

"Well . . . I—I just wanted to offer my assistance to you in this case. I'd like to see it solved."

"Obviously, I would as well." He was quickly losing his patience with me. I saw that same look on my mother's face at least twice a week.

Casting aside the newspaper, I sat forward in the worn armchair, "Have you ever solved a murder in a Basque boardinghouse?"

His voice was dry. "It doesn't happen regularly. So, no."

"It's a good thing it doesn't. Because if people were getting murdered all the time then less people would stay at boardinghouses. And then my mother wouldn't have anyone to cook for."

"Listen, kid. Stop yappin' and tell me what you want."

"You're going to need a translator."

"Excuse me?"

"Someone to help you learn about the hotel, interview witnesses and the boarders. I can do that. Do you have any Basque translators on retainer at the sheriff's office?"

"You know I don't."

"Well, then it's all settled."

"Not really, no. It is most definitely not settled. While I agree that I will need some assistance with some of this, I don't think it will be you. You are a kid."

"I'm much more mature than I look. I know how to shoot a gun and how to make a really good Picon. I also know how to drive."

"Excuse me?" His eyebrow rose.

"Never mind," I added hastily.

The sheriff sighed and ran a hand through his hair. "Fine. You can help. But, only with translating the interviews."

"Deal!" I extended my hand to shake his.

"We'll start with the person that found the body."

Witness Interview
(Property of the Douglas County Sheriff)

Case No: 22-43
Date: Mon, 12/20/43
Time: 10:15am
Witness: Teresa Harguindeguy (Anna Elissetche, interpreter)
Interviewing Officer: H. Williams

HW: I understand you were the last person to see Jean Larralde alive. Is that correct?

AE: *We call him Joanes, not Jean.*

HW: Okay. I understand you were the last person to see **Joanes** Larralde alive?

AE: *I just want you to have it correct in your record.*

HW: Fine. Okay. Will you ask her the question now?

AE: *Yes.*

TH: I was the last person to see Joanes alive, yes.

HW: Now what time was this?

TH: I brought up a dinner tray to his room at around 7pm. Just after we served dinner to the party guests.

HW: How did Mr. Larralde seem to you when you saw him? What was his demeanor like?

AE: *I don't know the word for 'demeanor' in Basque.*

HW: Well, then just use another word.

TH: When I saw him, Joanes seemed angry. He's often cranky, but this time he was more so. And his breath stunk of whiskey more than usual. I could smell it when he opened the door.

HW: Did you see anyone else upstairs?

TH: No, I saw no one else. Everyone was at the party.

HW: How many guests were at the party?

TH: We served 54 for dinner.

HW: Mr. Larralde was also a boarder in this hotel, is that correct?

TH: Yes.

HW: How many boarders live here?

TH: There are eight rooms for boarders. Right now, one is empty. But the Goytia brothers share a room, so there are eight boarders. Well, there are only seven now that Joanes is gone.

HW: You were the person to discover his body earlier this morning. Is that correct?

TH: Yes.

HW: Can you tell me about that?

AE: *She screamed so loud that I thought she was the one being murdered.*

HW: Miss Elissetche, can you please refrain from editorializing?

AE: *What do you mean?*

HW: It means that you need to just translate our words. That's it. Not do or say <u>anything</u> else. Can you do that?

AE: *Yes.*

HW: Are you sure? Because I might be able to get someone down from Reno to translate for me instead.

AE: *No! Please don't. I can do it. Promise.*

TH: I found the body when I took up a plate of breakfast to his room. He had asked me last night to bring another plate since he wouldn't be coming down for breakfast. When he didn't answer my knock, I pushed the door open to put the plate inside his room.

HW: Can I get you a tissue, Miss Teresa? I'm sure this is very upsetting.

AE: *I think she needs more whiskey.*

HW: What?

AE: *Ama gave Teresa a shot of whiskey before you arrived because she almost passed out from the shock.*

HW: I see.

TH: I could not believe what I saw. It was horrible.

HW: Yes. It is tragic. How long have you worked at the hotel?

TH: Three years. I started when I came to live with my uncle and aunt. They own this hotel.

HW: So, how well do you know Mr. Larralde? What kind of person was he?

TH: I don't really know him well. I help Maite in the kitchen with the cooking and I help carrying out the platters and bowls during meals. Other than that, I don't speak to him.

HW: But what is your impression of him? You seem like a perceptive young lady. What have you noticed about him?

TH: He has a habit of rubbing people the wrong way.

HW: I see. Do you think there are people who may have wished him harm?

TH: There were few people who didn't.

From Anna Elissetche's Secret Murder Journal

(Still hidden under her mattress.)

It's Still Wednesday
December 22, 1943

I think I just overheard something I wasn't meant to hear. After I hid my journal under my mattress and was heading out to help Ama with breakfast (since Teresa wasn't coming), I heard a low, anxious voice talking to my mother. I had my hand on the doorknob to the kitchen. Dropping my hand, I pressed my ear to the door.

"Tomas, you need to calm down."

"What am I going to do? I'm going to go to prison. Or, worse, get deported back to Urepel."

"What's wrong with Urepel? It's a completely fine place to be from. It's not like it's a boiling desert or one of those terrible places in Russia where the ground is always frozen and the men have to grow large beards just to keep their faces warm."

"You only say that because you didn't have to live in Sagasti with my Aita."

"Was it so bad?"

"My ipurdia got beat every day for just breathing, so, yes, it was bad. Aita made cider for a restaurant in Donibane Garazi, but he drank more than he sold. When she was just 16, my sister, Michou, got a job as a nanny in Bordeaux just to get away from him. I left as soon as I was old enough, too."

"What did your father say when you decided to leave?"

"I didn't tell him. Since I was underage, I needed his signature on the documents, but I forged them myself. One day, when Aita sent me to take a load of cider to Garazi—he was too hungover to do it himself—I just never went back home. I used the money the restaurant gave for the shipment to help pay for my trip to America."

"Alcohol has ruined too many men."

"Sometimes I think Aita was ruined from the start."

50

"What about your Ama? What did she say?"

Tomas's voice grew sad, and he sounded remorseful now, "I worried about leaving my mother behind there. And my little brother and sister, too. But I was only 16; I couldn't really help them, could I? I could barely help myself get away."

"I understand. We do what we must sometimes."

"Now you know why I can't go back to Urepel. Prison would be better than that. But I still refuse to go to prison. I will run before that happens. I've done it before, I'll do it again."

"You are not going to prison. You need to just tell the truth about what you saw and what you know about Joanes. That's it."

"Let me use the phone to call my sister? Maybe I can stay in Bakersfield for a while." Determination had edged into his voice.

"You cannot run away. That is what guilty people do," Ama reasoned.

"Let me use the phone." Tomas was insistent.

"Tomas, sit down and drink your coffee. Nothing will be solved by you acting like an idiota." I had heard that tone from Ama many times. He was better off doing what she said.

"Fine. Don't help me, then."

Their voices stopped. When a few minutes passed where all I could hear were the sounds of cooking, I cautiously opened the door. Tomas was gone. Ama was alone in the room, slicing up bacon for the skillet. As always, she was standing on an orange crate so she could reach the counter.

"Morning, Ama." I went to make myself a cup of kafesnea for breakfast. I liked a little kafea, but a lot of esnea. It was a good way to distract me from my whirling thoughts about Tomas.

"Good morning, coucou," Ama replied. "Your colors look better. Is the gripa leaving?"

"Yes, finally. How about Victor?"

"He seems better. But his hearing is even worse now. I think the medikua needed to clean out his big ears with those water hoses that the amerikano firemen use."

"I bet you would enjoy doing that, Ama." It was just the thing my mother would relish. She also loved squeezing the blackheads that started appearing on my nose last year. A look would enter her eyes when she spotted one on me, and she'd approach with her strong fingers extended towards me, making a pinching motion like a scary praying mantis. It was no use trying to run away. Ama always won in the end.

Laying out the slices in the skillet, Ama turned to me, "Last night I spoke with

Louise. She wanted to offer that you could stay over at their house for a few days. At least until all this sheriff business is over. She said you could stay in Patricia's room since she's not coming home for the holiday."

"Wait. What? No!" I knew I was sputtering, but I didn't care. This would ruin all my plans. This could not happen.

"It's not a bad idea. Maybe it would be good if you were away. I don't think it's appropriate that you be a part of this."

"The Cedarrys live two blocks away. I'd be just as much a part of this there, as I am here." I tried to keep my voice calm and even. Like I wasn't as invested in her decision as I was. As if the kafesnea in my stomach didn't suddenly churn into a ball of nerves.

"I suppose. What kind of sheriff is this man anyway, letting you help him? Ba," Ama tsked and grumbled, which was her automatic response to anything that a man did that was silly, unreasonable, or stupid. Which obviously happened a lot.

"The sooner the investigation is over, the sooner this will all go away, and we can go back to our normal lives. Me helping him will make that go faster." I was shocked at how quickly these explanations were coming to me. My brain was on fire.

All the reading I had done in my life was paying off.

She slid the bacon onto a plate and cracked a few eggs into the bacon grease in the skillet. "That's true," Ama allowed.

I switched tactics to make sure Ama relented, "Besides, it's Christmas. I want to be home with you at Christmas."

With a long-suffering sigh, my mother surrendered. I had to squelch a cheer. Then Ama held up a spatula and pointed it at me, "But, if one more crazy thing happens, you are off to the Cedarrys!"

I knew to quit while I was ahead. "Okay. Yes. Fine."

<u>Witness Interview</u>
(Property of the Douglas County Sheriff)

Case No: 22-43
Date: Mon, 12/20/43
Time: 3:00pm
Witness: Thomas Hardoy (*Anna Elissetche, interpreter*)
Interviewing Officer: H. Williams

HW: What do you do for a living?

TH: I do all sorts of things.

HW: What kind of things?

TH: Sometimes I shear sheep. Other times, I haul feed for ranchers.

HW: You don't have a steady job?

TH: I don't like staying in one place too long.

HW: Do you have a hard time getting along with people?

AE: *Uhm . . . He's getting mad, sheriff.*

HW: Just ask the question, Anna.

TH: Everyone has a hard time getting along with people sometimes.

HW: Do they?

AE: *Sheriff . . .*

HW: Anna, you promised not to interfere with my questions.

TH: I've got a temper just like any man does. What's the big deal?

HW: Fair enough. But did Mr. Larralde ever give your temper a specific reason to . . . flare?

HW: Mr. Hardoy?

HW: Anna, tell him that he has to answer the question.

TH: Of course, he did. Joanes Larralde was a liar.

HW: What do you mean by that?

TH: He promised he would pay something, and then he didn't pay it.

HW: So, did he owe you money?

TH: Yes.

HW: Did this make you angry?

AE: Uhm, sir . . .

HW: Anna, for Pete's sake, ask the question!

TH: Yes, I was angry. And you would be, too.

HW: I see.

TH: Are we done now?

HW: Just a few more questions for now. Is that alright?

TH: Not really. But, okay.

HW: Did you attend the Christmas party last night?

TH: No, I did not.

HW: Why is that?

TH: I didn't feel very much like a Christmas party. So, I went to the casino in Carson City, instead.

HW: Is that all you did?

TH: Well, if you must know, I went to an establishment on the out-skirts of town that young ladies are not supposed to know about. I can tell you more about it, but I don't think you'd want me to, considering.

HW: Point noted.

AE: *What does he mean by that?*

HW: Never mind, Anna. Now what time did you return to the boardinghouse that night, Mr. Hardoy?

TH: It was very late. I was quite drunk and I don't remember the time.

HW: Did anyone see you get back?

TH: The party was over. Some girls were cleaning up the dining room and Antton was wiping off the bar. He did make me one last drink before I went up to bed.

HW: Did you see anyone when you went upstairs?

TH: No.

HW: Are you sure?

TH: Yes.

HW: I may want to ask you a few more questions in the coming days. Would that be alright?

TH: Do I have a choice?

HW: Not really, no.

From Anna Elissetche's Secret Murder Journal

(Still hidden under her mattress.)

Wednesday Night
December 22, 1943

It's funny how everyone thinks that I don't know what a whorehouse is. I live in Nevada. Of course, I know what it is.

And, if I didn't, I would have probably already have learned about it by now in one of the books I snuck borrowed from the library.

Anyway, Tomas Hardoy is digging himself quite a hole. At this point, I'm about 55% sure that he killed Joanes Larralde. But the case is definitely far from over.

Plus, I'm not very good at math. It's why Ama doesn't let me do any measurements. I always lose track during the middle of counting flour scoops. (It's a miracle my Thanksgiving pies turned into real pies and not meteorites.)

This afternoon, I saw Tomas settling his weekly bar and boarding tab with Benat. Tomas had a wad of bills that he pulled from the pocket of his jacket. I had never seen Tomas with so much money before. Especially considering he had been to the whorehouse. I knew those places weren't cheap.

Even Benat seemed surprised. Where did Tomas get that money? It couldn't be from the casino. No one won money at the casino. Not really. It was a place that usually took money from the boarders silly enough to go there—leaving them to beg Benat for an extension on their boarder fees. He'd usually agree if it was the first time the man had done it. Those casinos could be very enticing to young sheepherders who had never seen anything so fancy in all their lives. But, if the man made a habit of it, Benat would give the poor idiota the boot from the boardinghouse.

So, if Tomas didn't get his money from the casino (which, of course, he didn't), then where did he get it?

Tomorrow, I think it's time for me to look a little deeper into Tomas Hardoy.

Thursday
December 23, 1943

Basque men like to say that it's women who love to gossip, but I'm pretty sure it's the other way around. It's not women I see gathered around the dining room table on long afternoons, playing mus and drinking out of a brown mug that has more brandy than coffee in it. It's the older men who can spend thirty minutes arguing over which pilotari was the best in the summer of 1911—and whether that man had two illegitimate children, or just one, hiding in Zuberoa. It's the old men who know which rancher is broke, and which one is hiding all his money in an iron box by the Washoe River because he thinks Uncle Sam is going to steal it.

The women are far too busy to do these things, despite what the ruddy-faced men think.

Now that The Sierra Hotel has become the most exciting crime scene in Douglas County, all the Basque men decided that it was the place to come this morning for a cup of coffee on a cold December day. They filtered through the door like curious ferrets with bushy eyebrows and long noses—sniffing out gossip like a worm in the ground.

The dining room was officially closed to outside guests (other than the boarders), but that didn't stop the men from coming anyway. Antton fired up the coffee pot, opened a bottle (or two!) of brandy, and prepared to spend the morning learning about why the Basque men all knew that Joanes Larralde would eventually meet a terrible end. If it hadn't been now, then it would <u>definitely</u> have been soon. Probably before that Nazi with the scrawny mustache could be sent back to Alemania (seen as the worst country in the world by 82% of all Basque men).

So, when it was time to get the skinny on Tomas Hardoy, I knew just where to go. Not surprisingly, Tomas didn't much care for the old men—his temper didn't abide the teasing and ribbing that comes with their company. Plus, he preferred to lose $5 at the casino table than lose 50¢ to Ignacio Zubillaga's dobleak with two kings. Therefore, I could ask all the questions I wanted without worrying that Tomas Hardoy would overhear me.

I was very happy about this. I didn't want his temper turned on me—which would cause Ama to send me to the Cedarrys until I was old enough to vote. Or maybe longer.

Puffing on hand-rolled cigarettes that dropped tiny ashes all over the dining room table, the four older men picked up their cards—eying each other suspiciously to make sure no one was sending a sign to his partner. Ignacio Zubillaga—with his curly shock of salt and pepper hair—was sitting diagonally from Benat Cedarry, his mus partner for the morning. Ignacio had bright red suspenders that he liked to flick when he had three of a kind, or better. This habit was unnoticed by Victor Arrossa who tended to bet the whole game on a pair of aces if he'd had too much wine the night before. The foursome was rounded out by Michel Lassa—a white-haired retired masonry worker who was missing one finger after an Italian dropped a 50-pound brick on top of it. I was told that his scream could be heard two blocks away. To this day, Michel has refused to eat spaghetti—or anything made with marinara.

I approached the table with a platter of day-old bread, apple slices, and dried Monterey Jack cheese—the slim offerings that I could find in the kitchen after Ama agreed to feed the "nosy gizonak that shouldn't be here, anyway."

As they discarded unwanted cards, and waited for new ones, Ignacio's deep voice mused, "So, who do you think did it, anyway?"

Michel sat up straighter in his chair, clearly happy that the subject had been raised, without having to do it himself, "Oh, it must be that Hardoy boy. He's trouble, that one. I heard he got arrested in Fresno for punching a polizia in a bar. Spent three days in jail before his poor sister bailed him out."

"We had polizia here all week!" Victor added loudly, not hearing the rest of their conversation because of the zikina in his ears. "The sheriff is tall! He has a lot of questions. Talked to everyone but me, so far." He paused and scratched his head, "I don't know why."

Chuckling affectionately at his old boarder, Benat pivoted the conversation back on track, "I don't know. Hardoy seems pretty harmless. Pays mostly on time. That's a good sign. Says something about a man. But I could be wrong, I suppose."

Michel persisted, "I heard that wasn't the only time Hardoy's been in jail. I heard that he can't ever go back to Oregon because there's a warrant for his arrest because he stole a toolbox from a German farmer he worked for."

"Aleman putak!" Victor spewed a bit of apple flying from his mouth to land on the chips in the middle of the table.

I snorted before I could stop it.

"Victor!" Ignacio chided, casting an embarrassed glance my way. "We're sorry, neska. We're rude old men with nasty mouths."

Benat winked, "Oh, Anna has heard much worse than that over the years."

Michel clearly wasn't finished talking about the murder, though. "If you don't think it was Hardoy, who do you think it was?"

Losing his patience, Benat picked up his cards, "If I knew that, I could become a famous detective. I could sell this hotel and not have to share my brandy with you three!"

Ignacio took a sip of coffee, "There was a dining room full of Bascos that night. Including all of us. It could have been anyone there. I don't envy that sheriff."

"He was so tall!" Victor interjected.

Ignacio wasn't finished, "But, my money is on it being someone quieter. Hardoy is a loud, obnoxious fool. It could be him, yes, of course it could. It could be Victor, at that rate!"

"There's no way it was Victor," I mumbled.

Tapping his cards on the table, Ignacio added, "But you're forgetting the person with the most motive. The one that has a reason to kill Larralde. And he's clever and quiet enough to get the job done quickly and easily."

Michel leaned forward, enthralled as if this were a radio show, "Who? Who do you mean?"

Ignacio gave him an exasperated look.

"Domingo Echeveste."

Witness Interview
(Property of the Douglas County Sheriff)

Case No: 22-43
Date: Mon, 12/20/43
Time: 3:30pm
Witness: Domingo Echeveste *(Anna Elissetche, interpreter)*
Interviewing Officer: H. Williams

HW: I understand you are an employee of Mr. Larralde.

DE: Yes. I have worked for him for five years. I started as a sheep-herder, and now I am camp-tender.

HW: What does a camp-tender do?

AE: *The camp-tender helps run supplies to the sheepherders and manages—*

HW: I wasn't talking to you.

AE: *Sorry, I keep forgetting that.*

DE: The camp-tender manages the sheepherders for the owner. It's like being a foreman, but a little different.

HW: What did you do before you worked for Mr. Larralde?

DE: I picked oranges and fruit in Southern California for a season before making my way north to the Central Valley. I heard about local sheepmen needing workers when I had lunch at the Pyrenees Hotel one day in Stockton. Pierre Elissetche hired me. He was partnered with Joanes at the time. I've worked for them ever since.

HW: Where were you born?

DE: I come from Basauri. It's in Bizkaia.

AE: *That's in Spain . . . not far from Bilbao. Do you know where that is?*

HW: No, but I'm sure I can find a map or something. We have a bunch of National Geographic magazines laying around the sheriff's office.

AE: *I love National Geographic! Sometimes I steal them from the library.*

HW: I'm sorry, you what?

AE: *I meant that I borrow them. I always take them back, though. Always. It's just that Mrs. McGillicuddy thinks it's inappropriate for a young girl to read about "heathen people from faraway places that don't wear enough clothes." Those were her words, not mine.*

HW: Clearly. I doubt you're much fazed by that.

AE: *Of course not. After all, I grew up seeing men castrate lambs using only their teeth.*

HW: I really don't know what to say now.

AE: *Don't worry. There's far less blood than you'd think.*

HW: Anyway, Mr. Echeveste, when did you immigrate to America?

DE: In 1937. I took a ship to Mexico and then traveled north from there.

HW: Why Mexico?

DE: It was easier for me.

HW: Was there a reason why you left Spain? Did you have a job waiting for you here?

AE: *That's a silly question.*

HW: Why is that a silly question? Seems perfectly reasonable to me.

AE: *Why does any immigrant come to America? To work to build a better life than the one they left behind. Obviously. Where did your family come from?*

HW: I don't know. Probably England or something.

AE: *You don't know?*

HW: No, not really.

AE: *Don't you think that you should know? I doubt your family dropped fully-formed from the sky. Unless you are like the Greek goddess Athena who exploded out of her dad Zeus's head wearing a suit of armor and carrying a sword?*

HW: Jesus, I think you read too much.

AE: *Why do people keep telling me that?*

HW: Anyway, Mr. Echeveste, tell me about your employer. What was he like?

DE: There's not much to tell. He's like any other sheepman, I guess. He could be mean and cranky, but what old Basque man isn't?

HW: Did you get along with him?

DE: For the most part. I just did my job, and that's it. I don't like to make trouble or cause problems. I have no interest in any of that. Or getting involved in the fights and arguments that other sheepherders get into.

HW: Are you planning to keep managing the sheep now?

DE: Yes. It will need to be done until Mr. Larralde's family decides what to do with the business. I haven't thought much about it. The man has been dead less than a day.

HW: Were you at the Christmas party last evening?

DE: Yes, I was there with my fiancée Catalina.

HW: Did you see Mr. Larralde yesterday evening?

DE: No, he did not attend the party.

HW: Did you remain at the gathering the entire evening?

DE: Not the whole evening.

HW: Where did you go?

DE: I had to drop off Catalina to the house where she lives before it got too late. She helps take care of an old lady and she lives there with her. The poor lady worries if Catalina isn't home early enough.

HW: So, you didn't go upstairs at all that evening?

DE: No, I did. I had to get our coats which I had left in my room. It was a cold night and I didn't want Catalina to get sick.

HW: Did you see anyone upstairs?

DE: Not that I remember. Maybe just that French boarder, though? I think he was coming from the toilet? I don't quite remember.

HW: About what time was this?

DE: Maybe a little after 10pm?

HW: Thank you for your time. If I have more questions, can I reach out to you again?

DE: Of course. I have nothing to hide.

	INVENTORY REPORT
CASE NO: 22-43	DOUGLAS COUNTY SHERIFF
	STATE OF NEVADA

NAME OF DECEASED: Larralde, Jean

RESIDENCE OF DECEASED: The Sierra Hotel, Hwy 395, Gardnerville

DATE OF DEATH: est 12/19/43, body found 12/20/43

Cataloged items removed by investigators, 12/20/43, from scene

From Dresser:

—Top Drawer
Chesterfield cigarettes, brown boot polish, black boot polish, 2 combs, 1 straight razor
bar of shaving soap, 1 bottle of Old Spice aftershave lotion, 1 bottle of aspirin
1 toothbrush, 1 unopened tube of Colgate dental creme
6 white undershirts, 6 pairs of cotton briefs, 6 pairs of black socks
8 red cotton handkerchiefs, 1 clip-on tie, 1 empty trinket box

—Middle Drawer
3 pairs of size large Levi denim blue jeans, 2 pairs of black trousers size large
1 pair of gray trousers size large, 5 misc cotton western-style shirts large
3 flannel button-down shirts large, 2 white linen dress shirts, 1 black dress jacket
1 Colt 45 Revolver, loaded

—Bottom Drawer
El Principal cigar box filled with misc papers, receipts, and opened bills/mail
Including:
 — $119.66 bill from Carson Valley Hospital for patient Thomas Haraday
 — $11.97 invoice from Sears, Roebuck & Co
 — $47.87 income tax bill due 12/31/43
 — $89.76 receipt from Virginia Jewelers
 — $59.84 invoice from Laramie Insurance
 — $100.00 US war bond, maturation date 1/1/52
 — $75.00 US war bond, maturation date 1/1/52
 — quarterly statement from Wells Fargo Bank, Genoa. Total in deposit as of 9/30/43, $14,959.76

signed, 12/21/43

Hiram Williams

Hiram Williams
Sheriff
Douglas County, Nevada

Witness Interview
(Property of the Douglas County Sheriff)

Case No: 22-43
Date: Tues, 12/21/43
Time: 2:20pm
Witness: Matthieu Dallut-Bec (*Anna Elissetche,*
    interpreter)
Interviewing Officer: H. Williams

HW: I understand you've just been staying a short while at the boardinghouse.

MDB: Oui. Just a few weeks. I'm working on the altar at the church. I'm a sculptor and woodworker.

HW: Have you been to Nevada before?

MDB: Non, monsieur, this is the first time.

HW: So, you had never met any of these people before you began staying at the boardinghouse?

MDB: Non, I hadn't.

HW: Did you attend the Christmas party?

MDB: Oui. For a short while. I was getting over an illness, so I just listened to some of the music and went to bed early.

HW: About what time was that?

MDB: It was about 9:30.

HW: Did you see anyone upstairs when you went to bed?

MDB: Non. But I did see someone coming up the stairs when I went to the toilet a little later.

HW: Who did you see?

MDB: Domingo Echeveste.

HW: What time was this?

MDB: I'm not certain. But not too long after I went to bed.

HW: Did you speak to him? What did he say?

MDB: I wished him a good evening. He did the same. That's it.

HW: Did Mr. Echeveste seem agitated?

MDB: What does that word mean?

HW: Anna, please explain what I mean.

AE: *I don't really speak French.*

HW: I thought you did.

AE: *I don't. Basque people are not French. And they aren't Spanish, either. We're an odd kind of creature. Like a penguin that lives in a desert.*

HW: Penguins don't live in deserts. They live in cold places.

AE: *Well, Basque people can live in deserts OR in cold places.*

HW: Please stop.

AE: *I'm just saying . . .*

HW: Okay, if you don't speak French, then why are you here?

AE: *I thought you'd need my help.*

HW: With what?

AE: *With non-French related things. Like detective things.*

HW: You need to leave now.

From Anna Elissetche's Secret Murder Journal

(Hidden under her mattress, but this is probably not the best place, anymore.)

Thursday Night
December 23, 1943

Holy moly. I found a piece of evidence. I'm certain that I need to tell the sheriff AS SOON AS POSSIBLE because I think withholding evidence is a crime and I don't want to go to jail. I'm not sure they would actually send me to jail, but Ama would definitely take away my books for interfering in all this, and that would be the same thing as jail.

Maybe worse.

Okay, so, yes. I will tell Sheriff Williams about this first thing in the morning. But first I have to write all about it here.

This afternoon, Catalina asked me to help her strip and change the linens from the beds in the boarder rooms. She was collecting them for Mr. Li—who owns a laundry in Genoa and picks up the dirty linens each Friday. He returns them the following Friday when he makes his rounds into Gardnerville.

When I went into Tomas Hardoy's room at the end of the hall, I found that he was surprisingly messy for a person who had only been back in town for a few days. Pulling the linens from the bed, I had to yank extra hard on the bottom sheet. When it finally gave way, I fell forward onto the bed frame and bumped my shin. The pain was sharp, and it made me cry out. Frustrated, I sat on the bed and rubbed my leg for a few moments. When I stood, I heard a small thump under the bed. Looking underneath, I saw that I had dislodged a worn leather wallet that had been wedged between the bed boards.

It sat on the wooden floor next to a half dozen dust bunnies.

I grabbed the wallet and stood up. The pain in my leg was forgotten. The wallet looked familiar, and I turned it over in my hand. Nervousness stole over me as I sensed that this was very important.

With tingling fingers, I opened the wallet flap. There was no money in the main compartment, but the card sections had a few yellowed documents sticking upward. I pulled the first card out. It was a small index card with the logo of Wells Fargo Bank in Genoa. With a five-digit account number on it.

I pulled the second card behind that one.

It was a United States of America Permanent Resident Card.

In the name of Jean Larralde.

I dropped the wallet on the floor like it was on fire. My fingers were burning in a hellfire of guilt and shame. The kind of inferno that those Southern preachers on the radio talk about before they try to get everyone to send them money. (I generally change the radio station at this point because Ama says that half of all priests are crooks and the other half have illegitimate children with the housekeeper. I've told her that priests and preachers are two different things. But Ama insists that there is only one God, so preachers and priests are basically the same thing—they just wear different outfits.)

I picked up the wallet, my hands trembling.

"Anna?" Catalina's voice drifted from the hallway. Panicked, I shoved the wallet into the pocket of my corduroy trousers. I straightened my sweater to cover the small lump at my hip.

"Just finishing up. I'm coming."

My mind is still whirling from this discovery—even though it was several hours ago. I don't know how I made it through dinner—although helping Ama make tripota, boiled potatoes with butter, and canned peas didn't take much mental energy. Even still, I cut my finger on the tin can, cursed loud enough to cause Ama to frown at me, and didn't notice that blood was trickling down onto my apron. I was a bit of a mess. Even Antton asked me if I was okay after I didn't hear him ask me to pass the black pepper at the dinner table, even though he was sitting directly across from me.

I managed to go the entire dinner hour without making eye contact with Tomas Hardoy who was nursing a hangover by drinking more highballs. He was subdued. His eyes were glassy and bloodshot.

He looked terrible. And far older than just twenty-two.

But I think I know why.

Tomas Hardoy had the murdered man's wallet hidden in his room. Tomas had stolen the money from the wallet to keep for himself. I saw him with the wad of money just <u>yesterday</u>! Everyone had seen Tomas confront Joanes last week about the hospital bill he didn't pay. Everyone. It attracted enough attention in the busy dining room that Benat could have charged extra for the show. Why, Tomas had been mad enough to strangle Larralde with his own belt! (Understandably so.)

Maybe Michel Lassa was right, after all.

Tomas Hardoy must be the murderer.

Right?

A little later the same night

Okay. I will definitely be turning the wallet over to Sheriff Williams tomorrow. I know I said I was FOR SURE going to do it, but now it's a given because Ama just saw the wallet.

Curtains closed to the darkness outside and lying in bed in my warm flannel pajamas, I had the wallet in my hands. I was examining Joanes's green card, and the sharp, dark edges of his signature on the back, when the accordion door to my room suddenly opened. Ama was standing there with two mugs in her hands, "I got some of that chocolate amerikano. The Ovaltine. We shall try it. It won't be good—those Americans have terrible tastes."

She sat on the side of my bed and extended one of the steaming mugs to me. The hot milk and Ovaltine powder swirled together in the depths of the chipped brown mug. With no choice but to grab the drink, I tried tucking the wallet in my blanket (out of sight), but my mother's eyes were sharp.

"What is that?" Ama took a sip of Ovaltine and gave a noncommittal shake of her head. She didn't love it. But she didn't hate it, either. For Ama, that was a fairly good review.

The warm Ovaltine was soothing. Casting about for the right words, I took my time in responding. "It's—it's a wallet."

Brows furrowing behind her glasses, Ama set the mug down on the nightstand. "Who does it belong to?"

"Well—uh—" I faltered until Ama snatched the wallet.

Her face tightened when she saw the name inside. Even though no one was around to hear our conversation, Ama lowered her voice to a whisper, "Where did you find this?"

I told Ama what had happened, leaving nothing out.

"Haurra, we must give this to the sheriff. Tomorrow." Ama was angry. Picking up her mug, she downed the contents in one big swig. "I don't like you being involved in this mess. Stay away from it. Just help the sheriff with his questions, don't involve yourself more than necessary. A man is dead. We don't know what else may happen."

"You don't think we're in danger, do you Ama?"

She reached out and squeezed my hand, "I don't think so. Joanes had many enemies. That's a fact. But we can never know what people may do. Or what goes on inside their heads. So we must be careful."

I pondered that for a few moments, and then Ama stood, "It's time for bed.

It's been a long week for everyone. I will keep this wallet in my room until we can give it to the sheriff tomorrow. Get some sleep, haurra."

I slid down into my blankets, "Tomorrow night is Christmas Eve. Maybe we need to go to church. Seems like we have a lot to pray about."

"Bai, we do."

Witness Interview
(Property of the Douglas County Sheriff)

Case No: 22-43
Date: Mon, 12/20/43
Time: 11:45am
Witness: Bernard Cedarry *(Anna Elissetche, interpreter)*
Interviewing Officer: H. Williams

HW: Mr. Cedarry, how long have you known the deceased?

BC: About 25 years. But, for most of that time I didn't know him well at all. He was the sort of guy you saw at a dinner or a besta. And you said hello to him. Talked about mutual friends. Not much more than that. He began boarding here during the seasons he pastured his sheep in the Carson Valley. He did this more so in recent years.

HW: Tell me about Mr. Larralde.

BC: Joanes was born in Donibane Garazi, but he was raised in Luzaide, where his mother was from. I think his father got into some problems with the polizia in France and had to move the family to Spain. It happened sometimes in those days.

HW: When did he immigrate to America?

BC: Because he had French citizenship, he was expected to go into the service in 1914. Like many guys, he didn't want to go fight the Germans in those terrible trenches, so he came to America instead. The French didn't treat the Bascos well, either, so why should they fight and die for a country that didn't care about them?

HW: Do you know what he did when he immigrated? Where did he work? What did he do?

BC: I don't know all the places he worked, but I know that he worked in the mines for a while, then as a sheepherder in California. Eventually, with a partner, he got his own sheep. When his partner died, he bought out his share and continued to run the business.

HW: Who was the partner?

BC: Pierre Elissetche.

HW: Wait . . . Is that? . . .

AE: *It was my father.*

HW: Really. How . . . surprising.

AE: *Not really. All Basques know each other. It's like having a bunch of nosy neighbors that know everything about you.*

HW: Okay. Anyway . . . maybe we'll chat more about that later.

AE: *Not much to tell. My Aita got hit by a train on a foggy day during a supply trip to Stockton. And he died.*

HW: I'm sorry to hear that.

AE: *My mother and I moved to the boardinghouse after that. Benat and Louise offered Ama a job.*

HW: I see.

BC: Do you have more questions for me?

HW: Yes. Sorry. From what you know of Mr. Larralde, and from his past, can you imagine anyone having a reason to do something like this? Commit murder?

BC: Joanes always paid his boarding fees on time, he never gave me any problems, really. But I noticed things and heard other things . . .

HW: Like what?

BC: Larralde was tight with money. Didn't much care to pay debts if he could find a way out of it. I heard that he cheated some of his workers out of wages. This is just talk, of course.

HW: You must know more details than that.

BC: I don't like to gossip.

AE: *He doesn't dislike gossip, either.*

BC: I can understand you, neska!

HW: Wait, you speak English?

BC: Of course I do. I've owned this hotel for 25 years.

HW: Why didn't you say something sooner?

BC: I don't like to lay all my cards on the table.

AE: *Unless they are better than Michel Lassa's cards.*

BC: Oy yoy, Anna! I'm going to tell your mother you are interfering.

AE: *No, please don't, I'll stop now.*

HW: I don't like being lied to.

BC: Well, you better get used to it. Because Bascos don't like telling tales to outsiders.

From Anna Elissetche's Secret Murder Journal

(<u>Not</u> hidden under her mattress. It's now buried under a stack of sanitary napkins. Maite bought them when that stupid blood started flowing from Anna's body every few weeks.)

Friday
December 24, 1943

It doesn't feel much like Christmas Eve. Even the shiny garland hanging in the hotel looks dreary. While it could be my imagination (Ama says things often <u>are</u> all in my imagination), the red and green tinsel seems sad and limp—which is exactly how Pintto looks after he eats all the leftover pigs' feet.

Ama and I are going to Mass later after supper, though. Louise and Teresa are coming, as well. I might ask Catalina if she wants to join us. Apparently, the men don't like going to Mass. Along with cooking and cleaning for them, the men feel it's a woman's job to pray for them, too.

I'm not sure if praying the rosary is transferable, though. If a woman prays an extra two rosaries, can she pass credit for praying those rosaries to another person? Like it's a savings bond or a Buick? I'm not sure. I would think it's a different story if you are praying for someone who's in need or is sick or has died. But transferring credit for praying the rosary to a person who has NO EXCUSE to not go to church himself (other than needing to finish a bottle of wine before it "goes bad") does not seem fair.

I would probably know the answers to these questions if I paid more attention in catechism. But the catechism books are just <u>so</u> much more boring than a mystery novel where an embezzling archbishop gets killed when a church organ falls on top of him.

Now that's a book I would read.

Anyway, I just got back from the butcher. Ama ordered four chickens to make soup for tonight—and then to make chicken and rice for tomorrow. Fred had the full order this time, plus I got two beef tongues, too, because it's my ABSOLUTE

FAVORITE and I'm going to force Ama to make it for Christmas lunch tomorrow. I can almost taste the garlic and parsley and the wine vinaigrette.

My mouth just filled up with saliva.

I just left a message for Sheriff Williams. He should be here soon to get the wallet. Ama made me call as soon as I got back. It makes her nervous to have the wallet, too, as if it's going to scald us like hot xingarra grease.

I saw Tomas Hardoy earlier getting a cup of coffee in the kitchen. He didn't seem to have noticed that the wallet wasn't under his bed anymore. If he had, I doubt he'd have been keen to lounge around the scene of the crime, drinking coffee. Coffee <u>without</u> all the things that make it so good—which includes two spoons of sugar and enough cream to make it the color of a golden retriever.

I just realized that I am writing about food nearly as much as I'm writing about murder in this journal. I don't know how I feel about that. While Miss Gleason says that journals can be about <u>whatever</u> you want them to be about, I had said at the outset that this would be a murder journal.

Yet, this murder feels very Basque. Therefore, it smells a lot like garlic.

Thirty minutes later . . .

The sheriff is here . . . He's waiting in the bar for Tomas Hardoy to return from the store so we can question him. Er . . . I mean so that Sheriff Williams can question him. I need to stop saying "we" because the sheriff says I'm not an actual detective but an "unpaid civilian assistant." He emphasizes the "unpaid" part because the other day I asked if the government would pay me for helping him. I didn't see the problem with asking this. But it REALLY annoyed him because then he said, "The government barely pays me, so why the <insert expletive here> would they pay a 14-year-old who already breaks the law when she drives down Highway 395?"

We shouldn't have to wait too long for Tomas. After all, Antton said he had just gone to buy cigarettes. Tomas didn't want to run out after the mercantile in Minden closed for Christmas.

I'm sitting on the other side of the bar, writing in my journal at the table by the window—the table that Victor Arrossa prefers to use when he falls asleep after breakfast. "Naps that are taken in a bar don't count as real naps," he said when I asked him why he didn't take a nap in his room like a normal person. I guess there's some logic in this theory. Plus, Antton doesn't mind the old man snoring in the bar, because then he gets double the tips. Victor tips Antton once <u>before</u> his nap and then again <u>after</u> because he usually forgets about the first tip.

Sheriff Williams is nursing his cup of coffee at the bar. He is glaring at me as I write in here. I think he knows I'm writing about him, because when I look up at him, his eyes narrow even more. He's not the only one suspicious about my journal . . . Ama asked me about it the other day, too. But I just told her that Miss Gleason asked us to write several pages a day so that we don't forget how to write complete sentences over Christmas vacation. This maybe isn't a complete fabrication because I once read an article in *The Ladies' Home Journal* that eating too many candy canes will make a child's brain rot.

Wait . . . I see Tomas pulling his truck into the boardinghouse.

Will write more soon.

Witness Interview #2
(Property of the Douglas County Sheriff)

Case No: 22-43
Date: Fri, 12/24/43
Time: 9:45am
Witness: Thomas Hardoy (*Anna Elissetche, interpreter*)
Interviewing Officer: H. Williams

HW: Have you ever seen this wallet before?

HW: Mr. Hardoy?

HW: Anna, please tell him that if he doesn't cooperate, it won't reflect well on him.

AE: *I really don't want to get involved more than absolutely necessary.*

HW: Since when?

AE: *Since . . . now?*

HW: Ha! I don't believe you.

AE: *I thought that was very believable. I even practiced saying it before you got here.*

HW: Why say something so obviously not true?

AE: *Ama made me say it. She doesn't like that I'm helping you.*

HW: Well, I don't like that you're helping me, either. So, I guess we have something in common.

TH: Excuse me . . . What is going on? Am I going to jail, or not?

HW: That remains to be seen. Please answer this question: Have you seen this wallet before?

TH: Maybe.

HW: Mr. Hardoy, this wallet was in your room. How did you gain possession of the deceased's wallet?

HW: Please answer me.

TH: I found it.

HW: Where?

TH: On the ground. Outside.

HW: When?

TH: The night of the murder. I found it when I got back from the whorehouse. I mean, when I got back from the bar.

AE: *I'm not an idiot. I know what a whorehouse is.*

HW: Hush, Anna. We're finally getting somewhere.

AE: *If you say so.*

HW: What . . . you don't believe him?

AE: *Not really.*

HW: Why?

AE: *I think he stole the wallet. He took the money from inside it. I saw him with a bunch of money a couple days ago. A person isn't going to dump a wallet full of money on the ground for someone else to take.*

HW: Hmm . . .

TH: Stop talking about me like I'm not here. Either arrest me or let me go.

AE: *He's getting really irritated. He just called me a silly girl that should be slapped on my butt and locked in my room.*

HW: He's not wrong, really.

AE: *Don't be mean. You're just mad that you haven't solved this case, yet.*

HW: Says you. Anyway, ask him what he did with the wallet after he found it.

TH: I kept the money from inside it. Then I hid the wallet under my bed.

HW: How much money did you take? What did you do with the money?

TH: I used it to pay my boarding fees with Benat. The rest I spent on cigarettes and whiskey at the market. There was about forty dollars in it.

AE: *I bet there was way more than forty dollars in there. I heard that Joanes hoarded money like a squirrel. Plus, I think Thomas is wearing new boots right now. I don't remember seeing those before. I think he got these to make him look taller. He's very sensitive about his shortness.*

HW: Anna, what did I say about editorializing?

AE: Sorry.

AE: Oops, Thomas is getting mad at me again. He knows I'm talking about his new boots.

HW: Mr. Hardoy, so you admit to stealing Joanes Larralde's wallet? How do I know that you didn't kill him to get it?

TH: Listen, I've said all I have to say. I didn't kill Joanes Larralde. I swear.

From Anna Elissetche's Secret Murder & Food Journal

(Hidden inside the waistband of her corduroy pants
because she hasn't had time to put it anywhere else.)

It's Still Friday
December 24, 1943

Tomas left after our interview with Sheriff Williams. His new boots echoed on the hardwood floors of the bar as he stomped out.

The sheriff told him to remain available for further questioning in the coming days. If Tomas didn't cooperate, Sheriff Williams would be forced to arrest him for hampering a murder investigation. I didn't know the Basque word for 'hampering' so I just told Tomas that the sheriff would send him to Alcatraz if he pretended <u>not</u> to know things (when he <u>did</u> know things). Tomas got very irritated at me when I said this. I'm quite glad that he likes Ama's lamb stew so much, because otherwise I think he'd have locked me in the linen closet upstairs and thrown the key in Lake Tahoe.

I mean, he still could do that, but I'll just make sure to stay ten feet away from the linen closet because I don't think he could carry me farther than that without someone else noticing.

Plus, I'm stronger than I look. (And I know how to kick and bite if I have to.)

Anyway, as I make my notes in my journal, the sheriff is making notes in a small notepad at the bar. My journal is bigger than his notepad. This makes me concerned about the state of his investigation.

He stopped writing . . .

Now he's glaring at me again . . .

He's asking to see my diary . . .

79

I told him it's a journal, not a diary. I also told him that even if it was a diary, it's very impolite to ask to see a woman's diary . . .

He's saying I'm a girl, and not a woman, so it's <u>not</u> rude to ask me this . . .

I just told him that I got my first period a few months ago, so technically I <u>am</u> a woman . . .

Now his face is getting red and he's looking away. He just told me that it's inappropriate to talk about those things . . .

Okay, now he's leaving . . .

He said he'll be back later . . .

As he walked out the front door (his limp more pronounced than usual), I think I heard him grumble under his breath that he hopes my pen runs out of ink . . .

Silly man. I have six more in my room.

Two hours later

As I write this, I can smell the chicken soup simmering in the kitchen and the gas fumes from Tomas Hardoy's beat-up truck as he speeds away down Highway 395.

Perhaps I should back up a little.

After the sheriff left, I stuffed my journal under the front waistband of my corduroy pants and went off to the kitchen to help Ama. I've decided that the contents of my journal are too sensitive to keep hiding it in random places. I'll have to come up with a new place to keep it, because Ama will notice the suspicious lump in my pants. I <u>really</u> don't want her to think she has to send me to a nunnery in Navarra. Although, she really should know me better than that because the boys at Douglas High School are not very interesting.

With the soup safely bubbling away, and the beef tongue boiling in another pot to prepare for tomorrow (yippee!), Ama said that I should rest in my room for a while before supper—otherwise she'll make me take some of the medicine that the doctor in Carson City gave Victor. The pills are bigger than lamb testicles. Since I absolutely refuse to eat those (I don't care how good Ama's recipe is), I also reject all pills of similar size.

I burrowed in my bed for a while, dozing in and out of sleep until I heard shuffling, booted steps in the gravel outside my window. I leaned up from my window to look for the source of the sound.

Tomas Hardoy was wearing a heavy jacket and carrying a large canvas sack over one shoulder. He had a smaller leather satchel over his other shoulder and was trudging towards his truck which was parked on this side of the hotel. My heart started to pound.

His movements were rushed as he opened the passenger side of the truck and tossed his bags inside. Slamming the rusted door shut, Tomas began walking around to the driver's side, when I saw Antton walking briskly towards the truck—with a forgotten cigarette dangling from his lips.

Antton began gesturing wildly. Nearly falling down in my haste to get off my bed, I slowly rolled the lever to open my window a crack. In that moment, I was thankful to have inherited my father's large ears and not my mother's smaller ones. The cold December air rushed through the cracked window and made me shiver.

"Tomas, it isn't a good idea to run. It really isn't. You don't want to give that polizia any more reason to think you are guilty."

"I did not kill Joanes."

"Great. So stay and wait for the sheriff to do his job."

"I am not going to jail for this. If I go to jail again, they are going to deport me. And I can't go back to Urepel, I just can't."

"Come on, Urepel isn't so bad."

"Garai, you are not going to change my mind."

"Fine. But don't be hasty. My Amatxi Xaharra used to say that regret always came from choices made by angry or drunk men."

"Save your breath. It's no use. That polizia is turning his eyes to me. It won't be long before he arrests me."

"I thought you said you didn't kill Larralde."

"I didn't. But the only reason I couldn't kill him was because he was already dead."

Tomas's words hung in the cold air as Antton's arms fell uselessly to his sides. The bartender was momentarily speechless, which was unusual for him. His throat worked convulsively as a million thoughts and words must have fought their way around inside of him.

Tomas continued, "You'd best be careful, Antton. I know you hated Joanes, too. So, that sheriff might come for you next. Get inside so you can't say that you saw me leave."

Antton didn't reply, he just stood for a few minutes before reluctantly turning around and heading around to the rear door of the boardinghouse.

Tomas walked around his truck, kicking the tires with his new boots. As if sensing someone watching him, he looked up. Eyes narrowing in annoyance, he gazed straight at me. His lips quivered as if suppressing a smile. Climbing in his truck, he raised one arm up in the air before he closed the driver side door.

He had flipped me off.

It was so rude. I had never done anything bad to Tomas Hardoy before. Well, not really. Other than assist in the investigation that could find him guilty of murder. But that's not so bad.

Right?

Nonetheless, I had <u>never</u> been flipped off before. So, I wasn't quite sure how to respond. Yelling at him seemed useless, as did flipping him off in return. (I don't think I have the right flair necessary for such a gesture.) Therefore, I did the next best thing.

I waved goodbye.

With a screech of his tires, Tomas drove away, kicking up gravel in the yard. I watched him speed south down the highway, taking with him the answers to the questions/revelations/thoughts I suddenly had:

Tomas Hardoy has just admitted to <u>wanting</u> to kill Joanes . . . he had <u>intended</u> to do it . . . but found him <u>already</u> dead?

This means that Tomas knew Larralde was dead before Teresa found the body the next morning.

Why wouldn't he admit all this to the sheriff?

If Tomas Hardoy didn't kill Joanes Larralde, then who did?

Ugh. My head is starting to hurt. I think I need a snack.

One piece of bread and cheese later . . . .

As I stuffed cheese into a piece of bread and held it under the broiler, Ama watched me as she peeled the thick membrane off the beef tongues. "Don't spoil your supper, haurra," she said as she yanked the fibrous tissue off to get to the tender meat beneath.

"I won't, don't worry," I blew air through my teeth as the cheese burned my mouth.

"Be careful or you won't be able to taste your supper either," Ama warned me with a chuckle.

A firm knock sounded on the wooden frame by the back door to the kitchen. I opened the door with one hand, my grilled sandwich in the other. It was Sheriff Williams.

Without waiting to be invited inside, he demanded, "Where is Tomas Hardoy's truck?"

"Uh . . . well . . . I suppose . . ."

He crossed his arms over his chest, and sighed heavily—the weight of the world on his shoulders, "Did he take off?"

"It's hard to speculate . . . well . . . uh . . ." I stuffed my snack into my mouth to delay the words that I knew the sheriff didn't want to hear.

"He did, didn't he?" he said flatly.

I licked the last of the cheese from my fingertips, "All evidence points in that direction, yes."

"What evidence?"

"I saw him drive away with all his belongings earlier. After he flipped me off."

"He flipped you off?"

"You don't have to sound happy about it."

"Well, if he wasn't my chief murder suspect, I think I could actually like the guy."

Ama tapped her spoon on the pot to draw our attention to her. Then she asked me what this was all about. I told her in Basque, while the sheriff sniffed the pot of chicken soup in appreciation.

"Remember what I said, haurra. Help the polizia, yes, but don't involve yourself in this more than you need to," Ama said in a low voice, even though he couldn't understand her. Although I could have sworn his ears perked when she said the word "polizia." Some words translate, anyway, I supposed, no matter how unusual and rare Basque was 99% of the time.

"Which direction was he heading?"

"He went south," I replied.

"I suppose I'm going to have to issue a warrant for his arrest now," Sheriff Williams sounded disgruntled, "My wife isn't going to be happy if I'm late for dinner on Christmas Eve."

He seemed to be talking to himself more than to me, so I didn't respond. I had enough on my mind, as it was.

Should I tell the sheriff what I had overheard? Would it make any difference? Or, would Ama just get upset that I was inferring more than I needed to?

I didn't know what to do.

The sheriff asked, "Did Hardoy say anything before he left?"

"I . . . I just saw him through the window. We . . . we didn't speak."

This was technically true. But, with that, I seemed to have made my choice to withhold the full story of the afternoon. Guilt burned at my ears.

"Can you ask your mother if she overheard anything, or if she has anything to add to our interview from the other day? I can see she's busy cooking, but she maybe knows something?"

I passed along the question to Ama. After a few moments to gather her thoughts, she had me translate this reply:

"I have nothing to add, really, to our talk the other day. I stay very busy in the kitchen, so I don't have time for much else. Tomas has a temper and is quick to run away. It's probably why he doesn't keep a job for too long. But some men are free spirits like that. Whether he killed Joanes, or not, I really have no opinion on that. I have a hard time imagining he did, though. As the saying goes, I think he has 'more bark than bite.' Does that help answer your question?"

The sheriff thanked her with a nod, wished them both a good day, and prepared to leave. As he reached for the doorknob, Ama called out to him, "Salda?" She gestured to the chicken soup and made a drinking gesture with her hand.

"Really?" he asked in surprise. "That sounds good, thank you."

A few minutes later, Sheriff Williams was on his way with a paper cup of soup in one hand, and no murder suspect in the other.

Witness Interview
(Property of the Douglas County Sheriff)

Case No: 22-43
Date: Tues, 12/21/43
Time: 4:15pm
Witness: Maite Elissetche *(Anna Elissetche, interpreter)*
Interviewing Officer: H. Williams

HW: Thank you for taking the time to speak with me. I know you're busy preparing dinner, so I'll try to keep this as brief as possible.

ME: I'm glad to help how I can. This has been a difficult time for everyone . . . especially my daughter, she is so young to be around such a . . . mess.

HW: She seems to be doing just fine. She's quite helpful and enthusiastic.

ME: Yes, that's part of the problem.

AE: *My mother thinks that I read too many books. And that I don't know that books and real life are two different things.*

HW: Well, . . . do you?

AE: *Of course, I know the difference between novels and real life! For example, Nancy Drew is not a real person. Whereas Jack the Ripper was a real person—even though I once read a book about those cases. So, just because something is in a book, that doesn't mean it's not "real life." There's fiction, and then there's nonfiction.*

HW: Good God, why did you bring Jack the Ripper into this?

AE: *It's the most recent nonfiction book that I read. So, it's the freshest in my mind.*

HW: Jesus Christ Almighty.

AE: *Speaking of Jesus, the Bible could be called nonfiction or fiction. It really depends on who you ask. It seems to me to be equal parts of both, but Sister Mary Evangeline got really irritated when I said that a few weeks ago at catechism. So she made me go to confession.*

HW: I really don't know how to respond to any of this. Plus, I'm scared to even contemplate the sins you confessed to doing.

AE: *I just made a few things up to sound more interesting than I am. I figured the priest gets bored listening to confessions all day.*

HW: Just stop now. Your mother looks like she's getting mad at me.

AE: *She looks like that a lot, but she really doesn't mean it. It's how she's survived cooking and caring for rowdy sheepherders all these years.*

HW: Anyway, let's proceed. Mrs. Elissetche, how long have you known the deceased?

ME: Oh, so you finally have a question for me?

HW: See, I told you she's mad at me. My wife looks at me that way at least twice a week.

HW: Wait . . . Anna, don't translate that!

ME: I've known Joanes since I married my late husband, Pierre. They had immigrated on the same ship. They saw each other from time to time and a few years after we were married, Larralde was looking for a partner to buy some sheep with, and he asked Pierre to join with him. It made sense at the time because Pierre was ready to start his own business rather than continuing to work for another sheepman.

HW: What were your impressions of him during this time?

ME: My husband spent more time with him than I did. So, my opinion probably isn't helpful.

HW: Please, tell me anyway. You have thoughts, I'm sure.

ME: It's not polite to speak badly of the dead.

HW: Yes, that is true. But this conversation is just between us. And your daughter, apparently.

AE: *I can be discreet.*

HW: If you say so.

AE: *I do say so.*

ME: Should I answer your question now? Or wait a little longer?

HW: Sorry, yes. Do continue.

ME: Joanes was . . . well, a little lazy. He left more work for my husband to do, which, of course, I was not always happy about.

HW: Did Mr. Larralde and your late husband ever have any disagreements over their business?

ME: From time to time, which is expected when you run a business. One person wants to do one thing, while the other wants to do another. They usually worked it out—my husband was an even-tempered man. Which, honestly, was probably the only reason their partnership actually lasted. Joanes could be difficult sometimes.

HW: How do you mean?

ME: He could be rude. Many people didn't care for him. He could be rough with the employees—not treat them the most fairly. My husband didn't care for that. Well, I didn't either.

HW: What happened when your husband died? Anna mentioned he died in a tragic accident. I'm sorry for your loss. It must have been difficult.

ME: As I did not want to run a sheep business, and I had a young daughter to care for, it made the most sense to sell my husband's share to Joanes after he died. Joanes handled the details of all that.

HW: How did you come to live here at the boardinghouse?

ME: For some months after Pierre died, I worked cleaning houses and harvesting apricots and cherries in the Central Valley. I took the jobs I could find. I needed to save the money from the sale of the sheep to keep a roof over our heads. It was hard. But Benat and Louise Cedarry are also from Bidarray—the same village in the Basque Country as I am from. So, when Louise began to have trouble with her rheumatism and needed help here in the kitchen, they decided to offer a job to me. I know that they meant it as a kindness, initially, but it has all worked out in the end.

HW: I am glad for that. Truly. So, how did Joanes Larralde end up boarding here at The Sierra Hotel? I thought your business was in California?

ME: Well, it was mostly. But sheep get pastured in different places depending upon the season. Joanes has pastured the sheep more frequently in the Carson Valley in the last few years.

HW: Do you know why that is?

ME: I couldn't really say. I left the sheep matters to my husband, but I know there are a lot of things that go into those decisions.

HW: Do you know any of the other boarders from your years before you came here?

ME: Just Domingo. But, only for a short while. He began to work for Joanes and my husband the year before he died. He continued working for Joanes, of course, afterward. He's now the camp-tender . . . like a foreman.

HW: Tell me what you know of Mr. Echeveste.

ME: He came from Bizkaia in Spain. Domingo is a hard worker and I always thought he seemed like a good young man. He's serious, but there's nothing wrong with that. My husband thought well of him, too. I think working for Pierre and Joanes was one of his first jobs when he immigrated. I don't know much else about him.

HW: Would you say Mr. Echeveste had a temper? Or got angry easily?

ME: No, not at all. Like I said, he is serious, but he's polite and reasonable.

HW: Do you know any of the other boarders?

ME: Other than in the time they've spent here? No, not really. I met Victor Arrossa once at a dinner at the Pyrenees in Stockton years ago with my husband, but Victor was already retired from sheepherding by then, I think.

HW: You said that you know Benat and Louise Cedarry from back in France. What can you tell me about Mr. Cedarry?

ME: Benat and Louise are some of the finest people I know. I will not gossip about them because they don't deserve that. And that's all I have to say about it.

HW: Okay, okay. That's fine.

ME: Are we finished? I have to check on the stew. I don't want our dinner ruined.

HW: Perhaps we can talk another time?

ME: If you must, yes.

AE: *Ama isn't happy*

HW: Yeah, I caught that.

POST MORTEM EXAMINATION REPORT
OFFICE OF THE CORONER
DOUGLAS COUNTY
STATE OF NEVADA

CASE NO: 22-43

NAME OF DECEASED: Larralde, Jean

RESIDENCE OF DECEASED: The Sierra Hotel, Hwy 395, Gardnerville

AGE: 55   SEX: Male   RACE: White   HEIGHT: 5'7   WEIGHT: 185lbs

DATE OF DEATH: est 12/19/43, body found 12/20/43.

TIME OF DEATH: est btw 9:00pm/11:00pm, 12/19/43

CAUSE OF DEATH: Homicide, exsanguination due to damage to carotid and jugular vessels

OTHER SIGNIFICANT CONDITIONS PRESENT: 1) Minor bruising to left shoulder, left elbow, and left side of face, indicating deceased sustained fall or trauma before death. 2) Deceased consumed alcohol prior to death, the scent permeated body and internal organs. 3) Hepatic decay indicative of early stages of compensated cirrhosis. 4) All other organ systems appeared normal and unremarkable.

signed, 12/23/43

E.H. Clarke

ELIAS HOWARD CLARKE
Coroner
Douglas County, Nevada

From Anna Elissetche's
Murder & Food Cuisine Journal

(Hidden inside the extra blanket in the trunk at the foot of her bed.)

Friday Evening
December 24, 1943

It's been quite a long day, but I'll try to fill you in on the rest of it before I fall asleep. We just got home from mass and Ama let me have a glass of the real eggnog that Louise made. Meaning the eggnog with the brandy in it. My fingers feel loose and liquidy (I know this isn't a word, but I don't care).

I think I love eggnog. Truly. Really. <u>Really</u>.

Anyway, after the sheriff left, I helped Ama in the kitchen. Since we were going to mass afterward, Ama kept dinner simple—just a few pintxos and chicken soup. We made a tortilla de patata with pimentos and mushrooms. I separated the baked omelette into little wedges and Ama spooned some homemade piperade over the top of each small serving before we served it. To go alongside, Ama made some pâté using chicken livers that she had been collecting in the pantry freezer for Christmas. It's important to note that Ama never, ever throws anything away. She calls it a sin, which I think I agree with because missing out on that heavenly pâté would be a CRIME against the God that created chickens to begin with.

I just realized that eggnog makes my ~~food~~ cuisine descriptions even BETTER, so maybe I should have eggnog more often.

Anyway, I toasted some buttered bread for us to serve with the pâté and I almost burned the toast because I left the broiler unattended while I gave Pintto some attention. He loves when I massage the top of his head. He drools when I do that, which led to me having to wipe up his slobber from the kitchen floor, which is why I almost burned the bread. Ama wasn't happy about that (or the sheepdog drool) since the bakery was closed for Christmas and she couldn't send me to go get more bread.

Louise brought an almond cake, roasted chestnuts, and the WONDERFUL EGGNOG, which I've already talked about, but warrants more talking about. Before dinner, the boarders (minus Tomas, of course!)—along with Louise, Benat, Teresa, and Catalina—had a drink in the bar, along with the warm chestnuts. Antton had the radio on, and Bing Crosby's new hit "White Christmas" played every 18.5 minutes.

Victor gobbled chestnuts like he hadn't eaten since last week. Bits of the nutty flesh sputtered from his mouth as he raved, "Oh boy, Louise! Gaztainak goxoak dira." Unaware that he was talking louder than a bull could bellow, Victor continued, "I haven't had gaztainak since back home in Landibar. My brother and I stole some from the tree by the church one day, but the apeza caught us. He tried chasing us away with a stick, but we still came away with our pockets full. It was a great day until the apeza told our mother and she slapped us with a kanabera." White hair sticking up around his large ears, Victor reflected, "It was still worth it, though."

Sitting next to the old boarder at the table by the window, Benat laughed and saluted him with his Picon.

At the bar, the Goytia brothers played dice with Antton, throwing pennies on the table as each tried to outbid the other. They both wore blue plaid shirts that they clearly bought from the same place. There are only so many mail-order catalogs delivered to western Nevada, so you see the sheepherders wearing the same eight or nine shirt styles at each event.

Mr. Dallut-Bec spoke to Louise at the next table—sharing stories of the stone projects he had worked on in San Francisco and back in his apprenticeship days in Amiens, outside of Paris. He had been an expert on "medieval gargoyle restoration," which was an arrangement of words that I had never heard used in one sentence. Just as I was about to ask him what that actually meant, the front door to the hotel opened and Mitchell Lauden stepped inside, his shiny dark cane clicking on the wood floor. He swept the brown fedora from his sandy head and called out, "Merry Christmas! Are you open for a drink? I'm a thirsty man headed to a long and boring Christmas Dinner."

Benat stood and went to shake the young lawyer's hand, "For you? Always!" He gestured to the bar, "You are welcome anytime."

As Antton made Mitchell his usual Manhattan, I said hello and offered him some chestnuts, which I had to pry out of Victor's sticky hands.

"So, Miss Anna, how are things? I left a message yesterday for the sheriff for an update on the investigation but haven't heard back yet. You all aren't getting hassled too much, are you?" Mitchell's face was earnest and concerned.

He really was a very nice man.

Antton slid the drink to Mitchell, "That polizia has been here every day. Asking many questions. No answers, yet."

I leaned close to the men, "Tomas Hardoy, one of the boarders, ran off earlier today. Joanes Larralde's wallet had been found in his room. Hidden under the bed. I was the one that found it while helping Catalina change the linens in the rooms."

"It was you that found the wallet?" Antton's mouth had dropped open in shock.

"Umm, yes?" I said it as a question, even though it was a definitive fact. As definitive as the fact that the sun rose in the east and that mint jelly should NEVER be served with lamb chops. Ever. I don't care what the amerikanoak say.

Domingo Echeveste and Catalina were enjoying a drink just a few feet down the bar. The foreman's ears perked up, "Hardoy had Larralde's wallet? Is that why he took off?" He asked his question in a low voice, in Basque.

"Wait, what did he say?" Mitchell looked to Antton to translate.

Antton brushed off the question, "Domingo is just surprised. As we all are that Tomas ran off like this."

"It doesn't look good for Hardoy, that's for sure." The lawyer took a large sip of his cocktail. "But that's not enough for a conviction. The sheriff would need more than that. So, his investigation will continue, I assume."

"Really?" Domingo's strong face was impassive. But I caught a tightening of his cheek—only because I've known him since I was 9 when he first started working for Aita and Joanes. Domingo cared more about the conversation than he was letting on.

I thought this was interesting, but also, not terribly surprising. Joanes had been Domingo's employer. Of course, Domingo cared about the investigation. He did have a stake in its outcome.

A little voice in the back of my head (the voice that once read three Agatha Christie books in one week) whispered: Domingo nearly killed Joanes right in the middle of the dining room.

Just a week ago.

Catalina tsked her disapproval of the conversation from down the bar, "Compañeros, es Navidad. No quiero tristeza hoy. ¿Acordado?"

Domingo reached over to kiss her on the cheek, "You are right, Catalina."

"Do forgive me," Mitchell nodded in her direction and raised his glass, "Feliz Navidad!"

When Catalina raised her glass in return, Mitchell suddenly exclaimed with a burst of joy, "Look—what a lovely ring! When is the happy occasion?"

I was shocked I hadn't noticed the gold and diamond ring on Catalina's finger. I gasped, "W—w—when did you get that?" I ran to forcefully grab her hand and pull it towards me—nearly yanking her off the bar stool in the process. I wasn't sure how I hadn't spotted the engagement ring sooner. I prided myself on my observational skills—which were essential in any (and all) sleuthing.

Agatha <u>would</u> be so disappointed in me.

The gold band shone prettily against Catalina's caramel skin—the tiny diamonds glittering in the low light of the bar. The ring was slightly big on her hand, but that could be fixed by a jeweler. "It's beautiful, Catalina!" I gave her a big hug.

Just then, Ama came into the bar with a platter of pintxos—the pâté spread upon the toast that I had nearly burned. "Ama," I exclaimed, "Come look!"

I yanked Catalina's hand in Ama's direction so hard that the young woman laughed, "Anna, mi amiga, cálmate! You are going to break my arm."

"Sorry, I can't help myself."

And I couldn't. I really, really couldn't.

Smiling, Ama set the platter on the bar and came to admire the ring. Taking the young bride-to-be's hand in her slightly larger one, Ama pushed her glasses higher on her nose to get a good look at it. And she looked at it. And she looked at it some more.

"It's—it's very, very lovely," Ama's words were slow to come forth, and an odd expression crossed her face. One I couldn't quite make out. Then, she hugged Catalina tightly, a gleam of wetness in her eye, "I am so happy for you. No one deserves this more than you."

Louise had bustled over to join in the excitement. She clapped her hands, "This is wonderful! Antton, the champagne, please!"

"I think that's my cue to leave." Mitchell downed the last of his Manhattan and tucked his hat back on his head, "Mother will be unhappy if I'm late for the appetizers she didn't make. Congratulations to both . . . and Merry Christmas to everyone else! Antton, will you be open for a drink later on my way home?"

Antton popped the cork on a bottle of champagne, "Yes. Of course. Have a good dinner with your familia."

We waved the young lawyer off with festive cheers as the champagne glasses were passed around. Ama approached Domingo and pulled him down for a kiss on each cheek, "Zorionak, I am happy for you." After a pause, she added, "That—that ring . . . It's very nice."

Domingo's smile froze, "M—mil esker."

Ama gave his arm a reassuring squeeze, "You deserve it. And more." Then, she reached up to hold his stubbly chin so he couldn't look away from her face, "Do you understand me?"

An emotion crossed his face that I couldn't read, but he nodded.

While Domingo seemed to understand, I really didn't.

Of course, Domingo and Catalina deserved each other. That went without saying. They are two of my favorite people. This statistic includes the many fictional people that I know, as well, which is really saying a lot—because I have read a lot of books. (Even the ones that Mrs. McGillicuddy doesn't know I have stolen borrowed.)

The joy was interrupted when a news bulletin came over the radio, the Christmas music paused for a short while. The words were seared in my memory—like grill marks on the side of a crispy pork chop:

Three German U-Boats were sunk this week by naval forces, while President Roosevelt just announced that General Eisenhower has been promoted to lead the Allied invasion of Europe which is expected to come sometime in the new year. In local news, the Douglas County Sheriff has issued a warrant for a Thomas Harday—who is wanted for questioning in the murder of local sheepman, Gene Larald. If you have any information about Mr. Harday's whereabouts, or any other information which may be helpful in the investigation, you are asked to contact the sheriff's office. And, with that, it's time to get back to Mr. Crosby . . . let's hear "White Christmas" one more time!

Conversation stopped. Everyone in the bar stared into their drinks, the festive cheer evaporating. Even Victor Arrossa sensed the change in the air, for he stopped eating chestnuts long enough to whisper (it really wasn't a whisper) to Mr. Dallut-Bec to ask him what was wrong.

The Frenchman didn't need to answer because Ama swept up the tray of pintxos and made for the dining room, "Come for dinner. I don't want the salda to get cold."

The soup was on the stove. It wasn't going to get cold. Everyone knew that. But they all followed my mother, anyway. Sometimes pretending something didn't happen was better than admitting that it did.

Basques could be really good at that.

Witness Interview
(Property of the Douglas County Sheriff)

Case No: 22-43
Date: Mon, 12/20/43
Time: 4:00pm
Witness: Fermin Goytia *(Anna Elissetche, interpreter)*
Interviewing Officer: H. Williams

HW: Mr. Goytia, thank you for meeting with me. Any help or answers you can give me would be appreciated.

FG: It's no problem.

HW: How long have you boarded here at the hotel?

FG: Off and on, for about two years.

HW: And when you aren't here, where do you live?

FG: When I'm out with sheep, I'll spend weeks living out in a small etxola, which is a wagon trailer with a canvas tent over the top. Sometimes I spend time at the Achaval ranch, but mostly I'm here when I'm not with the sheep.

HW: Who is your employer? And how long have you worked for him?

FG: Santiago Achaval. He's a big sheepman here in the Carson Valley. He needed sheepherders, so my brother and I heard about the jobs from an agent in Donostia. Achaval sponsored our trip and we both immigrated two years ago. We've worked for him since then.

HW: Where did you immigrate from?

FG: We are from Tolosa in Gipuzkoa.

AE: *That's in Spain.*

HW: How long did you know Mr. Larralde?

FG: I met him when I first boarded here, but I wouldn't say I really knew him. Or spent much time with him. My brother and I keep mostly to ourselves. It's less trouble that way.

HW: It seems like a wise idea. Especially considering what happened today.

FG: It's very shocking. I felt terrible for that Teresa girl that found the body. She screamed like the Devil himself had shown up.

AE: *See, I told you it was a terrible sound!*

HW: Yes, okay fine. Anyway, Mr. Goytia, what were your impressions of the deceased? What did you think of him?

FG: Honestly, not much. He could be rude. And he always took the last lamb chop, even if he had already taken seconds. My Amuma would have said that was a sign of a selfish man. A man that would turn on his friends. Or stab them in the back. Amuma was usually right about these things.

HW: I see.

AE: *This is true. Amatxis and Amumas do know everything. Like Sherlock Holmes knows everything. Too bad you can't be more like him, Sheriff Williams. He was a genius.*

HW: I can't decide if I should be insulted. Or just confused that you are complaining because I'm not like a fictional detective. One that injected himself with cocaine? And drove poor Mr. Watson crazy?

AE: *Oh my gosh, you've read Sherlock Holmes?!*

HW: Of course I have. I can read, you know.

AE: *That surprises me.*

HW: Okay, now I am insulted.

AE: *Sorry I didn't really mean it like that.*

HW: Didn't you?

HW: So . . . Anyway, Mr. Goytia, did you ever have any disagreements with the deceased? Or know anyone who did?

FG: I haven't, no. But there seemed to be many who have. Why, just last week, Hardoy confronted Larralde right in the middle of the crowded hotel because he owed him money for some debt he was to pay. My brother was ready to bet me a quarter that Hardoy was going to rip out Larralde's lying tongue and feed it to a sheepdog. And, honestly, I didn't take the bet because I really thought he was going to do it.

HW: Now, your boss, Mr. Achaval, is also a sheepman. How did he get along with the deceased?

FG: Well. I shouldn't say, because I don't want to tell stories on my boss.

HW: This interview will stay between us, of course.

AE: *Fermin is giving me a weird look. Like he doesn't trust me. But it's not like Achaval's dislike of Joanes is a big secret. Everyone knows about it.*

HW: Well, I didn't know about it.

AE: *Oh.*

HW: Mr. Goytia, please tell me about the disagreement between your employer and the deceased. I've had information from various sources that have mentioned it.

AE: *He knows that it was me. He just called me a chatterbox.*

HW: Mr. Goytia?

FG: Two seasons ago, Larralde snuck his sheep in pastures that Mr. Achaval had used for many years. Without warning or talking to him about it. It's not acceptable to do that in this business. My boss was very upset because all the best grass was eaten by Larralde's sheep. Then, this season, Larralde tried to steal a grazing lease that Achaval had with the state. My boss was angry, of course. What sheepman wouldn't be?

HW: I see.

AE: *Fermin is right. It's very dishonest for a sheepman to do something like that. My father would have never agreed to do that when he was alive.*

HW: Did Mr. Achaval attend the Christmas party here last evening?

AE: *I don't know I couldn't go. I was still sick.*

HW: I wasn't asking you.

AE: *Oh, yeah.*

FG: Yes, of course. Mr. Achaval was here with his wife Joseba, and his two children. Many of the Basques in the area were here. Mr. Achaval bought the dinner and drinks for my brother and me. So, I'm afraid that we probably drank too much. I don't remember much after the music started. I still have a little headache.

HW: I was young once like you. So, I can imagine.

AE: *That must have been a long time ago.*

HW: A man is in no danger of getting a big head around you.

AE: *What do you mean by that?*

HW: Anyway . . . Mr. Goytia, if I want to speak to your boss, where could I find him?

FG: You want to speak to Mr. Achaval? Why?

HW: I'm sure he knows many people in the area. And has information that could be helpful to me.

AE: *Fermin seems nervous. Maybe he's worried Mr. Achaval will get mad at him?*

HW: Don't worry, young man. This is all protocol. I'll be sure to tell your boss that. It has nothing to do with what you've told me. I won't mention you or your brother at all.

AE: *I'm not sure he believes that.*

HW: It's probably because of you and your chattering.

FG: Mr. Achaval's ranch is on the way to Genoa.

HW: Thank you for your cooperation, Mr. Goytia. It is appreciated. Can you send in your brother now?

Witness Interview
(Property of the Douglas County Sheriff)

Case No: 22-43
Date: Mon, 12/20/43
Time: 4:25pm
Witness: Manuel Goytia *(Anna Elissetche, interpreter)*
Interviewing Officer: H. Williams

HW: Thank you for speaking with me.

MG: Sure.

HW: How are you feeling today? I heard that you had quite an evening of celebrating.

MG: I'm doing fine now. Waking up to a dead body being found across the hall will sober you up very fast.

HW: Yes, I can imagine.

MG: I don't know how much I can really tell you, though. It was all a shock. I'll never forget that girl's scream as long as I live. The hairs on the back of my neck stood up and the whiskey in my belly squeezed up to my throat.

HW: Last night, what time did you go to bed?

MG: I really couldn't tell you. Fermin and I stayed in the bar until Antton stopped serving drinks. Who knows what time that was . . . Midnight, maybe?

HW: Did Antton bartend the entire evening?

MG: Most of it. He took a break to eat dinner and to play the accordion for a little while. Mrs. Sagouspe played for most of the dancing, but she needed a little break, too. When Antton wasn't in the bar, Fermin and I made the drinks. The cocktails we made were probably too strong, but we were too cheerful and drunk to notice.

HW: Did you see anyone else upstairs when you went to bed? Hear anything?

MG: No, not that I can remember. I was very drunk, though. I did hear Victor's snoring, but he does that every single day. For such a small man, he's got a large snore.

HW: What was your opinion of Joanes Larralde?

MG: He was a man with few friends. So, that really says a lot about him.

HW: Can you think of a reason why someone would want to kill him?

MG: I can think of a few reasons why someone would punch him, yes. But cutting his throat? I don't know.

HW: What are some reasons why someone would punch him, then?

MG: Both Hardoy and Domingo Echeveste had good cause to give him a black eye. That is for sure. Both disagreements had to do with money, of course, because Larralde was known to not want to part with one single dollar—even if he owed it.

HW: What reason did Mr. Echeveste have?

MG: I figured you already knew?

HW: Please, tell me your version of the story.

MG: I don't want to cause trouble for Domingo. He's a good guy— although I don't really know him well. He doesn't get too mad when Fermin and I take his pennies at dice, so he can't be half bad. And that's even with Fermin cheating sometimes.

AE: *Manuel cheats, too.*

HW: Anyway . . . What happened to make Mr. Echeveste upset?

MG: Well, Larralde was supposed to have invested some of his wages, but it seems like he made off with the money instead. When Domingo asked for the savings the other day, Larralde said he didn't have it. It was a lot of money, I understand. Domingo was outraged. I cannot blame him.

HW: What happened then?

MG: This was just the day before yesterday. I heard Mr. Cedarry broke up the fight before it got too bad. He told Larralde he had to leave the hotel before the week was out. But now, well . . . Larralde's dead. So.

HW: Mr. Cedarry was going to evict Larralde from the boardinghouse?

AE: *I thought you knew that.*

HW: No, I didn't. Honestly, you people don't tell me anything.

From Anna Elissetche's Murder & Eggnog Journal

(Still hidden inside the extra blanket in the trunk at the foot of her bed.)

Saturday, Christmas Day
December 25, 1943

While it's not the most pleasant thing to write about on Christmas Day, I forgot to make note that the sheriff gave the Cedarrys permission to clean up Larralde's room a couple days ago. After the coroner removed the body, they took all of Joanes's belongings for "thorough examination for potential evidence." Benat and Louise didn't want anyone else to have to clean the terrible and horrible mess, so they did it themselves. When I offered to help, Benat yelled at me to get my "ipurdia away from the room." He had never sounded so stern or so upset. This must have been what it felt like to be their daughter when he tried to stop Patricia from going to Holy Cross.

Speaking of Patricia, I got a letter from her again yesterday. She was shocked at Joanes's murder. But honestly, she seemed to be more upset to have missed all the excitement while she was stuck in San Francisco babysitting small children who liked to stick candy canes up their noses. Yes, they actually did this. She told me all about it in her letter. Little Frankie had to be taken to the doctor on Parnassus Avenue to have a piece of it pulled out with skinny forceps. This is the danger that comes from being Basque. Our noses are so big that if we stick something too far in, we need a search party and a flashlight to get it out again.

Don't believe me? Well, Patricia said that Frankie was still smelling peppermint four days later.

Anyway, Patricia also sent me a Christmas present that I was not allowed to open until today. So, I just opened it and it is the latest Agatha Christie novel, *The Moving Finger*. I'm so excited to read it, but I've got my nose (excuse the pun!) so far into our mystery here that I can smell the bleach fumes that are still wafting down from upstairs.

Speaking of Christmas presents, Ama got me a new lilac-colored dress with a plum cardigan. It's almost too pretty to wear to Douglas High School, because most of the freshman boys still spend half the time throwing clods of dry Nevada dirt at each other like idiots. And I definitely don't want this dress to get dirty.

Anyway, Louise got me a pastry cookbook and a bar of jasmine soap. She wrote a note inside the cookbook that said it's to help me continue to make delicious pies and treats for her to eat in her old age. (Hopefully those Thanksgiving pies weren't a fluke . . . the pressure is now on!)

The Cedarrys and Teresa and Catalina joined us, and the boarders, for Christmas breakfast this morning—chorizos, xingarra, patatak, and fried eggs with edges so brown and crispy that you knew the stove was screaming hot when they were made.

Just how I like them.

By late morning, there was light snow falling. But that didn't stop some of the most curious Basques from coming to the hotel for coffee (brandy), gossip, and mus. And by most curious, I mean Michel Lassa and Ignacio Zubillaga. Of course, this was in direct violation of the sign that still hung outside the front door indicating that the hotel was closed to outside guests. But I suppose "outside guests" really meant people who didn't speak Basque and who didn't appreciate the wonders of a mozkorsalda so strong that your breath could kill a vampire as far away as Denver.

But, nonetheless, Benat announced at breakfast that the hotel would reopen for lunch and dinner guests on Monday. He also announced that he'd had a call from Grace Ansolabehere, Joanes's older sister from Buffalo, Wyoming, that the county was releasing the body for burial on Tuesday. As his next of kin, she had to make all the arrangements. I remember meeting Mrs. Ansolabehere once at Aita's funeral. The only reason I remember her is because her nose had a large mole with six hairs sticking out of it like a porcupine. I suppose it was rude of me to be shocked by this at the time, but I was only 10 and I didn't know that humans who were not witches could also have moles on their nose.

Mrs. Ansolabehere also told Benat that a graveside service was going to be held on Thursday morning at 9am. She didn't want a big funeral because she knew what we all knew to be true . . .

That every Basque person west of Albuquerque would come to the funeral—through rain, sleet, hail, and snow (just like the US Mail!)—to have a chance to learn some unknown secret about Joanes Larralde's murder.

Mrs. Ansolabehere's daughter and son-in-law were joining her on the long drive. Benat offered to host the family for a small lunch after the burial, but the woman said (and this is a direct quote from Benat):

"I never want to step foot in your horrible hotel ever again. My brother's ghost is probably haunting all of you."

This statement made the Goytia brothers turn whiter than the snow on the mountains nearby. And then the brothers crossed themselves twice before taking a big sip of coffee with shaking hands (either caused by fear or the hangover they still had from drinking too many highballs last night).

But, okay, I'm going to be honest . . . this comment from Mrs. Ansolabehere seems a little extreme coming from a woman who actually looks like a witch and would do some haunting of her own. Yes, I know that I probably need to say some Hail Marys for even thinking such a thing. But, come on, The Sierra Hotel was originally built in 1889 . . . If there were ghosts here, we'd at least have one or two that had already taken residence by now.

And I haven't heard or seen any ghosts.

Unless the years and years of garlic have scared them away. Which is possible, I suppose. The Cedarrys have owned the place for a long while, after all.

Anyway, Joanes's sister extended an invite to the graveside service to Ama and I, and, out of obligation I suspect, to Benat and Louise. A couple of Larralde cousins from Fresno were expected, too. But that was it.

I didn't want to go, but Ama insisted that we must. Joanes had been Aita's sheep partner and, even though he hadn't been Ama's favorite person, going to the service to pay our respects was the right thing to do.

Ugh, why were amas always right?

Later the same night . . .

Sorry, I had to help Ama with supper and the dishes. Ama let me have the last two cups of eggnog after supper. This is some wonderful stuff. I wish we could have eggnog all year, not just at Christmas. People would be much happier and they'd have less reason to murder each other. This would be WAY better for my real life, but not for my fictional life (obviously).

Everyone went to bed early this evening—Domingo seemed extra quiet after he returned from dropping Catalina back at Mrs. Frunz's house. Domingo is often quiet, but this time it was different. He seemed heavy. Sad. Overwhelmed. You know, like he was carrying one of those big rocks that the giant, strong Basques like to throw around in those crazy competitions they have when they drink too much wine?

I asked Domingo what was wrong, but he just gave me a sad smile and said he was just tired from the Christmas celebrating. I'm not sure I believe him.

Speaking of Domingo, for Christmas, Catalina embroidered a white hand-kerchief for me with little purple flowers and my initials in green. It's really lovely. She's so sweet. I really, really, really hope that Domingo didn't murder Joanes. I've been thinking about it all evening . . . even while eating my favorite food at supper—tongue with garlic parsley vinaigrette.

Because Domingo <u>can't</u> go to jail. He just can't. Because then who will take care of Catalina and the baby???? It makes me cry thinking about it.

In fact, I'm crying right now as I write this.

Maybe I shouldn't drink eggnog after all.

Witness Interview #2
(Property of the Douglas County Sheriff)

Case No: 22-43
Date: Wed, 12/22/43
Time: 9:15am
Witness: Bernard Cedarry
Interviewing Officer: H. Williams

HW: I'm sorry for bothering you at home. But I thought it best if we spoke away from the boardinghouse.

BC: Would you like a cup of coffee? Louise can make you one.

HW: No but thank you.

BC: How can I help you?

HW: I understand that there was an altercation between the deceased and Mr. Echeveste?

BC: What means 'altacaccion?'

HW: I'm sorry for not being clear. Altercation means fight or argument. Did Mr. Larralde and Mr. Echeveste have a fight recently?

BC: Yes. Just the day before the Christmas besta.

HW: What happened?

BC: Domingo asked for the money that Joanes had invested for him over the years. From his pay. Domingo and Catalina are getting married, you see. He needs the money to find a place for them to live because she can't have a baby living in my hotel with a bunch of men. My Louise says that no woman wants to live with stinky men.

HW: My wife would say the same thing.

BC: Joanes told Domingo he didn't have any money for him. That the money was lost when the investment went bad. But I think he just kept Domingo's money for himself.

HW: I bet Mr. Echeveste was angry.

BC: Diós, yes!

HW: What happened then?

BC: Domingo pulled Joanes and nearly punched him. I stopped the fight because Anna was nearby, and I didn't want her to see that. That girl sees too much already. I worry about her. She doesn't have a papa to protect her, you know.

HW: Yes, I understand. I have a daughter, too, but she recently married and is living in Reno. I still worry about her, even still. Anyway, what did you do after you stopped the fight between the two men?

BC: I was disgusted by what Joanes had done. It was a bad thing. To do that to your own worker? A good, hardworking man? It is wrong. He deserved to get punched and kicked. I almost let Domingo do it. I really did. But I don't want trouble in my hotel. So, I told Joanes he had to find another place to live.

HW: You would have kicked him out?

BC: Yes. I may be an old man, but I can still throw a man out the door if I have to. And Joanes deserved it.

HW: You aren't old.

BC: I'm older than you.

HW: Not by too much. My wife keeps telling me to retire before this hip of mine gives out on me completely. Maybe after this damn war is over.

BC: Aleman putak.

HW: I'm sorry, what?

BC: Never mind.

HW: Anyway, tell me about what happened between the deceased and Mr. Santiago Achaval.

BC: Oy yoy, that got ugly. Joanes stole some pastures from Achaval and that's a sin when you are a sheepman. Then, he overbid the state to get some of the leases that Achaval had already been promised. Achaval filed a lawsuit against Joanes, but I don't think it had made it to court, yet.

HW: Is that all that happened?

BC: Well, I really shouldn't tell stories that I can't say for sure are true, but . . .

HW: Please. This is just between you and me. Anna is not here to take notes about us in her diary.

BC: Ayyy, that silly girl. She's going to get herself into more trouble than she can handle if she's not careful.

HW: Anyway, what happened next?

BC: Well, just a few weeks ago, Xavier—that's Achaval's son—was in an accident in one of the ranch trucks. He's seventeen and finishes school next year. Xavier was dropping off some supplies for the foreman and he lost control out on Kingsbury Grade. He survived with only some bruises and cuts, thank God, but Achaval was positive that someone had sabotaged the truck. I don't know why he thought this, but he did.

HW: Where did you hear this?

BC: You hear many stories in a Basque hotel bar. Only about half of them are true. So, take this "with a grain of salt" as the amerikanoak say.

HW: Did Mr. Achaval think that Mr. Larralde was involved in this?

BC: Yes. As revenge for the lawsuit he had filed against him.

HW: Do you know if Mr. Achaval had any evidence of this? It's a very serious accusation to make. And difficult to prove.

BC: I don't know. I only heard this secondhand. Or, it could have been thirdhand. Or fourth-hand. Who knows! Sheepherders are only good at counting sheep, not much else.

HW: Do you think it's possible it could be true? From what you know of Mr. Larralde?

BC: If you had asked me this question six month ago, I say no. But a man who would steal from his own worker? A man like that would do anything. So, I do not know what to say to this.

HW: I appreciate the time, Mr. Cedarry. I will let you get back to your day. By the way, the coroner is getting ready to release his report, so there is no need to preserve the crime scene any longer. You can have the room cleaned now, if you like. I'm sure it's a terrible, terrible sight. Would you like me to refer a cleaning service to you to handle it? I know there's one in Reno with experience.

BC: No, no. But thank you. My Louise and I will take care of it. We Basques always clean up our own messes.

HW: Why do I have the feeling you aren't just talking about dirty rooms?

Witness Interview #2
(Property of the Douglas County Sheriff)

Case No: 22-43
Date: Wed, 12/22/43
Time: 5:00pm
Witness: Domingo Echeveste *(Bernard Cedarry interpreter)*
Interviewing Officer: H. Williams

HW: I was on my way home for the day and thought I'd stop in for a few more questions. I hope that is okay.

DE: Yes.

HW: Anna is busy with dinner?

BC: *Bai. She is helping Maite. Did you want me to get her? I was just about to go home, myself.*

HW: No, it's fine. This shouldn't take long. If you don't mind?

BC: *No, it is fine.*

HW: Mr. Echeveste, you mentioned in our last talk that you immigrated in '37. I made a couple telephone calls and I couldn't find any records of you . . . anywhere. Do you know why that could be?

DE: I do not know.

HW: Perhaps you have a different full name? Or I have some information wrong?

DE: I know nothing of these things. But Domingo Echeveste is my name.

HW: I don't want to cause trouble for you, after all, you seem like a solid young man. But I just want to make sure you've told me all that I need to know.

BC: *Sheriff, I am sure that he has. Domingo is a good man. You know how these Americans destroy our beautiful Basque names! I bet they changed his name in the paperwork because they didn't know how to spell it.*

HW: Perhaps. But please know, Mr. Echeveste, I just want answers. Did the deceased find out something about your past that you didn't want anyone to know?

BC: *What means 'deceased?'*

HW: It means the dead person.

BC: *Then why didn't you just say that to begin with?*

HW: I honestly don't know.

BC: *Ha! Silly amerikarra.*

HW: You know, I thought you'd be easier than Anna. But I guess all Basques are contrarians.

BC: *What means that?*

HW: Umm . . . Never mind.

HW: Mr. Echeveste, I just want to help. If you know anything that can help me solve this case, please tell me. I am not in the business of immigration, deportation, or anything like that. I do not care about any it.

BC: *The man has told you all he knows. But, if he learns more, we know where to find you. We don't have to look far because you show up here every day like kukusuak on a xakurra.*

HW: Wait, what?

BC: *You say "never mind," so I say never mind, too.*

HW: Well, okay then. So . . . I better let you get to your dinner. I'm sure mine is waiting for me at home, too.

BC: *Yes. Goodnight, Sheriff.*

HW: See you tomorrow, probably.

BC: *Watch out for the kukusuak. They bite.*

HW: You people make me tired.

From Anna Elissetche's
Murder & Eavesdropping Journal

(Just shoved inside the drawer in the nightstand next to her to bed.
Not a good place to keep it.)

It's Still Christmas (Barely)

I guess not everyone is asleep. I just got up to get a glass of water because my eggnog mouth feels dry and cottonish. Padding to the small bathroom, I heard low murmurs coming from the kitchen. At first, my sleep-addled brain thought it was the grumbly sounds that Pintto makes when he's dreaming about his younger days chasing sheep with Aita. But then I remembered that Pintto was not in the kitchen. His doghouse is an old wine barrel with Aita's old jacket as his bed. It sits next to the back door. (I've tried to convince Ama to let Pintto sleep in my room, but she says that while having a dog with fleas is one thing, having a daughter with kukusuak is quite another.)

The voices in the kitchen were so low that I knew the conversation was not meant for my ears. This, of course, made me six times more likely to want to hear it. So, I tiptoed to the kitchen door and pressed my ear to the wood. I felt like one of those spies in the detective stories they play on the radio sometimes on Saturday night. I love them, but Ama usually wants to listen to polka music, so we compromise. She gets to pick the radio show one day, and I get to pick the next time. This means that I hear about half the episodes of any show—so I only know about half the clues I need to solve the case.

Why does it feel like the same thing is happening to me now?

I cupped my hands around my ear to amplify the sound. I had to strain very hard to make out any words. It sounded like Domingo's deep voice was confiding to my mother.

"With Tomas gone, and only Jesus knows when or if he'll come back, that polizia needs to find someone to put in jail. And I think it's going to be me."

"Domingo, we don't know that. The amerikano seems to be fair and do things right. I don't think he's going to put someone in jail just . . . because."

"I had the most reason to kill him. It is no secret what he did to me. Whether I did kill him, or I didn't, it won't matter."

"You make me nervous when you talk like this. Tomas sounded like you, and now look what he's done. The idiot boy."

"You know I'm right, Maite."

"I know nothing of the kind! If that polizia decides to jail you, he'd have to jail half the Bascos around. More people disliked Joanes, than liked him. Use your head!"

"You sound like my Ama."

"She'd tell you the same thing I'm saying right now."

"You know, I really miss her."

"I'm sure you do. But you never talk about your home. About your time before America. I've always wondered why. Usually, sheepherders will share every single thing about home. About the village they are from, the house they were born in, and even which of their apple trees makes the best cider. Some of the talkative ones will even admit which village girls could be sweet-talked into putting a ladder outside their bedroom window at night. Ostia, as if I really needed to know about that!"

Side Note: Okay, I'm not ashamed to admit that I really wanted to know about what Ama was talking about. But I needed to stay focused.

Domingo began, as if the words were slowly dribbling like molasses, "You know I'm from Basauri."

"Well, yes. Of course. But, not much else. Did something happen back home? Is that why you don't mention it?"

I didn't think it was possible, but Domingo's voice got even lower, "I . . . left home in 1937. I know you know what happened in April of that year."

My brain thought back—I couldn't put my finger on it just then. But Ama knew. Her voice got sad, "I had a feeling it had something to do with that terrible, terrible thing."

"When those alemanak bombed Gernika, I was just 17. I had a bigger temper then, and the feeling of needing to do something—anything!—to avenge those many lives lost, it was overwhelming. So much anger. It was a difficult time. A few friends and I joined a group affiliated with Eusko Gudarostea to resist the frankistak. One night in early summer, we set fire to a home in Bilbao that was owned by a frankista. Then, a few days later, we tried it again to a villa in Donostia. The dirty garda must have known we were coming because they were waiting for us."

Domingo paused and I held my breath, riveted by every word he had uttered—which was burned into my brain like a brand on a steer.

He continued, "I managed to get away because I knew the area better than the other rebels. My Amuma's sister lived in Donostia, so I had visited before. I knew my way around. So, when I ran away from the villa, I knew exactly where to go. I hid in Tia Rosi's house for three days until word came from my Aita. The polizia nazionalista had been to Basauri looking for me. I could not return home, or they'd send me to prison, or worse. They made that clear when they threatened Aita."

There was another long pause. My heart was thumping in my chest. I was afraid they could hear it through the door.

Domingo added, "I knew then that I had to leave Euskadi. I didn't want trouble for my family. For my Aita. He worked at a factory, and I didn't want him to lose his job. So, my Tia Rosi gave me some money and her son-in-law got me on a boat headed to Lisbon. From there, I booked a passage to Veracruz. I made my way north and crossed the border at Tijuana. I decided to use the name Echeveste in honor of my Amuma and my Tia Rosi. Their father's name was Echeveste. My real name is Juan Domingo Gallatabeitia."

My mother's voice was stern, yet gentle when she replied, "I am very glad to meet you Juan Domingo Gallatabeitia." She added, "Those zozoak deserved to be punished for siding with that Franco. I understand how you felt. But it wasn't safe for you to do what you did. Yet, I'm happy you were brave enough to come here and make a life. Away from that terrible war that could have killed you."

"I may end up in prison anyway."

"Nonsense!" Ama tsked. She used the same tone with me when I thought there was a mamu living under my bed when I was seven.

"That amerikano sheriff knows that I don't have papers. He knows that my immigration wasn't legal. What if he sends me back to Spain? A prison here would be better than being in a prison guarded by dirty frankistak. Or being killed by one."

"A bigger war is happening now. I really don't think they are going to deport you. The amerikarrak have enough to worry about with those alemanak and japoniarrak."

"I pray you are right."

"I am always right. It makes Anna mad."

Domingo chuckled and the serious mood was broken. But then he added, "So, what do I do now, Maite?"

Ama took a few moments to collect her thoughts. I waited for what she would say next. I knew Ama would say the right thing. She usually did. (And she clearly wasn't modest enough <u>not</u> to admit it herself!)

"First of all, you're going to marry that sweet neska mexikarra before she is forced to have that baby right on this kitchen table." I could hear Ama knock lightly on the thick wood of the table. "Second, you are not going to run off like crazy Tomas. That was stupid of him to do. You must be smarter. You must cooperate with the polizia, but don't give more information than you must. Do you understand?"

"Bai."

"It's been a long week. I think it's time for bed. Yes?"

I heard wooden chairs scraping against the floor as they stood. The glass of water forgotten, I reared back from the door. Then, I dashed back into my room as quickly and as quietly as my stockinged feet would allow. As soon as I heard Ama enter her bedroom, I pulled out my journal and began to document what I had heard before the conversation evaporated from my eggnogged memory.

Tomorrow, I am going to be so tired. Hopefully Ama won't notice.

Sadly, she probably will.

From Anna Elissetche's
Murder & Hangover Journal

(Now hidden under her mattress because she's starting to lose track of
what is actually going on, let alone where she keeps this damn book.
She will never, ever admit it, but detective-ing is harder than she thought.)

Sunday
December 26, 1943

They say snails move at a slow pace, and I'd like to say that I can move like a
snail. I haven't given much thought to snails in my life, other than the rare
occasion that Ama finds them at a market and cooks them in garlic, parsley,
and oodles of butter. As the demand for snails among the amerikano popula-
tion of western Nevada is slim to "wait, you want me to eat <u>what</u>??," I don't
have them often.

In this post-Christmas, eggnog-hangover mood that I've been in most of the
day, I'm decidedly slow. Ama already gave me a hard time for taking five minutes
to wash one pot, but she doesn't understand how difficult it is to concentrate on
scrubbing off potato starches when your eyeballs are burning.

Why does eggnog make your eyeballs burn?

Why didn't anyone tell me that before?

Teresa came today to help tidy up the kitchen, guest restroom, and dining
room for the reopening of the restaurant tomorrow. When I woke up after 8am
and stumbled into the kitchen, Teresa was already there scrubbing the stove. Ama
couldn't resist commenting, "Oh, look, the mozkorra has decided to wake up."

It took all my effort not to grumble back—which would only prove her right
(which we have already determined happens too often!). Also, she wouldn't take
kindly to hear that I spent so much time scribbling in a journal about a murder that
she had already told me several times to not get mixed up in. Surely, I thought, I

116

need to find a better spot to hide this journal. Ama knows enough English that she'd piece together what this darned thing is about. Maybe tomorrow, after the cobwebs are cleared out of my brain, I will come up with an improved hiding place.

After sucking down a kafesnea like a thirsty calf at a bucket, I spent the rest of the morning helping Teresa. We scrubbed the kitchen, wiped down the dining room tables and chairs, and swept the floors. Before lunch, the guest bathroom and the boarder washroom were all that was left. While tidying up the boarder washroom, I felt my energy wane—and my scrubbing slowed to the speed of the snail I talked about earlier.

Talking seemed preferable.

"Teresa, what do you think about this whole thing?"

"What thing?"

"You know, the murder."

Standing from the counter of sinks, Teresa paled, and I realized my question might have been a little insensitive. Okay, a lot insensitive.

"I—I don't know," she muttered, looking away. She tucked a light brown strand of hair that had fallen into her face back into the band at her nape.

"I know it was awful for you," I rushed out, "I still can't believe it all myself."

Teresa didn't respond, so I continued, even though I probably shouldn't have. What can I say—I was tired and hungover (and did I mention the snail thing?).

"Do you have any idea who may have murdered Joanes?"

Teresa was quiet again, but her narrow chin tightened, ever so slightly.

I persisted, "I mean, it seems like there were many people who didn't like him."

Teresa turned back to the counter and began scrubbing, even harder this time. Finally, she answered, "With good reason."

"What makes you say that?" I leaned forward, then relaxed, trying to pretend like I didn't care much about the reply (even though I failed miserably!).

"He was not . . . . a good man."

"In what way?" I felt a peculiar ice dance across my skin.

"Do—can you promise not to say anything to anyone?"

Dear Lord, I was ready to expire from curiosity. "Of course, I can. Yes."

"A couple of months ago, Joanes came up from behind me while I was replacing linens in the storeroom upstairs. He grabbed my bottom and pulled me towards him. I could smell whiskey on his breath. It was sour and horrible. I tried pushing him away, but he was stronger than me."

Teresa paused, collecting her thoughts. I was dreading what she was going to say next, but I knew I needed to hear it.

"We scuffled for a while, and I thrust my elbow into his stomach. I was able to get away long enough to pull open the door before he pulled me back. Then he said, 'I will not take no for an answer again. Not today. Not again. You hear me?' "

Teresa hugged her arms to her middle, "He started to rip my dress when Antton appeared at the top of the staircase. He had a direct view into the storage room since I had managed to open the door."

Teresa took a shaky breath, "Antton called out my name in alarm. Joanes dropped his hands and took a step back. I managed to dash out of the storage room. I waited just outside, listening. But then, Joanes said the oddest thing to Antton."

"What did he say?"

"He said, 'Oh, it's just you.' "

"Wait, what?" I was so confused.

"Then, Joanes added, 'And if you know what's good for you, you'll keep your mouth shut about this. A man with secrets should know how to keep them. Bai?' "

The color began to return to Teresa's long face, "Antton looked ready to punch Joanes, but he didn't. He just stood there, his cheeks angry and red. As I started to run to the stairs, Joanes shouted, 'Neska, you misunderstand me. I was just saying hello. Don't embarrass your Otto Benat and Tantta Louise by trying to say this is anything else. A girl's reputation is a fragile thing—euskaldunak like to talk. Don't forget.' "

I felt my ears begin to burn as if I had witnessed the entire thing. Words came and went through my mind like water through my fingers—and I couldn't collect any of them to actually say aloud. "I—I don't know what to say."

Teresa stiffened her shoulders, picking up the rag and the bottle of white vinegar. She sprayed the vinegar on the mirror and began to wipe it down, "But, what is done, is done. And what Joanes said is right. Euskaldunak like to talk."

I finally found some words, "But, he needed to be punished for that! It was wrong!"

"Otto and Tantta were so kind to take me in after Ama died. Aita was lost and it hurt him to even see me and Marie-Batista, my little sister. So he sent me to America, and he sent Marie-Batista to live with Ama's cousin in Anglet. I didn't want to cause trouble. It was better to stay quiet. And Joanes pretended like nothing happened, so it was easy to pretend the same."

"Benat would have wanted to know. He would have been so angry." I was as sure of this as I was of the sun coming up tomorrow morning (if this hangover didn't kill me first).

"That's exactly why I didn't say anything. Otto's getting older now, and I didn't want him to hurt himself doing something he shouldn't. It wouldn't have helped matters, anyway."

"We don't know that," I insisted stubbornly.

Teresa's smile was sad, "Yes, we do. Remember when Otto tried to get that squirrel and he fell off the ladder? He nearly broke his neck in the process. Can you imagine what he would have done in this instance? After all, that was just a squirrel eating some of his cherries!"

I didn't like Teresa's logic at all. It offended every instinct that I had inside of me. But it was not my decision to make.

Right?

But she was correct about one thing: what was done, was done. And clearly nothing could be done about it now, anyway. After all, Joanes's body was currently lying in a freezer at the Douglas County Morgue. And at least, this way, Benat wasn't the cause of it.

Or . . .

Was he?

Puta, I am going to have to burn this journal, aren't I?

(Don't tell my Ama I said puta.)

Witness Interview
(Property of the Douglas County Sheriff)

Case No: 22-43
Date: Wed, 12/22/43
Time: 11:00am
Witness: Mitchell Lauden
Interviewing Officer: H. Williams

HW: I hope I'm not keeping you from an appointment with a client or a court appearance.

ML: No, not at all. It's fine. I'm catching up on my correspondence. My secretary has been getting on my case about it for weeks. She hates to see the pile of letters on my desk. She says it makes it look like she's not doing her job. I told her no, it makes it look like I'm not doing MY job.

HW: She better not see my desk at the station. I still have mail on it from '37.

ML: That makes me feel better. Anyway, I'm assuming you're here about the Larralde murder.

HW: Why, yes.

ML: What an awful business that is.

HW: Yes. And instead of having one decent lead, I have about four not-so-good ones.

ML: The job of a sheriff is never finished. And never appreciated.

HW: Ain't that the truth.

ML: I was actually at The Sierra Hotel for dinner the night before. For the Christmas dinner. I try to never miss an occasion when Maite makes oxtail stew. I know I shouldn't say this, but my mother is a bad cook. It's why she hires other people to do it for her. Even still, I'd never had a good meal in my entire life until I started going to dinner at Basque restaurants. I have lunch or dinner at the boardinghouse at least two or three times a week.

HW: Tell me about the Christmas dinner. Aside from the oxtails, which I'm sure were great. But I don't want to discuss food since I'm getting hungry for lunch.

ML: Ha! True. Anyway, there were about 50 or 60 people there, I'd say. The long tables in the dining room were full. While there were a few Americans, like me, it was mostly Basques in attendance.

HW: Did you know any of them?

ML: A few, yes. My family has lived in the area for a while, as you know, and my father knows, well . . . everyone.

HW: Did you see Mr. Larralde?

ML: No, I don't recall seeing him. Which is strange because the boarders usually always eat at the hotel.

HW: What time did you leave?

ML: It wasn't terribly late since I had to drive home. Maybe around 10pm? The music had already been playing for a while by that point.

HW: Did you see Santiago Achaval at the dinner?

ML: Why, yes, I did. I spoke to him for a while before dinner, and he bought me a drink. I've done some work for him in the past.

HW: What can you tell me about that lawsuit business with Larralde and Achaval?

ML: I'm not part of that case, so I don't know much. Achaval hired a lawyer out of Reno, I believe. Not sure what would have come out of it, though. Guess we won't know now. Unless Achaval tries to recover from Larralde's estate? Who knows! I do know that Achaval has enough stubbornness to try that, though. A man doesn't become the largest sheepman in the Carson Valley without some ruthlessness.

HW: That's true. Very true. Anything else I should know before talking to Mr. Achaval?

ML: Not really, no. But, if you are ever out to dinner with the man, never order beef.

From Anna Elissetche's Murder & Maybe-This-Wasn't-A-Good-Idea Journal

(Now hidden in a small tin box at the back of Pintto's doghouse. No one ever looks there. It's full of fleas, dirt, and drool.)

Sunday Evening
December 26, 1943

I snuck away after helping Ama clean up supper. I <u>had</u> to fill you in on the rest of the day's events. I'm beginning to feel like an ace reporter—like the kind played by Rosalind Russell in *His Girl Friday*. Which is also starring Cary Grant, who might be the most HANDSOME man in the world (aside from Antton Garai, of course). I saw the film with Patricia at the cinema in Carson City a couple years ago. She had just received her driver's license and it was the first time Patricia had legally driven a car anywhere. I felt quite grown to be going with her on the outing, but that didn't stop me from criticizing her driving skills which I thought were inferior to my own. Sure, she could see further than me over the steering wheel, but could she parallel park as well as I could? No.

Anyway, by early afternoon today, the typical Sunday lull commenced in the dining room. Ama forced me to practice my accordion which, I'm ashamed to admit, I only did halfheartedly. My jotas sounded like waltzes and my waltzes sounded like lullabies. The sound was drearier than the droopy Christmas decorations still hanging in the dining room. Victor still gave me a penny tip, anyway, even though he napped through three very, <u>very</u> slow Zazpi Jauziak.

Michel Lassa and Ignacio Zubillaga drifted into the bar after lunch, and soon parked themselves in the dining room for ~~coffee~~ brandy and mus with Victor and Benat. It wasn't long before Michel began to gloat, "See, I told you that Tomas Hardoy was guilty. He ran off at the first opportunity."

Ignacio tapped his cards on the table, "Oy yoy, Michel, just look at your cards already. Can't you wait five minutes before beginning to gossip like an old hen?"

Michel sourly picked up his cards, "Don't pretend that you don't want to hear about it. We all know you do."

Ignacio retorted, "At least I can be tactful about it. You are like a bull that chases five heifers at once!"

Michel waved him off, "Not five. Maybe three."

Benat rolled his eyes, "Are we playing these cards, going mus, or what? I don't have all day."

Victor called out, "Paso ttipi!"

Benat rubbed his hand over his face, "We aren't even on ttipia yet, Victor."

Ignacio turned to Michel and tapped the table again, "Mintza. Go."

The men proceeded to play, but it wasn't long before Michel turned the conversation back around again, like a dog picking up the scent of a jackrabbit, "So, any idea where Hardoy went? I heard the amerikarrak are looking for him."

Benat took a long breath, like he does when his patience is tested or he gets heartburn from too much tripota, "It's not like Tomas left us a note. Or a map. Or a confession. So, how would I know?"

"You seem to know everything else that goes on around here," Michel reasoned.

Ignacio pulled a chip from the middle of the table to the pile at his side, "You act like Cedarry works for BBC Radio. He doesn't, you know."

Michel shrugged, "I know that. He wouldn't be stuck in this place if he did."

"Hey! If someone else owned this place, would they let you drink <u>all</u> their brandy?" Benat retorted.

Michel went quiet and they resumed the game . . . at least until Victor said he had a pateak, which he turned out to <u>not</u> have, resulting in them having to start all over again.

Snapping his red suspenders as he yawned, Ignacio rose, declaring, "I need more coffee!" and headed to the bar. I weakly pecked at the chorus of "The Blue Danube" on my accordion. It sounded funereal. My playing was <u>not</u> what Strauss had in mind when he first wrote the song.

A few minutes later, Ignacio returned, "Garai is gone and there's no coffee. What do I do now?"

Benat spoke slowly, as if to a small child, "You <u>do</u> know how to make coffee, don't you, Ignacio?"

"But Antton usually does it. Or my wife."

"You poor man. Do they tie your shoes for you, too?" Benat replied dryly.

Michel chimed in, "It's a good thing he wears boots."

Ignacio grumbled, "Fine. I'll make the coffee. It can't be that hard if you idiotak can do it." He pivoted back to the bar.

Michel rubbed a hand over his white head, "Ach, are you sure you want him making the coffee, Cedarry? He might break the machine."

Benat quickly stood up, "Ostia, you're right!"

After he left to join Ignacio in the bar, I turned my attention more fully to my song. My playing slightly improved, but then Victor said, "Play a waltz, neska!"

"This is a waltz," I called out in frustration.

"It sounds like a funeral song for old soldiers that lost a leg," Michel grimaced.

"Then I'm not doing it right. It's supposed to be a happy song." My voice sounded surlier than I would have liked. I shoved the accordion straps further up on my shoulders, feeling defeated.

"Keep playing, neska!" Victor tried to encourage me, but I was pretty sure that a career as an accordionist wasn't in my future.

Just then, Ama emerged from the kitchen with a plate of leftover Christmas almond cake. She set it on the table where the men had been playing mus, and where Victor was clearly waiting to say "hordago" for a jokua he didn't even have.

"Haurra, why did you stop playing?" Ama asked. "Are you still mozkorra?"

Michel laughed, "Anna, are you mozkorra? Did you drink an entire bottle of Benat's whiskey last night?"

I felt my cheeks pink and I looked away, "No, I had some eggnog."

"You what?" Victor asked, a hand raised to his ear.

"She had that Christmas esnea that the amerikarrak like to drink," Ama answered for me. I said I wouldn't lie in this journal, so I won't. So, in that moment, I was very annoyed at Ama for ratting me out since she was the one who let me drink it to begin with. (And I told her so later on this evening!)

Victor tsked, "This is why you must only have good Basque drinks. Not these silly amerikano ones. Years ago in San Francisco, I had something called 'peppermint schnapps' at the Ligue Henri IV Christmas party. I got so sick that I couldn't eat anything with sugar in it for six days. Even now, the smell of peppermint gum makes my stomach turn—"

Thankfully, Victor's story was interrupted by the men returning from the bar. They were joined by Santiago Achaval and one of his foremen, Melchor Espinal (who was also his sister's son).

I did say that Basque people are all related to each other in one way, or another, right? We are like those interbred horses and show pigs that you see at the fair.

Anyway, Santiago was an imposing man with a barrel chest and thick strands of grey running through his black hair. He wore a denim jacket over a black button-up shirt open at his neck, revealing strong muscles in his shoulders—muscles far more developed than one normally saw in a man nearly sixty years of age. As a proper gentleman would, Mr. Achaval immediately greeted Ama with two kisses and wished her an "Eguberri On." (Merry Christmas.) He then told her that he'd be bringing his family in to eat sometime this week if she could save them a table.

Not since Santiago's disagreement with Joanes began some months ago had the Achavals been to eat here at the boardinghouse—without it being for a specific event, like a large party. It was notable and, well, odd, to see him here now.

Mr. Achaval gestured to his nephew, who had a chest as large as his, but weirdly, far less hair on top of his head. Melchor was in his late twenties. His round face had a few scars from a battle with acne that he had clearly lost. "Can we join you for mus?"

Benat was first to respond, "Sure. We can play sei mus since we have two more players."

The men settled at the table, threw kings to decide the partners, and started to play. Ama let me put away my accordion (thank goodness!) but made me fetch more ~~coffee~~ brandy from the bar for the men and two more slices of almond cake from the kitchen. I got three slices of cake—one for me—because I was feeling faint from my extraordinary accordion playing.

Accordions are heavy, don't let anyone pretend otherwise.

Anyway, Mr. Achaval had way more tact than Michel because he let nearly an entire game go by before he brought up the murder investigation.

This was why Santiago Achaval was such a successful businessman—while Michel Lassa spent half his life being mad at all Italians because a man named Giuseppe once dropped a brick on his finger.

"Cedarry, this whole murder investigation must have disrupted your business. I'm sorry you're having to go through this mess," Achaval clucked his tongue in sadness and dealt out the next hand of cards to the six players.

"We open again tomorrow, so things should turn around. I will be glad when this is all over," Benat replied, picking up his cards.

Michel's eyes darted back and forth between the two men. He squirmed slightly in his seat as if he longed to join the conversation, but also didn't want to impede its progress. Ignacio patiently took a sip of the coffee he had made, but then grimaced slightly as if the coffee wasn't quite as good as he had hoped. He set it down on the saucer and pushed it away. Melchor was shoving an entire piece of cake into his mouth as if he hadn't eaten cake since last Christmas.

But Victor interjected, "I'm mus."

Benat sighed, again, "We can't go mus, Victor, because we went hordago on the haundiak."

"Why did we do that?" Victor asked. "I don't have any kings."

Their other partner, Ignacio, slapped his forehead, "Oy yoy, Victor!"

Mr. Achaval smiled, and put a king, a queen, and a jack on the wooden table, "Kanta!"

Ignacio threw his cards down and stood up, "We need to make new coffee, this one is terrible. And I need better coffee if I'm going to keep losing like this."

Ignacio stomped off to the kitchen—probably to find Ama and ask her to make fresh coffee in there.

Men.

Mr. Achaval leaned back in his chair, "How is the investigation going?"

Benat shrugged his shoulders, "Slow, it seems. But, that polizia does ask a lot of questions. Not sure if any of the questions are helping, but what do I know?"

"Does he have any idea who did it?" Achaval asked, a curious note betraying his relaxed posture as he lounged in the wooden chair as if he didn't have a care in the world.

"Honestly, I don't think he does. He most likely suspects half of the Carson Valley since Larralde had more enemies than Napoleon."

Achaval didn't respond, but the muscles in his strong neck tightened.

"Anyway, I heard they are releasing his body for burial this week. Hopefully that brings us one step closer to having all of this behind us."

"I hope so."

"Did the sheriff interview you, yet?"

"No, why?" Achaval leaned forward, his dark brows lowering over his intense brown eyes, "What does he want with me?"

"Well, it's no secret that you and Joanes had a—" Benat tried using the tact and diplomacy that made him a good hotelier, "—disagreement."

"So?" A defensive edge entered the sheepman's voice.

"The polizia is being very thorough. He asked for a complete list of everyone that was at the Christmas party. Since you were there and you have a history with Joanes, I don't see how he won't be wanting to interview you."

"We'll see about that." Achaval crossed his arms over his chest, "I'm not talking to any polizia. I will call my lawyer tomorrow. I don't have time for this."

"But I don't know if you'll have a choice, Santiago," Benat reasoned.

"Oh, I <u>always</u> have a choice." He stood from the table and nodded to the men at the table, "Joseba will be expecting me home soon. Thank you for the game. Gero arte."

And, with that, Santiago Achaval stalked out. Before following him, Melchor grabbed one more piece of almond cake. With crumbs falling from his mouth, the younger man said goodbye.

I could feel that Michel and Benat were quite uncomfortable, and maybe a little concerned, about Mr. Achaval's response. Victor was not, of course, because the heaviness in the air didn't seem to bother him in the slightest. I picked up the empty plate of almond cake and swept up a few crumbs from the table, trying to appear busy and not the least bit interested in their conversation.

Ignacio returned from the kitchen holding a tray of fresh coffee. He halted in his tracks, "Wait, where did everyone go?"

Witness Interview
(Property of the Douglas County Sheriff)

Case No: 22-43
Date: Mon, 12/27/43
Time: 9:00am
Witness: Santiago Achaval
Interviewing Officer: H. Williams

HW: I'm sorry to bother you while you're working, Mr. Achaval. But I was told it would be the easiest to find you out here in the pasture.

SA: Who told you that?

HW: I first went to your house and your wife directed me out here.

SA: I ask that you not go to my wife with this.

HW: Of course, but I did need to find you. So, here I am.

SA: I don't know why you would need to talk to me.

HW: You were acquainted with Mr. Larralde?

SA: Everyone knew him. This is a small town.

HW: Well, yes. But I understand that you and the deceased had some disagreements in the past . . . over business?

SA: Who told you that?

HW: It doesn't seem to be a secret. It's general knowledge that you had a dispute over some pasture lands.

SA: I'd still like to know who told you this.

HW: How is that important?

SA: Was it the Goytias?

HW: Mr. Achaval, please. I just have some simple questions; it won't take long.

SA: I have nothing to say. I know nothing about this whole Larralde astakeria.

HW: Please—

SA: You can speak to my lawyer if you want. His name is Anderson Kepner and he's in Reno.

HW: Can I speak to your son, Xavier, or to your employee Mr. Espinal? I know they were also at the dinner party at the boardinghouse.

SA: Good morning to you. I have lambs to check now. This business doesn't run itself. I think you know the way back to the road. It's just down that trail right there.

HW: But—

SA: Adios, sheriff.

From Anna Elissetche's
Slightly Smelly Murder Journal

(Still hidden in a small tin box at the back of Pintto's doghouse.)

Monday
December 27, 1943

"I need to order as many non-German sausages as possible before Friday, Mr. Richter."

I said this earlier this morning to the butcher, Fred, while standing in front of his counter. In retrospect, perhaps my words were not the wisest if I didn't want to offend the man. After all, I was pretty sure he was at least 37.5% German on his father's side. The large man raised an eyebrow, "I'm sorry, what?"

"We are having a New Year's Eve dinner on Friday and Ama was thinking of frying up some sliced sausages and serving it with bread for the appetizer."

"Okay . . . and . . ." Fred patiently waited for me to continue.

"Well, as most of the attendees will be Basque, and given the . . . well, you know?" I gestured vaguely in the air as if my hand movement alone would indicate what I meant, "It might be best if the appetizer doesn't scream 'German.' "

"I'd like to think my food doesn't scream anything."

"It doesn't, of course." I paused and considered, "Well, unless we're talking about when it was still alive? Because then, yes, it would scream at that point. Because what pig would want to become another batch of chorizo?"

Fred leaned forward onto the counter, "Why would the pig want to be chorizo when it could be a frankfurter?" Amusement creased the corner of his eyes.

"See, I'd like to avoid having to tell people that we're serving frankfurters. It sounds way too Germanish."

"We could just call the sausage something else."

This idea had immediate appeal. "Like what?"

129

"I don't know. You're a clever girl who drives around town, I'm sure you can come up with something."

So, that led me to buying 20 pounds of assorted bratwursts and frankfurters. I've tentatively named them "Alpine Sausage," "Winter Sausage," and "Of-Course-No-Germans-Were-Involved-In-The-Making-Of-This Sausage."

It was Benat's idea to throw a New Year's Eve dinner. He wanted to show everyone that things are okay now at the boardinghouse and that none of the Basques should worry about getting murdered in the middle of eating their lamb roast—which is what Ama decided to cook for the dinner.

We don't know how many are coming to the dinner, but given what happened just a week ago, I doubt that many Basques would resist the opportunity for a good dinner and even better gossip.

Having loaded the sausages, I backed up the truck, and when I turned onto the road, I saw Antton walking by Mitchell Lauden's office to the corner store that sold cigarettes. He held a small envelope in his hand. I waved, but he didn't see me. He was wearing a dark blue shirt that complimented his dark hair that was still just a little too long.

He really is so very handsome.

If Patricia doesn't marry him, I will be so very disappointed, because there is no way Antton Garai will remain single long enough for me to be able to marry him. Time isn't on my side. I know enough math to figure that one out.

After returning to the boardinghouse, I helped Ama and Teresa with lunch. But now I am tucked in the corner of the bar with a pen, my secret journal, and my scuffed World History textbook (the only one big enough to hide my journal inside). If I place the journal between the chapters on the Dark Ages and the Renaissance, no one will be able to notice it is there. Victor is dozing at his usual table by the window, and Antton just made drinks for two amerikanoak at the bar. One has a small leather camera bag over his shoulder and the other has a thick notebook in his hand.

"Say, Mister, what can you tell me about that murder here last week?" The blond man with the notebook is tapping his tongue to a pen and looks poised to write.

"I no English. No English," Antton just pantomimed dramatically and shrugged his shoulders in the most Gallic way I have ever seen him do. I am biting back a smile.

"Shit." The blond man snapped his notebook shut. Then took a sip of his Picon. Then he grimaced. "This is disgusting. Try it, Lenny."

Pushing his camera bag further up his shoulder, the shorter man took a sip. He pursed his thin lips, "It's not terrible, but it's not good."

"Maybe we should talk to that old guy over there."

"He's sleeping."

"We'll wake him up. We don't have all day if we want to get back to the newsroom in Reno before dark. I have a date at 7:00. Taking Leonora to the pictures. And then hopefully to my place afterwards, if you get my meaning."

The camera guy rolled his eyes, "I have no idea how you get so many dates."

"It's because I'm so charming." The reporter has tossed a few coins on the bar and slid off the stool.

"It's definitely not that," the photo man replied dryly.

They are approaching Victor . . . The photographer has tapped the old man on his shoulder—causing Victor to lurch awake, and his rheumy eyes to turn glassy and unfocused, "Zer?"

"Excuse me, sir, may we ask you a few questions about the murder?" The reporter opened his notepad with a flick of his thumb.

"Nor zara?" Victor is giving him a distasteful look.

"THE MURDER?" The reporter yelled the words and swiped his hand across his own throat.

"Amerikar ergela."

Oh my. Okay. I have to intervene now. Be right back—

The American journalists from Reno just left.

After Victor began to curse the reporter for waking him, I closed my textbook over my journal with a large thump, directing their attention towards me.

"Where did you come from?" the photo man asked. He had a mustard stain on his tan blazer's lapel.

"I've been over here the entire time."

"Huh," the reporter ran a hand through his blond hair, "I didn't notice."

I crossed my hands over the textbook on the small table in front of me, "Wow. You must be an amazing reporter."

"I think she's being sarcastic," the photo man added.

"Yeah, I caught that," the reporter grumbled.

"They don't speak English, in case you haven't worked that out already. And yelling at a Basque person won't magically turn English into a language they can understand. This isn't the Tower of Babel, it's a boardinghouse."

The photo man laughed, "She's a sassy one."

"Okay fine, kid," the reporter plopped himself down in the chair across from me. "I don't want to go back to Reno with nothing to show for it. Other than a bad taste in my mouth from that Pecan thing."

"It's a Picon."

He was losing his patience, "Fine, fine. What can you tell me about the murder?"

"A man died."

"Yes, I know. Did you know him?" He spoke slowly like I was about four.

"A lot of people knew him."

He persisted, "What was he like?"

"He had dark hair, with some grey in it. He was about 5'7. Maybe 180 pounds. I'm not sure. I just weigh 95 pounds. So, that's just a guess." I was enjoying this more than I would ever admit to anyone.

The reporter sighed heavily, "What was he like as a person?"

"He didn't like milk and sugar in his coffee, which is crazy, because those are the best parts. But, other than that, I suppose he was like all the other Basque men who came into the hotel."

"Did he have any enemies?"

I pretended to give it some thought, "You mean like in the movie *Zorro*?"

The reporter rubbed his thumb over his temple slowly, "Sure, like Zorro."

"No. We don't know anyone who uses a sword," I shook my head innocently.

The reporter eyed me with suspicion, "You're not going to tell me anything, are you?"

"What could I possibly have to tell?"

He nodded to the textbook in front of me, "What's that?"

"A history book."

"Why do you have a history book in a bar in the middle of your Christmas holiday? What kind of kid are you, anyway? I threw my books in my room during vacations and never looked at them until I went back to school again."

The photographer winked in my direction. "He never looked at his books!"

The reporter gritted his teeth, "You. Are. Not. Helping."

"This is a waste of time, Jim," the photographer insisted, "We should just hit the road. I'll take a couple shots of the exterior on our way out."

"But the chief said he thinks there is a story here. We can't just leave without one. He's still mad at me that I missed the scoop on that arsonist in Spanish Springs."

I really wanted to ask about the arsonist in Spanish Springs, but I managed to restrain myself. Wouldn't it make a great title for a mystery novel?! *The Arsonist in Spanish Springs*. It had a nice ring to it.

"Maybe we should just give it another week. Wait until the investigation finishes up, or more information comes out. Or maybe they'll find that Thomas Haraday guy. He's probably the one that did it, anyway."

The reporter considered his partner's words for a few moments. Finally, he said, "Alright. We can try talking to the family or whoever the next of kin is next week. See what was in the man's will, maybe? One of these things will have a story, or if it doesn't, it doesn't. I'll just tell the Chief that we tried and that it's not my fault that these Basques are so boring."

We were NOT boring. But, as I wanted them to leave as quickly as possible, I held my tongue by biting the inside of my cheek. It was very difficult to do this. I tasted a little blood, which left a bad taste in my mouth that I would have to fix by eating a snack.

"Can we talk to your ma or pop before we go?" the photographer asked, "Maybe they can help us?"

"I don't think so. My father passed away. And my mother doesn't speak English, either. So, it's me or no one, I'm afraid."

"We're never going to get a story," the reporter lamented.

An hour later . . .

Pintto sniffed the melting cheese as I made myself a toasted sandwich. His black and white tail swinging happily, he grinned at me when I gave him the kaskoa from the end of the loaf. As he gnawed at it, Ama tsked and looked down the end of her glasses, "Haurra, Benat is going to be upset that you gave the kaskoa to the xakurra. That's his favorite part of the bread."

"They are coming for dinner tonight?" I asked.

"Bai. I'm making a big pot of beef stew, as you can see. But we don't know how many kuriosak will come tonight because it's the first day we're back open. Benat and Louise wanted to be here in case people ask questions."

"You know they will, Ama," I burned the tip of my finger on the bread and nearly dropped the whole sandwich on the floor. Pintto would have been thrilled. Ama, not so much.

Ama turned to me, suddenly serious, "Are you doing okay, haurra? This Joanes business is very upsetting for everyone. I don't like that you are around this. It must worry you."

"I guess it does. But I'm not scared or anything. Not really. I do want to find out what happened, though. It's like a book, in a way," I took a bite of my small sandwich and breathed in and out as the cheese scalded my tongue.

I really haven't ever learned to wait until it cools. Given how many times I've burned myself, you'd think I would have learned by now. But apparently not.

Ama squeezed my arm, her blue eyes concerned, "This is not a book, haurra. Not at all. Don't forget that."

"I understand," I assured her quickly. I took another bite of sandwich to cover my discomfort. I didn't like the intensity in her voice.

Antton interrupted our conversation when he opened the back door and stepped inside. He was carrying a small paper bag in one hand, a brown document envelope under his upper arm, and a heavy sack of vegetables in his other hand. He struggled not to drop the sack, "Maite, they only had these vegetables for you. The grocer said they will have more on Wednesday."

"That will barely be enough to make it to Wednesday," Ama frowned as she asked me to put the sack into the pantry and put the vegetables in their bins. I shoved the last bite of my sandwich into my mouth.

From the pantry, I heard Antton say, "I got the mail here and those papers for you. Where would you like them?"

"Oh, I'll take those. Thanks, Antton."

"Is that stew?" the bartender asked.

Ama's voice faded as she went into our apartment, "Yes. And don't worry, there will be plenty for you. I made enough to feed the entire amerikano army."

"The amerikarrak wouldn't appreciate your cooking the way I do," Antton called out in return.

"Ba! Those poor soldiers would probably appreciate even six-day-old bakailoa."

"That's true," Antton admitted.

When I entered the kitchen again, Antton was pulling out his purchases from the paper bag. He had a carton of cigarettes, a small collection of blank mail envelopes and stamps, butterscotch candies, lemon drops, and gumdrops. He held up the candy to me, "Which one do you want?"

"A little of each one, of course." It was the only way to answer a question like that.

"A girl after my own heart." Antton separated the candy into two piles and placed one pile back into his bag with his other purchases.

I eagerly scooped the remaining candy into the pockets of my woolen trousers as Ama returned to the kitchen.

"That will rot your stomach," Ama warned.

"No, it won't. It may rot my teeth, though."

"Wonderful," Ama rolled her eyes and stirred the pot of stew with a long wooden spoon, "Just what I've always wanted—a daughter with fewer teeth than Victor Arrossa."

Antton laughed and walked away.

"Anna, can you wipe down the tables in the dining room? Teresa should be here soon to help me with the rest of dinner."

I went to do as Ama asked, but it took me twice as long as it usually did because I kept stopping to eat candy. When I was wiping the last of the chairs, I heard the bottles clanking in the bar as Antton set to work.

I scooped up the candy wrappers I had abandoned on top of the table and went to throw them in the trash at the bar where Ama wouldn't see them. As I entered the bar, I saw the Goytia brothers shuffle into the front door. They wore their work clothes and heavy wool-lined coats. Frowns marred their matching faces, but Manuel looked ready to maybe . . . cry? Or punch a wall. It was hard to tell which.

Dirty boots shuffling along the worn floors, Fermin stalked to the bar, "Cervezas, please, Antton. We had a bad day."

Antton pulled out two bottles, snapped off the lids from the tops, and set them on top of the counter, "What happened?"

Dejected, Manuel sunk into his stool, "I think we got fired."

Fermin sat next to his brother. "Calm down, anaia. We didn't get fired. At least, it didn't quite sound like it." Rubbing his chin in thought, Fermin took a big swig of beer, "Let's not think the worse."

"You know what Achaval is like when he's angry. Grizzly bears are friendlier than he is." Shuddering in unease, Manuel drank another heavy swallow.

"True. But he's a fair man, really, let's remember that." Fermin pointed the neck of his beer in his brother's direction.

Antton asked, "But, why would he fire you?"

"His nephew, Melchor Espinal, told us they thought we had been the ones gossiping to the sheriff about the fight with Larralde. Espinal was very mad about it," Manuel replied.

"Ba!" Antton scoffed, "Every euskualduna from here to Elko knew about that. Even some of the amerikanoak, too. Mitchell Lauden asked me about it a few weeks ago because he heard about it from another lawyer."

"See, Manuel! I told you! This will all blow over—like one of those thunderstorms at Lake Tahoe."

"Do you think there's another reason he could be so angry?" My voice startled the men—who hadn't seemed to notice that I was there. Manuel looked confused, blinking owlishly. Fermin grew thoughtful. And Antton scrubbed the counter briskly with a rag—he bit his lip, as if he wanted to say something, but didn't.

"Are you saying that you think Santiago Achaval killed Larralde?" Manuel gazed at me like I had grown horns on top of my head.

Antton threw his rag on the bar top, "Ba! She's not saying that at all. Mano, drink your beer before you say something else crazy."

Fermin twisted his beer bottle between his two callused hands, then he said very slowly, "He didn't actually have to do the killing. Did he? Someone else could have done it for him. And we all know who that would have been."

Manuel quickly crossed himself like he wanted to ward off any evil spirits. Then, he stuttered, "M—M—Melchor."

Antton leaned forward onto the bar, losing his patience with the lot of them, "This is a ridiculous conversation." Then the bartender pointed to the Goytias, "And you two are worried about getting fired? This kind of talk won't help that. Use your head."

Antton pivoted to me. He grew intense, and his voice lowered, "Neska, this is serious. Nothing to play at. Unlike those books you read." Turning to the bar, he wiped a few bottles, "Maybe you should check if Maite needs help in the kitchen."

Feeling dismissed, I did as he instructed.

Although, I was still pretty sure I was right.

Witness Interview
(Property of the Douglas County Sheriff)

Case No: 22-43
Date: Mon, 12/20/43
Time: 5:00pm
Witness: Antoine Garai *(Anna Elissetche, interpreter)*
Interviewing Officer: H. Williams

HW: I know it's been a long, upsetting day for everyone here at the hotel. I'll try to keep my questions simple and brief, Mr. Garai.

AG: It's a terrible thing.

HW: Oh, you speak English?

AE: He does, but I'd best stay in case there is a certain word he doesn't understand.

AG: I will be fine—

AE: I don't mind staying.

HW: Let's just move on, okay? Mr. Garai, how long have you worked at The Sierra Hotel?

AG: I've been the bartender for the past five years.

HW: When did you immigrate and where did you come from?

AG: I came to America when I was 18. So, that was almost ten years ago. I was born in Estérençuby, a small village in Basse-Navarre.

AE: *That's right by the French border with Spain.*

HW: What was your first job when you came?

AG: My Otto on my mother's side found me a job as a sheepherder in Wyoming. I worked there for about two years, but I was a terrible sheepherder.

AE: *I'm sure you weren't that bad.*

AG: No, I was. I lost four lambs in one night, not because of snow or wolves . . . but because I sprained my ankle by tripping on my own sheepdog.

AE: *Ha! That didn't actually happen.*

AG: Yes, it did! Why else do you think I had to start working at the Basque hotels? It's not because my Picons are the best. It's because I can't be trusted to keep sheep alive.

HW: Do I need to be here for this interview, or are you just going to do it without me, Anna?

AE: *Sorry Sheriff.*

HW: By the way, he doesn't need a translator. His English is better than my sister's. And Agnes is a schoolteacher.

AG: Pardon, Sheriff. Please continue the questions. I know you are busy.

HW: Mr. Garai, how long have you known the murder victim?

AG: I first met Joanes briefly when I worked at a different Basque restaurant in Stockton, about maybe six years ago? Didn't know him, though. That hotel switched owners soon after that. They didn't need a bartender, so I moved here to Nevada for this job at the boardinghouse.

HW: What were your impressions of Mr. Larralde when you first met him?

AG: Honestly? He didn't tip much (if anything) to waitresses or bartenders. In my line of work, you notice that very fast.

HW: How did your opinion change when you got to know him better while working here?

AG: It didn't really change. Not really. He was a good businessman, could be interesting to talk to, but he could be . . . gaistoa.

HW: What does that mean?

AE: *It refers to a mean person. Or someone with a bad side.*

HW: Did you ever have an argument or confrontation with Mr. Larralde, yourself?

AG: I keep to myself, really. I don't want problems or to start fights with people. To be a bartender, you must be a peacekeeper. Alcohol and gaistoa men are not a good combination sometimes.

HW: Do you think that played a part in this crime?

AG: A man has been murdered. And it happened during a party where there was a lot of whiskey and wine. Maybe I made a drink for the murderer? I don't know. I did think about that a lot today.

HW: Last night, were you working behind the bar all evening?

AG: Most of the night, but not all of it. Mrs. Sagouspe played the accordion for the dancing, but Benat and Louise asked me to play for a short while so she could take a break and have a drink. The Goytia brothers bartended for me during that time.

AE: Antton is a great accordion player. He gives me lessons sometimes, but I'm not very good.

AG: You are doing well! You've gotten better in the last year.

AE: So, I just went from playing very badly, to just badly.

HW: May I continue?

AE: Oops. Yes, sorry.

HW: So, Mr. Garai, you went from the bar to the dining room? How long did you play music?

AG: About 30 minutes?

HW: You didn't go upstairs at all last night during the party, then?

AG: Well, I had to get my accordion. It was in my room.

HW: What time was that?

AG: I don't know the exact time. But I guess it was around 9pm? 9:30?

HW: Did you see anyone upstairs when you went to get your accordion?

AG: No.

HW: So, you went to get your accordion and then directly back downstairs?

AG: Well, no. While upstairs, I used the toilet and changed my shirt, too. I got grenadine on my sleeve from the Picons I made before dinner.

AE: *Grenadine can stain. And it is so sticky*

HW: We all know what grenadine is, Anna. Thank you for clarifying.

AE: *Just making sure.*

HW: Anna, I think I can finish this without you. I'm sure your mother needs your help now. It's almost supper time. I'll call you if I need you. Okay?

AE: *I guess so. I'll see you tomorrow?*

HW: Yes, I'm sure you will.

AG: Thank you for helping, neska.

HW: Fine. Now, then. Mr. Garai, you see and hear many things working in a bar, I'm sure. You probably learn more things about people than you wished to know. What can you tell me about Thomas Hardoy and Domingo Echeveste? Do you know them well?

AG: I haven't known Hardoy as long as I've known Domingo. Hardoy stays here when he's in town, but that's not very often. He's a younger, wilder sort—he prefers the casinos . . . and other places . . . much more than spending time in a Basque bar with old men who play mus and tell the same stories over and over again.

HW: What are your other impressions of Mr. Hardoy?

AG: Well, he has a temper. Yes. I've had to break up a few fights between him and others a few times. He gets an idea in his head, and it's hard to change his mind if he decides to do something.

HW: Would you say that he could be violent?

AG: I don't know if I would say that. It's one thing to get into a fight with a drunk amerikano that insulted you. It's quite another to murder someone. So, I don't really know how to answer that question.

HW: And what of Mr. Echeveste?

AG: Domingo is quiet. Serious. But he's a good man. And he's a much better sheepherder than I ever was! Hardworking. Again, more hard-working than I am! Ha! I've known him for most of the time I've worked here, and he's never gotten into a fight with anyone.

HW: Do you think he's capable of violence, though?

AG: I can't imagine it. Honestly, I can't.

HW: But, what about if he had the right motivation? I heard he argued with Mr. Larralde very recently.

AG: Yes, he did.

HW: It seems that what Mr. Larralde did to Mr. Echeveste would be enough to drive him to violence. Wouldn't it?

AG: I guess. It is the most upset that I've ever seen Domingo. He had a right to be mad. But, to say that he murdered Joanes? I don't know. It's possible. But . . .

HW: But, what?

AG: Never mind.

HW: Please, Mr. Garai. What were you going to say?

AG: Nothing. I don't want to cause problems for Domingo. It has nothing to do with any of this. I swear it.

HW: You do know that I am going to investigate it, don't you? It's easier if you just tell me.

AG: He's a good man. Leave him be.

HW: I have no interest in harming innocent people. I am a sheriff. I made an oath to protect others.

AG: Please don't forget that promise.

From Anna Elissetche's
Murder & Too-Many-Suspects Journal

(Tucked inside her schoolbag because she is too tired to take it out to Pintto's doghouse.)

Monday Night
December 27, 1943

I can barely keep my eyes open, but I'll try to write down how the evening went before I fade away into dreamland. First, it was an average crowd for dinner—meaning that there will be leftover beef stew for lunch tomorrow. I don't mind this because I'm of the opinion that leftover stew is sometimes better than freshly made stew. I am aware this position could be unpopular, but I still stand by it because I know I'm right.

Anyway, after the first small wave of early-bird guests (the ones mostly over 60 and/or the just <u>really</u> hungry ones), Mitchell Lauden arrived with the lovely Bridget Farquhar and his parents, the Senator and Mrs. Lauden.

I was coming from the dining room to scope out how many diners would be coming from the bar, when I saw the foursome bustling inside. Mrs. Emmaline Lauden held tightly to her husband's arm as they stepped toward the bar for a drink. Her light hair was curled around her face in such a perfect way that I knew that a beautician had been responsible for both the style and the color—which, at her late-to-middle age, should have had plenty of gray by now. Senator Lauden, a taller version of his son, had a ready grin and a perfectly pressed dinner jacket. His handshake was practiced, and firm, as he reached out to greet Benat, "Mr. Cedarry! It's been a while. How are you?"

"Senator! We are so happy to have you here with us. It is kind of you to come," Benat said warmly. Then, he turned to Mitchell, "Your son is one of our best customers. Maite loves to cook for men who appreciate it, and Mr. Lauden is always coming back for more."

Mitchell laughed and leaned on his cane, "I can sniff Maite's cooking from miles away. It calls to me like a dog."

Emmaline Lauden's brows furrowed, "Mitchell, darling, but you hardly eat anything at home."

"Uhh—" I nearly laughed when Mitchell desperately cast about for a change in subject, "Mr. Cedarry, have you met Bridget? Her dad is Daniel Farquhar out in Spanish Springs?"

Benat politely shook the young woman's hand, "Yes, I have. I never forget a beautiful face. Although, my Louise does not like it when I say that." He winked.

Bridget's light hair was pulled back into a ponytail and she wore a dark pink dress that matched her rosy cheeks. She laughed, "Well, you are a handsome and distinguished gentleman, so I can see why she'd get jealous."

"Ba!" Benat pulled off his black boneta to reveal a bald spot beneath it, "I'm not so handsome, anymore."

"I disagree," Bridget said defiantly.

"You need to bring this girl with you to my restaurant more often, young man, she is good for this old man's heart," Benat said to Mitchell, who had already turned to order drinks from Antton.

Antton pointed the young lawyer's attention back to Bridget, "You better do as Benat says, Mr. Lauden, or he won't ask Maite to save the best lamb chops for you anymore."

Mitchell turned back to his party and a flush had settled over his cheeks, "Y—yes, of course I will!" He smiled brightly . . . almost too brightly.

The senator looked at the young couple fondly, "I hope we'll be seeing more of Miss Farquhar, as well. Her father and I are very old friends."

Antton knocked over a glass and hurried to clean it up. I dashed forward to greet the newest arrivals, "Hello. Will it be just the four of you for dinner? I can make sure to get a table ready for you once you are done with your cocktails."

"Thank you," the senator smiled at me and asked, "Miss—?"

"My name is Anna."

"She's the daughter of the wonderful cook in the kitchen, Pops," Mitchell offered.

"Lovely," Emmaline Lauden said distractedly, as she gazed in slight disgust at the dark, rustic decor of the bar. I noticed a tightening in her lips. Mrs. McGillicuddy made the same look when I checked out "too many books." (What does that phrase even mean, anyway?! "Too many books." It should be blasphemy for a librarian to even say such a thing.)

Then the woman examined me a little more closely, "My, aren't you young to be working so hard in a place like this?"

Her words prickled at me. Really and truly. Like itchy poison oak. I had to scratch it. So, that's my only excuse for what I said next:

"Well, most people aren't fortunate enough to not work. So . . ." I let my words trail off to let everyone know what exactly I meant.

Mitchell guffawed and swallowed it with a cough. After passing Bridget a Mary Pickford cocktail, he handed his mother and father an Old Fashioned as he took a large gulp of his Manhattan, "Anyway, Mr. Cedarry, did you have a chance to finish reviewing those documents? If so, I can take them with me and finish them up later this week."

"Yes, I did. They are here in the office behind the bar if you'd like to come."

Emmaline pouted, "Must you conduct business . . . here?"

"But, your son is smart man. You must be so proud," Benat said diplomatically.

The senator slapped his son on the back, "We are very proud. And I think he has quite a future at the state house in Carson City, too. Just like his old man." He paused and considered, "Well, one can hope, right?"

Emmaline pulled off one of her white gloves, "Hurry up with your business, Mitchell, dear, it's not polite to keep your date waiting."

Bridget shook her head, "Oh, it's no bother. I'm still enjoying my drink, anyway."

"I won't keep him long, I promise," Benat said as he led Mitchell to the door behind the bar that led to the small office he kept there.

There was an uncomfortable lull that settled over the group as the two chattiest members of their conversation had left. The senator admired a deer that graced the wall of the bar. I had decorated the antlers with Christmas garland and a Santa Claus hat. "Does this fellow work at the North Pole?"

"Just in December," I felt an embarrassed flush come over my face. I was supposed to have taken the decorations down earlier today, but I forgot about the deer.

The senator chuckled, "I like it. My wife won't let me put one in our house, I'm afraid."

Emmaline sniffed, "That's because they are dirty and disgusting. No one wants to look at something like that."

I was beginning to like Mrs. Lauden less and less. How did such a nice man come out of a mother like that?

Even Bridget seemed embarrassed by the older woman's rudeness, but she clearly couldn't say anything. The senator smoothed over his wife's curtness by turning to Bridget, "Next time your father comes to town, I'm bringing him here for lunch."

"I'm sure he would love that, sir," Bridget replied.

"Oh, let's not do this 'sir' business, Bridget. We're practically family." The senator tossed back the remainder of his Old Fashioned as Benat and Mitchell returned.

Benat clapped his hands together as he rejoined the group, "Can we get you four a table now?" He gestured to the dining room with his arm.

The Laudens and Miss Farquhar followed Benat into the dining room and I stayed behind to help Antton clean up the empty cocktail glasses. When I placed them behind the bar and began to rinse them, I noticed that Antton had a cut on his finger. It was bleeding a little.

"Antton, what happened?"

"Ba! I cut myself on that glass I dropped. I'm a clumsy man." He shrugged his shoulders and turned away from me.

"Do you need a bandage? I can get one for you."

"I'll be fine. I've had wounds that hurt more than this." Handsome face flushed, Antton gave an odd laugh. He couldn't quite meet my gaze.

"Are you sure?" I persisted.

"Bai. Can you tell Maite I'm going to sneak over for some dinner soon? Not too many people here in the bar now." A lock of dark hair had fallen over his eye, and I longed to brush it back myself.

"S—Sure," I replied. I heard the hiccup in my own voice.

I hesitated for a moment before finally going to do what he wished.

But something was wrong. I just know it.

Witness Interview
(Property of the Douglas County Sheriff)

Case No: 22-43
Date: Mon, 12/27/43
Time: 10:15am
Witness: Catalina Rodriguez (*Anna Elissetche, interpreter*)
Interviewing Officer: H. Williams

HW: I meant to speak with you last week, but the days have gone by so fast. I can't believe Christmas has come and gone. Anyway, each time I've wanted to talk to you, it was when you were already gone for the day.

AE: Catalina just works a few hours a day, depending on her schedule with the older lady she takes care of.

HW: I see. Thank you. But please leave the questions for Miss Rodriguez to answer, alright?

AE: Right. Yes, sorry.

HW: Wait, you do speak Spanish, right? You're not going to pretend to speak it, and then spring it on me later that you actually don't?

AE: My Spanish is better than my French. At least I think it is. Well, I guess we'll find out.

HW: Great. Lovely.

AE: Are you being sarcastic?

HW: Anyway . . . Miss Rodriguez, how long have you been in the US?

CR: I came with my brother, Ernesto, about three years ago. We're from Juchitlán in Jalisco. We first came to our uncle's house in Reno. He found us jobs cleaning in the casinos.

HW: And how did you end up in Gardnerville?

CR: My cousin heard about an old lady that needed someone to be a live-in housekeeper and he recommended me for the job. I started working at the boardinghouse soon after that.

HW: And when was this?

AE: She started working here last fall.

HW: You did it again, Anna . . .

AE: Drats. I promise I'll do better from now on.

HW: Maybe in time for me to catch the next murderer?

AE: *Does this mean you're going to hire me, after all?*

HW: How many times do I need to tell you that we aren't going to pay you?

AE: *Just thought I'd check again.*

HW: Anyway . . . Miss Rodriguez, were you acquainted with the deceased?

CR: Not well at all. I clean the boarder rooms sometimes, so I would see him on occasion. Domingo knows him much better than I do, of course.

HW: Right. You are recently engaged to Mr. Echeveste?

CR: Yes. We plan to marry soon.

HW: Congratulations. That's a beautiful engagement ring.

CR: Thank you.

HW: What were your impressions of Mr. Larralde, though? You've worked here for over a year. You must have formed an opinion of the man.

CR: My mama taught me not to say bad things about the dead. It is bad luck.

HW: If it's the truth, you have nothing to worry about.

CR: Well . . . Mr. Larralde never said thank you. Or left a tip, or anything. The other boarders would express thanks, and sometimes leave a tip. I'm not saying I expect these things, of course. After all, the Cedarrys pay me fairly, but it says something about a man if he isn't polite to those who cook or clean for him.

HW: Yes. I understand. What else can you tell me about your inter-
actions with Mr. Larralde?

CR: I don't know. It is embarrassing for me to say this . . .

HW: I don't plan to share this information publicly, so you don't have
to worry about that. And, from what I know of Miss Elissetche
here, she probably already knows what you're going to tell me,
anyway.

AE: *You keep making it sound like I'm nosy*

HW: Aren't you?

CR: Well, Mr. Larralde used to stare at my—well, he used to stare.
And it made me uncomfortable. So, I didn't wish to spend any
time alone with him.

HW: I understand. It was wise of you to be careful, of course. Now,
did Mr. Echeveste know how you felt about his employer? Did you
share these things with him?

CR: No, I did not. What good would it have done? I didn't want to
cause problems for Domingo. He had a good job. Well, I guess he
still has a job? For now at least.

HW: Are you sure that Mr. Echeveste didn't know any of this? We
men can be more observant than women think sometimes.

CR: What are you trying to say?

HW: Nothing. It's just a question. Thought it would be helpful to know
if Domingo was aware of your feelings about Mr. Larralde. That
he made you uncomfortable.

CR: Do you think Domingo killed his boss?

HW: No—

CR: You do, don't you?

HW: I'm not saying that—

CR: Domingo would never do such a thing. Never. Never.

HW: It's just a simple question.

CR: I know what you are trying to do—

HW: I'm not—Wait, Miss Rodriguez, please don't cry . . . I'm sorry . . .

AE: *Wow. She's crying hard. Wait . . . now she just said that you're going to lock her fiancé in prison, and she and her baby will end up living in the streets . . . forever. And that they will probably die there like starving dogs.*

HW: I really, really hate this case.

From Anna Elissetche's
Murder & Milkshake Journal

(Tucked under the foot of her bed because she's afraid of letting it out of her sight.)

Tuesday
December 28, 1943

I stuck close to Catalina this morning. She arrived at her usual time of 8:30am (after she gave old Mrs. Frunz her breakfast at home). I felt so bad about how yesterday had gone with the sheriff that I was probably more helpful to her than I had ever been in my life. This doesn't mean much, I'm sure, because it probably just translated to me doing a task well enough that she didn't have to go behind me to do it again.

Her normally cheerful face was puffy from crying, and I could tell she hadn't had much sleep the night before. I chattered on like a deranged person—just so that Catalina would be distracted from thinking about the fact that the man she's going to marry might go to jail for murder.

Side Note: I don't want to think that this is going to happen. But it is increasingly looking like it is. I'm not convinced that Domingo actually killed Joanes, though. Is there a possibility that he did? Yes, of course. But Tomas Hardoy and Santiago Achaval had just as much of a reason to do it as Domingo did. However, there is a difference between them. The temperaments of Hardoy and Achaval are much more suited to the task. Plus, Achaval's nephew Melchor looks like the kind of guy who would kill someone just to have a Christmas almond cake all to himself. Therefore, here's where I'd place the murderer odds at this time:

Santiago Achaval (c/o Melchor Espinal), 40%

Tomas Hardoy, 35%

Domingo Echeveste, 20%

Jack the Ripper, 5%

I'm fully aware that Jack the Ripper is probably dead. But we don't know that for certain, and western Nevada is a great place to hide if you are trying to get away from the law. (Don't tell Sheriff Williams I said that. He would probably find it offensive.)

After Catalina finished up and went back to Mrs. Frunz's house, Ama and I went to Carson City to buy warmer stockings for Joanes's burial on Thursday morning. She left Teresa to start the pot of white beans for supper (we are serving pork chops and canned green beans to go with it). Of course, Ama didn't let me drive because she said, in her words, "We don't need to attract any more attention from any polizia by having my daughter drive 15 miles down the highway. The amerikano sheriff already thinks we're all ridiculous, anyway." I told Ama that I didn't think that the sheriff thought that at all. But I wasn't sure if that was true because, half the time, he looked at me like I had antennae coming out of my head.

I found a pair of black woolen stockings to wear under the only black dress that I own—which I last wore at Aita's funeral four years ago. It had been big on me at the time (Ama bought it secondhand because we couldn't afford anything new). Yesterday, Ama let out the seams and it still managed to fit me—barely. Ama told me to wear the new plum cardigan she got me for Christmas over the dress so that no one will notice that the dress is tight on my arms. Ama seemed very worried about what Mrs. Ansolabehere is going to think/say when we see her on Thursday. Ama said, and these were her words, "Gracianna has a vicious tongue, and I don't want her to tell everyone that we can't afford proper clothes."

To be honest, we can't really afford that many new clothes. But if Ama feels better by pretending that we can, that is fine by me. After all, she let me get a chocolate milkshake at the diner next to the clothing store in Carson City, so I was willing to go along with whatever she wanted.

Ama found warm black stockings, too, and a navy-blue shirt dress that was 50% off in the after-Christmas sale. She snatched the dress off the rack so fast that I thought she was going to pull a muscle in her shoulder. I hadn't seen Ama that happy since Fred Richter mistakenly gave her nine packages of veal chops instead of the six she had paid for a few months ago. (When Ama unpacked the crate, she gave a whoop of delight that you usually only hear at the Douglas High School baseball games.)

We made it home in time for Ama to finish dinner. Ama told me I could read for a while here in my room (she must have been really happy about the discount on that shirt dress), but I need to make my remaining library books last until I go back to school in January. So, I took the chance to catch you up here.

Two hours later . . .

Okay, so guess who came to dinner this evening. The Achavals. Santiago, Joseba, and their daughter Elena. Their son, Xavier, stayed on the ranch—I really don't know why.

I told Ama that I had a tummy ache and had to use the bathroom, but I've really locked myself in here so I can write down what I just overheard without being disturbed (there's no lock on the accordion door to my room).

Anyway, Ama sent me to find some more linens to dry the dishes. When I didn't find any in the storage room downstairs, I decided to try the linen closet upstairs. But, as I neared the top of the landing, I heard voices speaking in the boarders' sitting room.

"If you convince Grace Ansolabehere to sell the sheep to me for under seven dollars a head, I will give you a cut of the price. I understand that you need the money. There might be a job in it for you, too." It was Santiago Achaval. He was supposed to be having supper with his family downstairs.

Domingo's voice was hesitant, "But, the going price is $10 a head. The war has made everything higher. I doubt she'll sell for much less than that."

Achaval was persistent, "Well, you never know. It doesn't hurt to ask. And I'd be very thankful to you for this—I've wanted to get Larralde's sheep out of this area for some time. And I don't want another sheepman coming in—especially now that I've finally got the way cleared. At last."

Domingo's voice lowered to not much higher than a whisper. I had to strain to hear it. "I'm sorry. W—What do you mean?"

Achaval tried to sound reassuring, "Nothing, son. I'm just looking out for my business. Nothing more than that. It's important, though, that no one know we had this conversation. Especially that sheriff."

Domingo grew firm, "I—I don't want to be involved in anything . . . gaixtoa. I have enough problems of my own. That sheriff is already breathing down my neck like a hungry xakurra."

Achaval switched tactics, "What if I could make that disappear for you? You just deliver the Larralde flock for under seven dollars, and I take care of the rest?"

"I can't promise anything like that. I—I barely know Mrs. Ansolabehere. I only met her once at Pierre Elissetche's funeral. I doubt she remembers me or even cares that I work for her brother."

"Just think about what I've said. It would be very good for you if you did." Achaval's voice had an edge.

Domingo's tone grew anxious, "Maybe you should return to dinner with your family now, Mr. Achaval. They are probably wondering where you are."

"Fine, but think about it. We'll talk more another time."

"I—I don't think I'll be changing my mind. But thank you."

As his heavy boots walked to the stairs, Achaval chucked, "Oh, I think you will."

I tried to dash down the stairs, but my loafers were loud, and my legs were short—meaning I couldn't move very quickly. Seconds later, Santiago Achaval stood a few feet above me. His heavy, dark eyebrows quivered like caterpillars, "Neska, what are you doing here sneaking around like a thief?"

He looked at me as if I was another of his employees to boss around.

Ama said my stubbornness reminded her of her own—apparently it is a trait shared by women from the village of Bidarray. Therefore, it wasn't me, really, but my inherited stubbornness that was responsible for what I said next:

"I live here, so it's impossible for me to sneak anywhere. And you? I'm quite sure <u>you</u> don't live in this boardinghouse."

Achaval slowly stepped down the stairs, grimacing at me. If looks could stop one's heart, I would have perished right there on that creaky staircase. "Mind your own business, neska ttipia. There are many things you don't understand."

"I understand more than you think." I really shouldn't have said that, but . . . well, I did. And, as they say, it's impossible to put spilt esnea back into a jug—or into a cup of kafea.

The sheepman brushed past me, and when he did, he whispered, "Get back to your ama, where you belong. Before you say something you'll regret?"

I may be stubborn, but I'm not stupid. So, this time, I did as he suggested.

Boardinghouse Murder Still Unsolved

An immigrant boardinghouse down in Gardnerville was the scene of a horrific murder last week and the crime is still unsolved. Local sheepman, Jean Larralde, 55, was found dead on the floor of his room on the morning of Monday, December 20th, by an employee of the boardinghouse. The coroner's report indicates that Mr. Larralde, a native of the Basque region in France, perished from blood loss sustained from a neck laceration. Sheriff Hiram Williams, of Douglas County, is leading the investigation into the murder. No arrests have been made, at this time. There are no officially named suspects. It appears that language barriers between law enforcement and witnesses have hampered the progress of the investigation thus far. While Sheriff Williams was reluctant to comment on the record, he did admit that he has several promising leads, and an arrest should be forthcoming. He did, however, request that anyone with information about the case contact the Douglas County Sheriff's Office in Minden.

-Jim Calderman
Evening Gazette, Metro Desk

From Anna Elissetche's Murder & Love Triangle Journal

(Hidden under her mattress.)

Wednesday
December 29, 1943

While usually a staple on Fridays during Lent, on cold, dark days like these, Ama likes to make bakailoa with boiled potatoes and piperade on top. It is a simple dinner to prepare, meaning I didn't have to do much to help. (Which I like, of course.) Salted cod was on sale a few weeks ago, so Ama had saved it for a day such as this. Winter fog, mist, and bits of ice floated in the air, shadowing the mountain peaks just behind the boardinghouse. The gloom fit the mood that has settled over The Sierra Hotel. With the sheriff's unfinished investigation and Joanes's burial tomorrow, everything is . . . weird. Uneasy. Even Louise, who is usually cheerful and good-natured, snapped at poor Teresa at lunchtime when she dropped a couple dirty plates on the way to the kitchen. Clearly the older woman is worried, too.

Tomorrow the dining room will be closed. The Cedarrys thought it would be a mark of respect to the Larralde family and the polite thing to do. They are usually right about these things, of course. I am glad, too, that Ama won't have to cook after spending the morning trying to impress a woman who apparently cares if we have new stockings or not. I don't understand much of how things like that work, but it all seems a little silly to me.

Anyway, I spent most of my day in my room. I stuck Pintto inside the apartment from the door that leads directly outside (which we never use). He sat next to my bed, his tail thumping happily, as he watched me read. Sometimes Pintto would lick the book jacket to get my attention. This was a little gross, but I figured it wasn't as bad as the cigarette ash marks that dot the pages and the binding from other readers that have borrowed the book before me.

156

<u>Side Note</u>: It doesn't seem wise to smoke a cigarette while you're holding an extremely flammable object in your hand. If you fall asleep for just a moment, Charles Dickens could become the reason your entire house burns down.

Anyway, Antton popped into the apartment to say hi this afternoon, too. When he spotted Pintto next to the bed, he whispered dramatically, "Ayyy, Maite is not going to like this." Then he bent down to ruffle Pintto's thick fur, causing white and black hairs to poof into the air like the icy fog outside.

"You aren't going to tell her. Don't pretend like you are," I chastised him with a laugh. "I know you bring Pintto up to your room at night, too. I hear noises outside all the time."

An odd look crossed Antton's face. A long moment passed. Then, he covered his confusion with a grin that pulled at his shadowed dimples, "You caught me!"

I spotted a letter in his hand, "What's that?"

"Oh, this is for you! I just got the mail. It's from Patricia," Antton extended the envelope to me.

"Did you get a letter, too?"

"No," he gave a heavy, dramatic sigh, "She likes you better than she likes me."

"Ha!" I laughed, "That's not true and you know it."

Smiling, he shrugged and gave Pintto one last pet, "I better go check on Victor in the bar. Yesterday, he napped so soundly that he almost fell off his chair."

After Antton left, I tore open Patricia's letter. I decided to transcribe it here, so I don't miss anything:

"Dear Anna,

Merry Christmas! (Well, it's two days before Christmas as I write this, but the holiday should be over by the time you get this letter.) I have something to tell you. I've been wanting to tell SOMEONE, so I decided to write to you.

I met a man. A most wonderful, handsome, smart man. His name is Joaquin Yturriaga and he's in the Air Force. As some of the girls would say at Holy Cross, he's the <u>Bee's Knees</u>! Joe's a bomber pilot, but he was in San Francisco on leave from Moffett Field and he came to the Christmas dinner dance last night at Hotel Des Alpes. We danced together most of the night and he asked me to write to him. He's expecting to be sent off to Europe next month. I hope to see Joe again while he's on leave, but he's to spend time with his family down in the valley, so I'm not certain.

Oh, Anna. He wore his uniform to the dinner and I nearly <u>swooned</u>. I know we said that Antton was the most handsome man we've met, but I think Joe takes the prize now. His father is from Gipuzkoa and his mother is from Bizkaia. He's so wonderful that I *can't stop smiling. Cousin Genevieve saw us dancing and she's been winking and smirking at me all day today.*

I don't want to jinx it... but, between you and me, Anna, I'm telling you:
<u>*I'm going to marry this man.*</u>
But Anna... what will Antton say?!?
Tell me what to do.
Hugs & Pottak,
Patti"

I could feel Patricia's excitement vibrating through the pages of her Holy Cross stationary. This Joaquin Yturriaga must have been quite something to get her into such a state. There is something about a man in uniform—I had to admit that. And a pilot? Yes, that is note-worthy. This is quite a pickle, though. I'll have to think on this for a while to come up with a reply to her letter. My experience in these matters is . . . well, ZERO.

However, I do know one thing: this situation is called a "love triangle." Where two people hold a romantic interest for the same person. The reason I know this is that I once read a book where one man killed another man because he didn't want to lose the woman he loved. While I don't remember all the specifics, I think the murderer tried to make it look like a heart attack. But he put too much arsenic in the coffee cup—leaving proof behind for the detective to find. In the end, the detective solved the case and won the girl. So, I guess it all worked out, except for the guy that drank the arsenic. It wasn't great for him.

Anyway, I'd better go sneak Pintto back out before Ama finds him in here. Bye for now!

Much later the same night . . .

I'm very, very confused by what I just saw and heard.

I woke up to go to the bathroom just after midnight. When I got back to my room, I found Pintto's favorite pilota on the floor. He must have left it there earlier. Since Pintto likes to sleep with the ball between his paws, I decided to go outside to give it to him.

But, as I opened the outside door to our apartment, I heard low voices, and a hum of an engine in the darkness around the back. Even though the air was icy, my curiosity won out. Arms wrapped tightly around my middle, I tiptoed in my dark plaid pajamas to the back of the boardinghouse.

I saw two men talking inside a stylish coupe-style car. I recognized the car—I had seen it before. The engine was rumbling in neutral, and the headlights were on low. As there was almost no moonlight, there was just enough of a gleam from the headlights for me to make out the profiles of the men inside.

It was Mitchell Lauden and Antton.

Their voices were hushed, but I could tell the conversation was causing some upset. Their handsome faces were tense, and their hands were gesturing in the shadows. Perplexed, I moved forward in the darkness to hear what they were saying. The passenger window was rolled down and their voices drifted over the hum of the engine.

"No reason for you to do this now. We are safe. Joanes is gone. He can't blackmail us anymore."

"I have to, Antton. I don't have a choice."

"Ba! You always have a choice."

"No, I don't. And you know it."

My heart began to beat very fast. I felt my blood rush in my ears as panic settled inside of me. Immediately, I knew it had something to do with the murder. It just <u>had</u> to. But was Mitchell Lauden involved? Was he going to report something to the sheriff? Whatever it was, Antton was clearly not happy about it. And that, made me very nervous. My world, which had felt very secure—despite all the madness around me—suddenly felt unsteady. For the first time, it felt like something terrible was about to happen. To someone whom I very much cared about.

"Fine. There is nothing more to say." Antton turned to the door and opened it. He began to step outside when Mitchell's arm shot out to grab him by the shoulder.

"Wait—"

Antton tried to shake the young lawyer off and started to stand. But then Mitchell grabbed Antton's hand. And held it in his.

"Wait—" Mitchell repeated, still holding tightly to the bartender's hand.

"I don't know what you want from me," Antton's voice was sad. I had never heard it so sad.

"N—nothing has to change," Mitchell replied.

"Ba! That is not true."

Mitchell changed tactics, "We can make it work. I know we can."

Antton didn't answer right away. But, when he did, his voice was so soft, I almost couldn't hear it: "We said we would never tell lies. We will not start now."

Several moments passed. But then Mitchell let go of Antton's hand. The rumble of the car engine was the only sound to be heard. Watching them, I felt a deep sadness that I didn't quite understand. Tears prickled my eyes, but I didn't know where they had come from.

Antton closed the car door and leaned into the window, "Good luck."
And then he walked away.

I backed away into the shadows and made my way back to the side door to our apartment. I quietly entered and returned to my room. It was only then that I realized that I still had Pintto's pilota in my hand.

Thurs, Dec 30, 1943

Wedding Bells Imminent for Senator's Son

Mr. and Mrs. Daniel Farquhar of Spanish Springs have just announced the engagement of their daughter, Bridget Ann, to attorney Mr. Mitchell Lauden, Esq. of Gardnerville, Nevada. Mr. Lauden is the son of State Senator Harper Lauden and his wife Mrs. Emmaline Lauden. Senator Lauden represents the Carson Valley in the State House. There are rumors that the groom-to-be holds political aspirations of his own. As Mr. Farquhar is a successful rancher, this wedding is expected to be the biggest societal event of the coming year. The affianced couple plans to marry in June.

-Millie Conrad
Evening Gazette, Society Desk

Last Will and Testament

I, *Jean Larralde* (hereinafter referred to as "the Testator"), with a place of residence at The Sierra Hotel, Highway 395, Gardnerville, Nevada, being of sound mind and not acting under duress do hereby make and declare this document to be my Last Will and Testament, and hereby revoke any and all other wills and codicils heretofore made by me.

PERSONAL REPRESENTATIVE: I appoint MR. MITCHELL LAUDEN, ESQ., with a mailing address of 520 Douglas Ave, Gardnerville, Nevada as the Personal Representative of my Estate.

EXPENSES & TAXES: I direct that all my debts, funeral, burial expenses and taxes be paid as soon after my death as may be reasonably convenient, and I hereby authorize my Personal Representative to settle any claims made against my Estate.

DISPOSITION OF PROPERTY: I devise and bequeath my property, both real and personal and wherever situated, to the following Beneficiary: MRS. GRACE ANSOLABEHERE, who is my sister and is entitled to 100% of my entire Estate.

SPECIAL BEQUESTS: Aside from the main Beneficiary, the following individuals shall receive special bequests: MRS. MAITE ELISSETCHE, widow of my business partner, Mr. Pierre Elissetche, is to receive $2,000 from my Estate to assist in the care and well-being of their daughter, Miss Anna Elissetche. MR. DOMINGO ECHEVESTE is to receive $750 from my Estate in gratitude for his years of hard work.

I, the undersigned, *Jean Larralde*, do hereby declare that I signed and executed this instrument as my Last Will, that I signed it willingly in the presence of each of the undersigned witnesses, on this 14 day of January, 1942.

Signature: *Jean Larralde*

The above-named Testator signed, sealed and declared to be his LAST WILL AND TESTAMENT, in the presence of us and have hereunto subscribed our names as attesting witnesses thereto.

Witness Signature: *Bernard Cedarry*

Witness: MR. BERNARD CEDARRY, 1447 Douglas Ave, Gardnerville, Nevada

Witness Signature: *Louise Cedarry*

Witness: MRS. LOUISE CEDARRY, 1447 Douglas Ave, Gardnerville, Nevada

From Anna Elissetche's
Murder & Black Stockings Journal

(Hidden at the bottom of the trunk inside her bedroom.)

Thursday
December 30, 1943

It was cold and icy out at Garden Cemetery this morning. We arrived a half hour early because Ama didn't want to be late. The rotund mortician, wearing a somber black suit, stood near an open grave. A pine casket hovered above the hole, held in the air by a small metal platform. I stared hard at the box—knowing that Joanes Larralde's body was inside. A small arrangement of winter flowers lay on top of the casket, as did a beaded brown rosary—an item I had never seen Joanes hold in his hand or pray—ever. I briefly wondered where the rosary came from. Did the mortician have a box of rosaries in his office for exactly this purpose? The beads seemed too new to have seen any real amount of praying. I had seen older Basque ladies pray the rosary. Their wrinkled fingers rubbed the beads <u>so</u> hard that if the stones were clumps of carbon, they would have turned them to diamonds.

Two gravediggers stood to the side of the half dozen picnic chairs that were placed next to the grave. The gravediggers' expressions were bored and distracted; they smoked and flicked ashes into the icy, dormant brown grass. Digging graves every day must make a man immune to the emotions of the world.

Ama fussed with the black ribbon that was holding my dark hair away from my face. Strands of my hair kept falling out around my ears, and she chastised me quietly for not putting bobby pins in to secure the flyaways. Ama wore the same black chambray dress she wore to Aita's funeral, but she had on her warmest wool coat which covered most of the somber dress. On top of her short, wavy brown hair, Ama had fastened a small mantilla made of black Spanish lace.

It wasn't long before the rest of the burial attendees arrived at the cemetery,

162

as well. Benat and Louise stood beside Ama and me, while the picnic chairs were filled by the Larralde family. Grace Ansolabehere sat in the seat at the front; she wore a black mantilla on top of her head, too, but hers was larger and it looked like it was made of real silk. Probably from the cocoons of silkworms that spoke with fancy accents.

The priest began the simple graveside service, sprinkling holy water onto the casket that quickly froze in the air. I watched tiny icicles form on the top of the pine coffin. I shivered at the sight. Grace gave a muffled cry, and I immediately felt badly for not paying much attention to the service going on in front of me.

Straightening my back to force myself to alertness, I looked around the cemetery. Headstones dotted the grass like oversized chess pieces. Most of them were small, like pawns. A few were like bishops and knights. The ones that were like kings and queens stood out in the grey sky. Those buried there must have thought that having a large, impressive headstone would be more fashionable. But those stones had the most bird poop on them, so I'm not sure if it worked out the way they had planned.

It was then I spotted Sheriff Williams, hat in hand, standing a couple of rows away. He was stoic, but watchful. I would have paid money to know what he was thinking in that moment. (Okay, maybe I wouldn't have paid money, because I don't really have any. But you get what I mean.)

Anyway, a few minutes later, the priest completed the abbreviated service. After the attendees hugged and offered condolences to one another, the gravediggers descended to finish their work. At that point, our small gathering moved a little further away to avoid the obvious awkwardness of half-frozen dirt being flung on top of a pine box holding the body of a man that had been murdered.

Nonetheless, the pinging of dirt clods hitting the coffin still put a hamper on the conversation.

"I am so sorry for your loss, Gracie." Benat gave the woman two kisses, narrowly avoiding being pierced by the spiky hairs coming from the mole on her nose. It was still as large as I had remembered.

Did she not own tweezers? Or did those hairs have a superhuman quality that caused them to immediately regrow?

I felt guilty again for thinking these things when I should have been focused on being as polite and proper as possible. Ama would never let me buy a chocolate milkshake ever again if she knew what I had been thinking.

As Ama and I greeted Grace, the older woman held tight to Ama's arm, "Thank you for coming, Maite. I cannot believe how much your daughter has grown. Why, she'll need a whole new wardrobe soon!"

I understood enough of Nosy-Woman-Speak to know that Grace had just insinuated that my clothes are too small for me. While I would, under normal circumstances, have wished to bury my head in embarrassment, in that moment, I really didn't want to. I was proud of Ama for putting a roof over our heads. We had made it <u>despite</u> all that had happened. What did Grace Ansolabehere know, anyway? The hairy witch lady.

Ama didn't know what to say in response, but it was Louise that jumped in, "Our Anna is a lovely girl. And so hardworking and clever. A girl like her could wear a potato sack and still be beautiful."

While I appreciated her words, Louise was laying it on a little too thick.

"Oh, Maite. I wanted to talk to you. The lawyer brought a copy of Joanes's will to the hotel yesterday afternoon when we arrived in town. It lists a bequest to you for your daughter."

I was shocked. Joanes left us some money? Why would he do that? Joanes didn't give anyone anything. Ever. That fact was well established.

Then, the woman continued, "My brother was so noble to want to help you like this. It is just what he would do! What a saint! Nere anaia saindua!"

For a moment, it sounded like Louise snorted. But then she coughed and pulled her handkerchief from her pocket. She covered her face for a few moments.

"We are very thankful. It is generous and kind," Ama replied. Then she turned to me, "Isn't it, haurra?"

"Y—yes. Very kind. Thank you," I parroted. I added a nod to make sure I seemed as polite and sincere as possible.

"Well, I'm sure you can use it," Grace said in a whisper that really wasn't a whisper.

Benat's eyes darted back and forth between the two women. He was clearly fluent in Nosy-Woman-Speak, too.

Ama didn't respond. So, once again, Louise spoke over the sounds of the dirt hitting the coffin, "How long will you be staying, Gracie?"

"Through the end of next week. I want to see my brother's affairs settled by then," the woman answered.

"I hope we will see you again before you leave," Louise remarked, with more politeness than sincerity.

Grace shuddered and hugged her pudgy arms to her middle, "I will NOT ever set foot in that boardinghouse of yours again. Never. I still cannot think of what happened to my poor brother there. I cannot!" Tears filled her eyes, and I felt a burst of sympathy again. She thought her brother was about to be canonized by the Pope. It wasn't her fault that the brother who lived inside her head was very different than the one who lived on earth.

"We are very sorry about what you are going through," Benat rubbed the woman's back, and gave me a warning look that clearly said: <u>be nice</u>.

He should know me better than to think that I would kick a lady while she was down—and being delusional. It was just wrong. Even I knew that.

Grace wiped her dark eyes with her handkerchief, "They must catch this murderer right away! Do you have any idea who it is?"

No one said anything for a moment. Louise reached out to squeeze her arm, "It is a mystery, still, but that sheriff over there will sort it all out. Don't worry."

Her eyes still red from crying, Grace's face tightened, "My brother also left money to that Echeveste worker of his. One of the ones that could have killed him. I think he killed Joanes to get that money. It makes perfect sense to me."

Ama clucked her tongue. "No. Domingo is not the kind to do something like that. Not at all." Then she shook her head in sympathy, "But, I know how hard all of this is for you. When I lost my Pierre suddenly, I didn't see things clearly at the time, either."

"I'm going to have my son-in-law talk to the sheriff. That amerikano had better know what he is doing."

"Oh, he does!" The words came out of my mouth before I realized that they sounded very odd coming from my lips, "While I would never tell Sheriff Williams this directly because I don't want him to get a big head, he is actually very professional and smart."

Grace blinked at me like a confused owl with a hairy wart, "What are you talking about? What do you have to do with this?"

"Uhm, never mind."

Louise grabbed my hand and pulled me so hard that I nearly fell down, "Come walk with me, Anna. I want to show you the graves of my father's cousin." I had no choice but to follow her as she stomped through the frozen grass. Louise moved <u>really</u> fast for someone with rheumatism.

After we had gotten a dozen yards away, Louise hissed, "Watch what you say. You're going to ruin <u>everything</u>."

"What?" I nearly tripped on the headstone of a Martin Antchagno who was born in 1870 and died in 1917. Wincing, I carefully stepped around his grave and tried to catch up with the older woman, "What do you mean?"

Louise had paused in front of the grave of J.B. Borda—who had a bishop-sized headstone with a white angel on top. I thought the white angel had been a good choice because it didn't show the bird poop marks.

My attention went back to Louise as she took a long, long breath. Her stare was very Amatxi-like—half patience, half exasperation, "Anna, this is a serious time. And we must not make it harder for the people going through it. So, we must support them, but not be involved. Do you understand?"

"Why do people keep saying that to me?"

"Well, it's true. That's why."

I'm not sure if I believed her.

<u>Witness Interview #2</u>
(Property of the Douglas County Sheriff)

Case No: 22-43
Date: Thurs, 12/30/43
Time: 1:30pm
Witness: Maite Elissetche *(Bernard Cedarry, interpreter)*
Interviewing Officer: H. Williams

HW: Mrs. Elissetche, thank you for coming here to speak with me privately. I won't keep you long, I know you need to get back to your daughter.

ME: Yes, thank you for understanding. I told her I was going to the market to buy spaghetti. My Anna has much curiosity.

HW: Oh, yes, I know that very well! She is a special girl.

BC: *Forgive me for interrupting, but what is this regarding, sheriff? I don't want Mrs. Elissetche to go through any more than she needs to. She has been through much already in losing her husband and having to raise a child on her own.*

HW: I appreciate your concern and your care for them both. As a father myself, I understand where you are coming from.

BC: *We just want to put all of this behind us.*

HW: Me too. Believe me.

HW: Anyway, in Mr. Larralde's personal effects, there was a receipt in the amount of $89.76 from a Virginia Jewelers in Carson City. My deputy went to the jewelry store to inquire about the purchase. It turns out, it was for a gold engagement ring with a small cluster of diamonds—size 8 and 1/2. It was purchased on September 3rd of this year. However, there was no such ring to be found in Mr. Larralde's room—

BC: *I don't understand where you are going with this, sheriff.*

HW: Please let me finish. Now, my wife tells me that a size 8 and 1/2 ring is not the ring for a slender, flighty kind of girl. But, rather, a real sort of woman. A hardworking, strong woman that knows an honest day's work. You, Mrs. Elissetche, are exactly that kind of woman. My question is this: Did Mr. Larralde ever ask you to marry him?

BC: *What kind of question is that? This is ridiculous.*

HW: Mr. Cedarry, please relay my question. It's important.

ME: Yes, he did ask me to marry him.

HW: When was this?

ME: A couple months ago.

HW: What did you say?

ME: I said, no, of course.

HW: Why did you refuse his proposal?

ME: I did not want to remarry. My concern is for my daughter. I have no time for a new husband because I still grieve my late husband.

HW: I understand. When he proposed, did Mr. Larralde offer you a ring similar to the one I described?

ME: Yes—I believe so. Honestly, I barely looked at it.

HW: And you did not accept it?

ME: No, I did not accept. I already said as much.

HW: Do you know what he did with the ring afterward?

ME: I have no idea. Knowing what I know of Joanes, he probably immediately sold it to buy whiskey or flea dip for his sheep.

HW: And you have not seen that ring since that day?

ME: No.

HW: Was Mr. Larralde angry when you rejected him?

ME: Yes, of course.

HW: What did he say?

ME: That I would regret saying no.

HW: What did you believe he meant by that?

ME: That he thought that I would wish I had said yes at a later time. Once I had considered it more.

HW: And did you?

ME: No. Definitely not.

HW: You said he was angry . . . Did you feel threatened by this anger? That he meant you harm? That he would take revenge in some way?

ME: No, I did not think that at the time.

HW: How was your relationship with the deceased after you refused his offer of marriage?

ME: The same, I suppose. To be honest, I was surprised that he proposed to me at all. I had not given him any encouragement on that front. It came from nowhere.

HW: So why do you think he proposed to begin with?

ME: He wanted someone to cook and clean for him that he didn't have to pay? It's the only reason I can think of.

HW: I see. Well, I appreciate your speaking with me today. I know it was a long morning with the burial, so I'll let you get back to your day.

ME: I'd rather clean pig intestines for tripota every single day than have to do what you do. So, good luck.

HW: I'll take all the luck I can get.

From Anna Elissetche's
Murder & Spaghetti Journal

(Hidden in the trunk at the end of her bed.)

Thursday Night
December 30, 1943

Since outside guests (especially including Michel Lassa) would not be dining at The Sierra Hotel tonight, Ama decided to make something different for supper—spaghetti with meat sauce. She doesn't make it often, mostly because Michel Lassa tends to loudly recount the tale of how an Italian man was responsible for his missing finger. And he'd tell this story to every person within a 10-foot radius—no matter if they wanted to listen to it, or not.

However, spaghetti reminded me of the time when Aita was still alive, and we lived in California. There was an Italian restaurant in Stockton that we went to once. Ama loved the spaghetti so much that she decided to try to make it herself. That first time she made it for supper, Aita teased her that the noodles looked like worms. At first, Ama pretended to be insulted, but when Aita went on to say that he was going to save some of the spaghetti to catch trout in the river, Ama laughed and laughed.

This is one of my last memories of us together as a family before Aita died. Usually, Aita was busy with the sheep, or other people would be around. But, the night of the wormy spaghetti, it was just the three of us. I don't know why I'm telling you this story, but it feels good to write it here. Sad, but good.

I wonder if Ama thought of this, too, when she made the spaghetti earlier. I have a feeling she did. She was quiet this afternoon when we returned from the cemetery. I shouldn't be surprised she was quiet. Joanes was Aita's partner, and no doubt all of this made her think of Aita. How could it not?

Ama dashed off in the early afternoon to buy spaghetti noodles at the market when I was pretty sure she already had a package in the pantry. I didn't

170

say anything about it when she returned later, of course, because I didn't want to be too annoying.

I can be annoying enough without adding to it. It's the main reason she calls me "haurra" so much. Since we Basques don't fuss with middle names much, a Basque mother would never say, "Mary Dorothy Smith, clean your room right now!" Rather, she'd say, "Haurra, you are a pig."

Anyway, the boarders enjoyed Ama's spaghetti, especially the Goytia brothers who had seconds and then licked their plates. And, by licking their plate, I really mean it. The brothers picked up their plates and licked them with their actual tongues—the way Pintto licks his bowl after we give him scraps. The tip of Manuel's nose even had spaghetti sauce on it for several minutes before he realized it was there. And Ama didn't even tease him about it—so I know that her mind was elsewhere.

Domingo, however, just listlessly raked the spaghetti on his plate, creating furrowed rows of noodles that reminded me of a cut alfalfa field before it was going to be baled. Being a suspect in a murder investigation isn't the best for a person's appetite. I know that tomorrow Sheriff Williams will be back. And it doesn't look good for Domingo.

I know I've been told repeatedly not to get involved, but it's <u>hard</u> not to. So, when the sheriff stopped by earlier to talk to Domingo, I ran outside to speak to him privately before he left.

Darkness had fallen as I approached his car. Sitting behind the wheel, the sheriff was holding a flashlight with one hand, as he took furious notes in a notebook with the other.

"Sheriff?" I knocked on the driver's side window.

He swung the flashlight into my face and nearly blinded me. Then, he rolled down the window. "Oh, it's just you," he said.

"Ouch. My eyes hurt now." I rubbed my eyelids to get rid of the spots that were blocking my view of the sheriff's cranky face.

"Don't be so dramatic. What do you want, kid?"

"I have some information that might be helpful," I blinked at him slowly. The spots were finally receding.

"Okay. Then spill it. I don't have all night."

"Santiago Achaval is pressuring Domingo to get Grace Ansolabehere to sell Joanes's sheep to him for less than they are worth. Domingo refused, but Mr. Achaval doesn't seem to want to take no for an answer. He told Domingo that he could make his problems go away if he helped him."

The sheriff frowned, his gaze turning sharp, "How do you know all of this?"

"I overheard their conversation."

"When?"

"It was on Tuesday. The Achavals came for dinner. Mr. Achaval cornered Domingo upstairs in the sitting room."

"Anything else about the conversation that I should know about?"

"Mr. Achaval seemed very happy that Joanes is dead. He said that it was better for his business this way. Then he warned Domingo not to say anything to you about their talk."

"He said that?"

"Yes."

The sheriff's jaw tightened in thought. He turned back to his notebook, "Thank you for telling me. You better get back inside. It's cold out here and you're not wearing a coat."

"Wait, that's it? What are you going to do now? Are you going to the Achaval Ranch to question them?"

"Listen, kid, that's for me to worry about, not you." He suddenly looked tired. He rubbed a callused hand over his face, "Go inside. And stop eavesdropping all over the place like you're Miss Marple."

"You read Agatha Christie?!"

"Why do you always assume I can't read?"

"It's hard to imagine you in a library." I briefly imagined the large sheriff (with his shiny Colt 45) standing next to the aisle of romantic novels. It didn't compute in my mind. Like a chicken attending a picnic, or a kindergartener in a tobacco shop. "Wait . . . Do they even allow pistols in the library?" I paused to consider it for a moment, "I'll have to ask Mrs. McGillicuddy next time I go."

"Please don't." He closed his notebook and twisted the cap onto his pen. Tucking it into the pocket of his tan uniform shirt, he turned to me once more, "Goodnight, Anna." It was a clear dismissal.

I wasn't quite ready for him to go. I didn't long to return to the tense mood inside the boardinghouse. "Oh, by the way, we're having a New Year's Eve dinner tomorrow. Ama is making roast lamb. You should come! Ooo, bring your wife. I'd love to meet Mrs. Sheriff Williams."

He said under his breath, "I perish the thought."

I thought that was a little rude. I sniffed, "Why, you don't think she would like me?"

"No, I think she'd like you _too_ much," he admitted, "and that would just make you more insufferable than you already are."

"Well, now I _am_ insulted."

"Goodnight, Anna." The sheriff put the idling car into drive and gave me a final wave.

<u>Witness Interview #3</u>
(Property of the Douglas County Sheriff)

Case No: 22-43
Date: Thurs, 12/30/43
Time: 5:10pm
Witness: Domingo Echeveste *(Anna Elissetche, interpreter)*
Interviewing Officer: H. Williams

HW: I thought Mr. Cedarry would be here to assist me with the interview?

AE: *Benat and Louise aren't coming this evening because the dining room is closed to guests today because of Joanes's funeral. Or burial. Or memorial? Or whatever you want to call whatever that was this morning.*

HW: It really doesn't matter what we call it, Anna. The man is dead all the same.

AE: That's true.

HW: Mr. Echeveste, I have a few questions for you. I understand you are recently engaged to be married. Is that correct?

DE: Yes.

HW: To Miss Rodriguez?

AE: *Catalina is so nice. They are going to have a baby, too! Isn't that exciting? Oops, I wasn't supposed to tell anyone that.*

HW: Well, Anna, I'm sure people will figure it out, anyway, when suddenly there's a baby where there wasn't one before.

AE: *I already told her that she should name the baby after me, if it's a girl. I think that would be great.*

HW: I think there are enough Anna Elissetches in the world.

AE: *You know another Anna Elissetche?*

HW: No, just you. But that's enough.

AE: *I'm not sure if that's an insult or a compliment.*

HW: I'll leave that for you to decide. Anyway . . . Mr. Echeveste, I have a few questions about Miss Rodriguez's engagement ring. Where did you get it?

DE: I bought it at a store.

HW: Which store?

DE: A shop in Reno.

HW: Which one?

DE: It was off Virginia Street.

HW: Do you have a receipt for this purchase?

DE: I bought it at a pawn shop. Cash only.

HW: How much was it?

AE: *Why are you asking all these questions about Catalina's ring?*

HW: Never mind. Just ask the question.

DE: I don't remember, exactly. But I think it was $25?

HW: That's a nice ring for just $25. Quite a steal.

DE: I'm a sheepherder, what do I know about jewelry? It was a pretty ring, so I bought it. That's all I know.

HW: When did you buy it?

DE: A couple months ago.

HW: So, you planned to marry Miss Rodriguez already two months ago?

DE: Yes.

HW: I got the impression that your engagement was a sudden one.

DE: You shouldn't listen to gossip. It's usually wrong.

HW: Fair enough. Now, if I were to go to Reno tomorrow morning and speak to the pawn shop owner, they would corroborate your story?

DE: Do you think a pawn shop owner remembers every single person that comes into their store and buys something?

HW: I think they'd remember selling a diamond engagement ring for only $25.

AE: *Sheriff, what does this have to do with anything?*

HW: Mind your own business.

AE: *I hate when people say that.*

From Anna Elissetche's Murder & Please-Let-This-Be-Over-Soon Journal

(Hidden inside the tin box at the back of Pintto's doghouse.)

Friday
December 31, 1943

We're having potato salad and roasted carrots with the lamb roast for the New Year's Eve dinner tonight. So, I spent the morning peeling potatoes, and I peeled more than just the russets. It's important not to use a vegetable peeler when you are distracted because your knuckles end up looking like you put your hands into a barrel of angry cats.

Ama sent me away from the kitchen to put some ointment and bandages on the scrapes before "you bleed all over my potatoes."

It gave me more time to think about the mess around me that seemed to grow bigger every day. While I had already been worried about Domingo (and Catalina and the baby!!), now Antton was worrying me, too. What was the secret that Antton and Mitchell Lauden shared? There was a lot of emotion between them, which confused me, and I couldn't help but worry about it. While I first wondered if it was about the murder, now I'm not so sure.

Let's not forget everyone else I am worried about: Benat, Teresa, Ama, and even Sheriff Williams. (I am <u>not</u> worried about Santiago Achaval, however. That man will be just fine.)

In the small bathroom in our apartment, I rubbed soap on the abrasions on my hands. The suds burned, but the sensation was a relief from all that I was feeling. After drying my hands, I carefully put bandages on my knuckles. I glanced at my reflection in the small mirror above the sink. My shoulder-length dark hair was falling from the messy ponytail that I had fashioned this morning. My green eyes were bleary from lack of sleep and my skin wasn't as pink as it usually was. I think all of this was finally getting to me.

I was ready for it to be over. Over. <u>Over</u>.

There was a knock on the bathroom door, "Anna?" It was Louise. My heart began to beat faster, in alarm. What was she doing here? Had something happened?

I quickly opened the door. But Louise was just standing there in her apron holding a stack of folded clothes. Immediately, her eyes dimmed, "Anna, are you okay?"

"Yes, yes! Of course, I am."

She didn't appear convinced, but she let it go for a moment. She held out the clothes, "When I was putting away some of my Christmas things, I found these old clothes of Patricia's. They were from years ago when she was about your size. But they still have some wear left, and I think you would look nice in these. You're a little shorter than Patti was, so I hemmed the dresses a little for you."

I took the stack of clothes and stepped into the sitting room to examine them. I didn't recognize any of the clothes, so she must have worn them before we moved to Gardnerville. There were three dresses, a cream-colored cardigan, and a pair of chambray trousers in medium blue. "Thank you so much! I love them!" I gave Louise a big smile.

She reached for one of the dresses, which was a dark cranberry red with small white daisies printed on it, "I thought this one would be nice for dinner tonight. The red would go nice with your pretty dark hair."

I held up a hand to my messy ponytail, "My hair doesn't look so nice right now. I don't seem to do a very good job managing it."

"Ba!" Louise waved off my words with a huff and reached to tame my hair, "There are many women who would commit a crime to have this hair." She combed her fingers through it and refastened my ponytail tightly. "Voila!"

Scooping up my new clothes, Louise marched to my room, "Let's put these away." She draped the cranberry dress with the daisies across my bed and opened the trunk at the foot of my bed. She set the clothes at the top, her fingers brushing my murder journal. With a cry of recognition, Louise picked up the journal and turned to me with a satisfied look, "You're using it! I'm so glad."

Then, she absently opened the book, thumbing through the pages. I held my breath—my heart thumping in my chest. Louise held in her hand my most personal thoughts and observations from the last few weeks. While Louise's English wasn't perfect, she had been in America much longer than Ama, so she had a better grasp on the language.

What if . . . What if . . .

I almost couldn't fathom it.

Louise glanced down into the pages, and for a moment, I thought I noticed a tightening in her cheek as she did so. Then, she snapped the book shut, and tucked it back into the trunk.

I vowed to change my journal's hiding place <u>immediately</u>. Time for it to go in Pintto's doghouse again.

With a heavy sigh, Louise sat down on my bed, and she tapped the space beside her, "Come sit for a minute, neska maitea."

My stomach sank. It was the kind of thing a person did before they told you something you didn't want to hear. Good news was never delivered in this way. It was only bad stuff. Like when someone was dying of cancer. Or your cat got ran over by the milkman. Or that Cary Grant was never, <u>ever</u> going to marry you.

"This has been a very hard few weeks for everyone," the older woman began. "So much worry, and upset, and very serious things have been happening." She reached for my hand and squeezed it, "And you have been stuck right in the middle of it."

Inexplicably, I felt tears well behind my lids. My tummy clenched and I looked away from her perceptive blue eyes.

Louise continued, "But, I want you to know that everything is going to be fine. You are safe. We are safe. Your Ama is safe. And nothing is going to change that. Do you understand?"

I just nodded, finding that I couldn't speak. Louise reached up to pat me on the cheek, "Many people love you, don't forget that. And you have the best guardian angel of all—your Aita."

The tears I had been holding back spilled onto my cheeks. Louise wiped them away with her thumb, "So, you have no reason to worry. Okay?"

I nodded again, taking a big, shuddering breath to steady myself.

The older woman stood and straightened her apron, "Now then, I'm going to go help Maite with the dinner. Teresa is setting up the tables. When you finish in here, you can go and hang up the New Year's Eve decorations that I found at the drugstore earlier this week when I picked up my rheumatism cream. The decorations are in a bag on the bar."

Then, with a quick peck to my forehead, Louise left.

As I'm sure was her intention, I did feel better after the chat. Although, it really wasn't a chat—it was more her talking <u>at</u> me as I sat there in silence. Picking at one of the bandages on my finger, I nonetheless said a little prayer to Aita that everything Louise said would be true.

(Please, <u>please</u> let it be so.)

Later the same afternoon . . .

Okay, first of all, before I forget to mention it: When I went into the bar earlier this afternoon to get the decorations, I was met with the <u>weirdest</u> sight imaginable. Sheriff Williams was having a Picon with Victor Arrossa. I blinked my eyes. Then, I blinked them again. Then I rubbed my eyelids to make sure I wasn't hallucinating.

"Sheriff? Victor?" My eyes hopped from the two men like I was watching them play pilota on the north wall of the boardinghouse, "What are you doing?"

Victor reached up to pat the sheriff on his tall back. But his wizened arm only reached to his elbow, "A man needs a drink sometimes, neska ttipia. It is the way of things."

"Huh?" I knew my reply was inelegant, but some things were just too weird.

"You're gaping at me like a trout after it's been yanked out of the lake," the sheriff remarked.

"Trout is good. Fried with baratxuria," Victor mused.

"Fried with what?" the sheriff asked.

"Garlic," I answered automatically. Then I paused to consider the scene before me, "Wait, are you friends now?"

The sheriff took a swig of his Picon. "It's New Year's Eve. You do know that, right?" he said patiently.

"Well, yes," I admitted. I picked up the paper bag on the bar, "I've come to get these decorations, actually."

He saluted me with his glass, "I decided to have a New Year's Eve drink before I head home for the day." Then he looked down at me, a dark red, bushy eyebrow raised in amusement, "Is that okay with you?"

"I guess so."

"My goodness, you sound so enthusiastic." The sheriff's words were drier than parsley that had been in the pantry for too long.

Victor interrupted our exchange, setting his empty glass on the bar top with a thud, "Leave the polizia alone, neska ttipia." The old boarder then stretched his stiff back with a sigh that turned into a groan. He shuffled to his usual chair by the window, "It's time for my siesta. Isilik . . . no more talking."

Antton came from the storage room with a new bottle of Picon. He opened it and set it behind the bar. He pulled off the linen towel he had tucked into his brown belt and set it on the bar top. With a glance to the clock behind the bar, Antton rubbed the dark stubble on his chin, "I must go to the bank before it closes, and I need cigarettes and more shaving soap. It shouldn't take me long. The bar is ready for later. If someone comes for a drink before I get back, have Fermin or

Manuel come down to help." The bartender paused, and then gave me a pointed look, "You are not allowed to make drinks anymore. Not after you gave that amerikano a Sidecar made with tequila."

"She said she liked it!" I insisted. And, she really did say she liked it.

Antton rolled his eyes, "She was being polite." Stepping around the bar, he continued, "Besides, you could get us in trouble. You are not old enough to be a bartender. Right, Sheriff?"

"That is correct," he nodded in agreement. "She's not old enough to drive, either, but that doesn't seem to stop her," Sheriff Williams added.

"Isilik!" Victor grumbled from the corner. He opened one eye, "You are louder than sheep yelling for hay."

Antton held up his hands in apology, "Barkatu, Victor." Then, he added in a whisper, "I'll be back soon." Pulling on his denim jacket, Antton walked out the front door. His old truck was parked out back.

Tucking the bag of decorations under my arm, I decided to let Victor have his nap. I didn't want to be responsible for more crankiness at dinner later. It was better this way.

Sheriff Williams finished his drink and set the glass on the bar. Reaching for his hat that was sitting on one of the bar stools, he turned to me, his tanned face solemn . . . yet, kind, "Happy New Year, Anna. Here's hoping 1944 will be a better year."

"Happy New Year, Sheriff."

And, with that, he left.

Two hours before midnight . . .

There was a modest turnout at dinner this evening, and given the icy weather, everyone left early so they wouldn't have trouble driving home. It suited me just fine as I wasn't feeling especially festive. New Year's Eve has never been my favorite holiday—there is something sad and melancholy about it. As the last hoorah before the bleakness of Nevada winter settles in, it doesn't take us long to forget all the resolutions we've made. Like when we were silly enough to think that we could actually cut back on kafesnea. (Yes, I'm talking about me. And, no, I'm not going to even bother this year.

It's better to try goals that <u>might</u> be achievable. Like learning to juggle. Or not using as many adjectives in my writing. So, as I lay in bed and write in this book, here is my resolution for 1944:

I will absolutely, positively, <u>NOT</u> use as many adjectives in 1944.

Ha! We'll see how this one turns out. I'm not hopeful, but I suppose it's good to have goals that challenge us and make us try to be better people. Right?

Ooo, you know what would be fun?? Making a list of New Year's Resolutions for everyone here at The Sierra Hotel. (And maybe a few people who don't live at the boardinghouse, too.) No one will ever see this, anyway, so where's the harm? Besides, I'm better at telling other people what they should do than doing things myself. This might be related to my penchant for stubbornness—I'm not sure. (But probably.)

Side Note: I'm hiding this journal in Pintto's doghouse just as soon as I'm done writing this. One can never be too careful. Plus, Louise knows that I have a journal now. I saved Pintto a piece of roast lamb from dinner, anyway, so I'll give him that snack at the same time.

Anyway, okay, here goes:

New Year's Resolutions 1944

For Matthieu Dallut-Bec: "When I return to San Francisco, I'll try to remember the good times I spent at The Sierra Hotel. Not just the time I was really sick with influenza and then saw a dead body shortly afterward."

For Domingo Echeveste: "I resolve to marry Catalina in the next week. But first I will get a haircut and clean out my truck because it smells like 192 sheep took a poop inside of it."

For Teresa Harguindeguy: "My resolution is to tell my Otto and Tantta about what happened with Joanes and to not feel any guilt about it. I will also learn how to kick men in the barrabilak so that they scream like little babies."

For Fermin Goytia: "In 1944, I promise I will write to my mother in Gipuzkoa more often. I will also stop leaving my toenail clippings in a pile on the sink in the boarders' washroom."

For Victor Arrossa: "In 1944, I won't eat more than one piece of chorizo at a gathering where I will be within smelling distance of other people. I will also refrain from playing mus for money."

For Manuel Goytia: "Next year, I will drink less cerveza and change my socks more than once a week."

For Antton Garai: "My resolution is to avoid keeping secrets from the people who care about me. And also, to never grow a beard that covers the handsome dimple in my cheek."

For Tomas Hardoy: "In 1944, I will stop running away from my problems. And I will stop telling everyone Urepel is a bad place—when it isn't at all."

For <u>Sheriff Williams</u>: "In 1944, I will hire Anna as a part-time investigator—and pay her in real money. I will also see if I can get Mrs. McGillicuddy removed from her job as the Gardnerville librarian. There must be some kind of law that she has broken . . . right?"

For <u>Louise Cedarry</u>: "In 1944, I will make eggnog more often, even when it isn't Christmas."

For <u>Santiago Achaval</u>: "I promise I won't fire the Goytia brothers if they show up to work a little too mozkorra. I also resolve <u>not</u> to be a gaistoa—because in 1944, I don't want to be the person everyone wishes were dead."

For <u>Catalina Rodriguez</u>: "If my baby is a girl, I promise to name her Anna—after the nicest, sweetest, and cleverest girl I know . . . in the whole entire world."

For <u>Benat Cedarry</u>: "My resolution is to do what my wife tells me to do. I will also stop giving a hard time to my daughter for going to college, and I will do everything possible to prevent Victor from playing mus for money."

For <u>Maite Elissetche</u>: "My resolution is to let Anna read all the books she wants, and to not complain if she forgets to tell me that the truck is low on gasoline. I also promise to laugh more in 1944. Anna misses that."

Bye for now . . . Time to hide this in Pintto's doghouse.
Goodbye 1943, hello 1944!

From Anna Elissetche's Murder Journal

(Inside the tin box at the back of Pintto's doghouse.
All the previous entries have been torn out.)

Saturday
January 1, 1944

GUESS WHAT? My journal has been destroyed. Utterly ruined. It's a shell of its former self. A purple husk of leather flapping listlessly. As I write here, the torn edges of the binding are a reminder that every single word I wrote has been STOLEN. I know what this means. This was meant to be a warning. The person who did it WANTS me to know. Otherwise, the person would have just taken the whole goddamn journal—not just the pages. Yes, I said goddamn. And I'm not even sorry about it.

If they had stolen the whole journal, I might have thought that Pintto just buried it somewhere. Like he does with the soup bones that Ama gives him. We always find bones in the dirt around the boardinghouse—as if Pintto is preparing for the Doggy Apocalypse.

Honestly, it feels like the apocalypse right now.

That's because my words are OUT IN THE WORLD. My words, my theories, my thoughts, my EVERYTHING. My hand is shaking. Ugh, my penmanship is so bad that if this was an essay, Miss Gleason would make me write this out all over again.

Whoever did this wants me to stop investigating the murder. That is pretty clear. And it's someone close enough to me to notice that I have a journal—and where I hide it. Therefore, here are my top suspects. I've ranked them according to the Laws of Probability:

Ama, 10% (Pros: This is something Ama would do to prove a point to me. She told me not to get involved, I ignored her. Cons: Her English is not the best.)

Santiago Achaval, 15% (Pros: He's sneaky enough to do this. Meaning, he's sneaky enough to get someone <u>else</u> to do it for him. Cons: He doesn't live in the boardinghouse, so the only way he'd know about my journal is if the Goytia brothers told him.)

Louise Cedarry, 20% (Pros: She is the only person that has actually SEEN the inside of the journal. Her English is proficient. Cons: Her arthritic hands would struggle to tear the pages from the binding.)

Sheriff Williams, 20% (Pros: He's seen me writing in the journal. He knows it's about ~~our~~ <u>his</u> investigation. Cons: How on earth would he know I hide my journal in the doghouse?!)

Benat Cedarry: ~~20%~~ **35%** (Pros: He knows everything that goes on in the boardinghouse. Louise told him about my journal. Cons: Actually, I can't think of any reason why he <u>wouldn't</u> do this.)

All these numbers add up to one UNDENIABLE thing:

I am getting close to figuring out who murdered Joanes Larralde—and someone is trying to stop me.

Later this evening . . .

We had a very small crowd for dinner tonight, which suited my mood perfectly. I didn't want extra people hanging around. More people meant more suspects, and I had more than enough suspects to worry about. As it was, I had begun to look for paper cuts on everyone's hands. Because whoever had viciously destroyed my journal must have a paper cut. They BETTER have gotten a paper cut. If they didn't, then the world is a cruel and unfair place.

Ama served steak with soup and French fries. As I hacked at my steak, I imagined the same being done to my journal. My knife slipped onto my plate with a screech. From down the table, Benat commented, "Anna, that cow is already dead. You don't need to kill it again."

I narrowed my eyes at him, suspicious. "I bet you could just tear your steak with your hands. No need to even use a knife."

Confusion clouded his eyes. "Zer—what?"

I harrumphed and buried my head into a pile of French fries. He was clever to pretend like he didn't know what I was talking about.

Domingo and Catalina were subdued, and she kept reaching for his hand during dinner—as if squeezing it tightly would prevent him from being taken off to jail. The man from Basauri looked resigned—like he was counting the days until his own reckoning. It was hard to see. Especially since I wasn't convinced he had killed Joanes.

The Goytia brothers tended the bar tonight because Antton had gone to spend the day with his father's cousin in Reno. He had left a note in the bar this morning that he would return tonight or tomorrow—depending upon the weather. I saw snowflakes crusting the edges of my window, so I doubted Antton would return tonight.

I guess I'll wrap this up now. I'm going to try to read for a while before bed. I could use the distraction. And, if that doesn't work, I'll sneak Pintto into my room.

Witness Interview
(Property of the Douglas County Sheriff)

Case No: 22-43
Date: Thurs, 12/30/43
Time: 2:30pm
Witness: Louise Cedarry
Interviewing Officer: H. Williams

LC: I want to speak to you in private. I hope it's fine that I came to your office?

HW: Of course. Just making some notes here from my conversation with your husband and Mrs. Elissetche.

LC: I left my husband at home. He's taking a siesta. He snores loud. I doubt he heard me leave.

HW: My wife says the same thing about me.

LC: Sheriff, I came because . . . well . . . I'm not wanting to tell you how to do your job . . .

HW: Of course not.

LC: But you are doing everything wrong.

HW: Pardon me?

LC: Why do you let Anna help you? She is a little girl. You must stop.

HW: I understand your concern. But, language has been a barrier . . .

LC: Stop using such words. Ba! You can do your job without her. And then you leave us all alone. We don't know anything. Stop now.

HW: Mrs. Cedarry, please, I am doing my best to solve this case . . .

LC: No one cares who murdered Joanes Larralde. You just keep little Anna, and poor Maite, out of this.

HW: Could I ask you some questions, while you are here?

LC: You know everything there is to know already. My husband would not be happy if he knew I was here yelling at you.

HW: I understand how you feel, I do . . . but . . .

LC: I have to go. Benat will wake up soon. He won't believe me if I tell him I went to the merkatua to buy vegetables. He will guess that I am here. He only likes to pretend to be an idiota when it suits him.

HW: But Mrs. Cedarry . . .

LC: I say what I say. That is it. Goodbye.

From Anna Elissetche's Ruined Journal

(Shoved under her pillow. What's the use of hiding it now?)

Sunday Evening
January 2, 1944

Antton hasn't returned from Reno yet. It's snowing lightly, so maybe the roads are too icy. Fermin offered to bartend in his place today—he's saving up to buy a cowboy hat like Tex Ritter. He saw a movie poster for *Arizona Trail* and has been raving it about it ever since. The Goytia brothers are obsessed with Western films. All sheepherders are, really, as they were usually their first introduction to the English language. (I'm surprised more of them don't develop a drawl.)

I don't see the appeal in Western movies, though. It's not fun to watch folks get shot when you see the person who actually did it. Where's the mystery in that?

Monsieur Dallut-Bec announced at lunch that he's returning to San Francisco this week. He said he just has to complete the final touches, which involve "glaçure." I have no idea what this is, because I've avoided everything to do with art since 1938—when old Mrs. Svenssen said my drawing of the Easter Bunny looked like a cow.

I'm surprised that the Frenchman is leaving so soon. I was under the impression that his project was going to take a few more weeks. To be honest, this news made me a little suspicious of him. I hadn't given Dallut-Bec much thought, really, but now, I'm not so sure if I haven't underestimated him. The man works with stones, statues, and large pieces of art. He is strong enough to cut a man's throat—and unassuming enough to get away with it.

None of us had ever met him before he arrived several weeks ago, but that didn't mean that he didn't have cause to kill Larralde. After all, Joanes seemed to collect enemies faster than Ama could fry an egg—and she can fry an egg really fast.

I watched Matthieu Dallut-Bec deftly cut his food into neat little pieces. He smoothly slid one onto the back of his fork with his knife, lifting the bite to his mouth in reverse. I had never seen someone eat a piece of chicken that way. Even prissy Emmaline Lauden wasn't so fancy.

I looked at him in a new light. Maybe I had been examining this the wrong way the whole time. While perfectly nice, the Frenchman <u>was</u> a stranger. For all I knew, he had seven dead bodies in his basement back in San Francisco.

Could he be leaving early to avoid detection for Joanes's murder? Was that deceit I saw hiding in his finely trimmed mustache? I'm not certain, but I intend to find out.

Anyway, I'd better go for now. I probably should practice my accordion for a little while. Ama will bug me if I don't. Plus, maybe I can earn a penny from Victor if I play a waltz that doesn't sound like a funeral dirge.

One hour later . . .

I have no words. My heart is thumping and my ears flaming. I found something tucked inside the bellows of my accordion. It's so shocking that I don't know what to do or say . . . or feel. I know I'm rambling, but I just need to spill it.

It's a letter. From Antton. He's not in Reno at all. He's not waiting out the snowstorm before returning to the boardinghouse. He's run off. Left. <u>Gone</u>. Because . . .

Because he killed Joanes Larralde.

HE KILLED HIM!

Words have failed me. And that <u>never</u> happens to me. EVER.

So, I might as well just tell you what the letter says. Here it is:

Neska polita,

I couldn't leave without saying goodbye to you, my little friend. I hope you will understand why I left. I think you will, though, because you are the smartest girl I know. Joanes Larralde was a bad man and he deserved what was done to him—<u>what I did to him</u>. Never forget that.

I'm sorry I won't be around to watch you become the young woman I know you will be. Give the boys a lot of grief, neska, they need it! Don't settle for second best, when you should have the <u>best</u> of all.

Be good to Maite, she loves you more than you'll ever know. And don't quit playing this accordion—I know you want to quit, but don't. Promise me.

I am sorry I destroyed your journal. But it had to be done.

Pottak,

Antton

Can you believe it? I'd like to say that I can't. But, in the hour that I've been sittng numbly on my bed, with Antton's letter in my hand, I've had some time to think. Antton's words are spilling through me like a flash flood on the Washoe River:

"There's never enough of anything for that bastardoa."

"You'd best shut your mouth, Larralde. It's going to get you killed one day."

And, when I overheard Antton and Mitchell's conversation, Antton said, "We are safe. Joanes is gone. He can't blackmail us anymore."

That was Antton's motive. Joanes was blackmailing Antton . . . Of course he had reason to kill Larralde. Why didn't I connect the dots sooner?

I am a terrible detective. All the information was right in front of my face.

But, what now? Has Antton left . . . forever? The idea of never seeing him again makes my throat tighten. Where will he go? What will he do?

I don't know what to make of all of this. The secret is churning within me. I want to tell someone, but this information is so ENORMOUS that it seems wrong to let it escape into the world like a herd of elephants that could trample us all.

I won't be sleeping much tonight.

Aita, please tell me what to do . . .

CASE NO: 22-43

NAME OF DECEASED: Larralde, Jean

RESIDENCE OF DECEASED: The Sierra Hotel, Hwy 395, Gardnerville

DATE OF DEATH: est 12/19/43, body found 12/20/43.

<u>EXHIBIT A</u>

31 Decembre 1943

Sheriff Williams,

I am writing to tell you that I killed Joanes Larralde. I am not sorry that I did it, because he deserved it. He did many terrible things to people. And he was going to do more bad things. He threatened me when I tried to stop him. That is why I killed him. I have left Nevada because I do not want to go to prison for killing a bastardoa that deserved to be killed. I hope this explains for you and that you stop l'investigation.

Cordialemente,
Antoine Garai

**postmarked 12/31/43, received via US Mail on 1/3/44

AUTHENTICATED 1/3/44, SUBMITTED TO RECORD 1/4/44

From Anna Elissetche's Journal

Monday
January 3, 1944

I couldn't keep it inside any longer. It was eating me up. I didn't sleep at all last night. I tossed and turned in bed—like Pintto does in the dirt after I try to give him a bath.

With the moon still in the sky and only the slightest hue of violet in the eastern horizon, I climbed out of bed. I dressed and tucked Antton's letter in the band of my pants. Padding into the kitchen, I started the coffee brewing and stoked the wood stove to life. The warmth from the pot-bellied heater felt good on my chilled skin.

Ama was still abed. Teresa wasn't to be here for a couple of hours.

I wiped down the kitchen as the coffee bubbled in the corner. The busyness was calming. When the coffee was finished perking, I poured a mug and stirred in plenty of esnea and a heaping spoon of sugar. Sipping on it, I let the comfort settle into my bones.

The narrow door to our apartment creaked open. Ama's short brown hair was brushed, a paisley apron over her dark dress. She approached, "Haurra, why are you awake so early?"

It was the loving, familiar voice that finally broke the dam. And I cried. And cried.

In between hiccups, as Ama held me in tightly, I told her everything I had just discovered. I read her Antton's letter.

And she just listened. Her strong hand rubbing circles in my back.

When I was done, I asked her if we should tell the sheriff about the letter. Ama replied, "Antton's letter is addressed to you, not the sheriff. That is your business, not his. As it is, I suspect that polizia will find out soon enough on his own, anyway."

I agreed. Then Ama sternly sent me out of the kitchen, "Oy yoy, haurra! Go to bed. Your eyes are puffy like a mozkorra that had too much whiskey."

Outside my window, day is breaking. The edges of the window are laced with ice. Tiredness is pulling at me, draining all energy away. I think it's time to bring this investigation to a close. I'm done being a detective. It's time to move on.

But there is just <u>one</u> thing left to do.

(As her mother cooks breakfast, Anna tosses the remains of her journal inside the wooden heater and watches the flames shrivel the leather and paper into dust.)

Fri, Jan 7, 1944

Murder Case Closed, Suspect Fled

The investigation into the Dec 19th murder of Gardnerville sheepman, Jean Larralde, has officially been closed. Sources tell the Evening Gazette that the alleged murderer is Antoine Garai, a native of the Basque region of France. Mr. Garai was the bartender at The Sierra Hotel, the boardinghouse where the homicide occurred. Douglas County Sheriff Hiram Williams has issued the following statement to the press: "Our inquiry into the homicide of Mr. Larralde has concluded. Witness statements, and the evidence collected, corroborates our findings. However, the suspect, who has confessed to the crime, has fled the jurisdiction. It is believed he has sought refuge in South America. While a warrant has been issued for his immediate arrest, it is unlikely he will be detained for prosecution. Therefore, the case has been closed."

-Jim Calderman
Evening Gazette, Metro Desk

PART THREE

THE DEATH OF JOANES LARRALDE

Sunday, November 21, 1943

Sitting at the small escritoire in her bedroom, Maite's mind reeled from her conversation with Gregorio Sarratea earlier. After Anna had told her that the truck was not running as it should, Maite had asked Gregorio to take a look at it when he came to play mus with the other men today. Gregorio had worked as a mechanic in Minden for the past year—after moving to Nevada from the Stockton area with his wife and two young sons. He learned the crafts of the trade in California, apprenticing for a series of mechanics over the years, before striking out on his own.

As the light dimmed in that late afternoon, Gregorio slid under the Plymouth truck, a flashlight in his hands. Maite waited for the verdict—praying it was a simple repair that could be identified easily. They didn't have much money to spare—and she hated to think where they'd find the cash if something expensive needed to be done. She squeezed her hands together tightly.

A few moments later, Gregorio emerged—an odd look on his mustached face. Sitting up, he scratched his brown hair, making it stick up in tufts, "Well, Maite, I think I know what's wrong with the truck." He paused, and then stood up, "There are holes in the brake line."

Maite knew very little about cars and trucks. "What does that mean?"

"The holes cause a slow leak in the fluids. This can make the brakes stop working suddenly."

"How does that happen?"

The mechanic's chin tightened, "Most often, cracks in the brake line are accidental. But I'm not certain if that's the case here." His dark eyes probing hers, he added, "You don't usually see holes in a brake line like this. In fact, I've only ever seen this twice before."

Maite was confused, "When was that?"

"The first was a couple years ago, back in Stockton. I was working on a Dodge that needed a lot of repairs. This was right before we moved to Nevada. Anyway, my boss sent me to the junkyard to find some Dodge parts. There were a couple in the junkyard, and I managed to salvage enough out of them for what I needed. But, when I was working on one of the wrecked Dodges, I noticed that the brake line had holes in it, similar to the ones I see here. And I remember thinking at the time, 'No wonder this truck got wrecked. It was an accident waiting to happen.' "

A needle of unease pressed upon Maite's stomach. She pressed her hands into her apron, holding her feelings in. Her Pierre had a Dodge pickup. "Can you remember anything else about that truck?"

"Yes, I can. On the inside of the cab, which had been smashed very badly, there were small wooden pieces, painted in brown, pink, and white."

Maite's heart started to beat like a drum, "What did you think those pieces were from?"

"It looked like it came from a girl's toy. Like something a girl would play with, with her dolls." Gregorio shrugged, "Emelia and I only have *semeak*. So, I'm not familiar with girl toys."

Maite's vision narrowed until she only saw the man in front of her. All other sensations vanished. Horror had enveloped her. She swallowed reflexively, "When was the other time you saw a truck with a brake line like this?"

Gregorio put his hands on his hips, "You know, it was just a couple weeks ago. Xavier Achaval had a crash out on Kingsbury Grade, and Santiago sent the truck to my shop. I found that the holes in the line had most likely caused his brakes to fail. He was lucky the damage wasn't worse. And that the boy didn't get seriously hurt."

A realization was taking shape in Maite's mind. A terrible, sickening realization. There was a common thread in all these incidents. It could not be denied. "Are these holes accidents? Can they happen naturally when driving?"

Gregorio considered the question, "Most likely, yes. Sharp rocks, driving over rough terrain—many things can damage a brake line. That is very true."

"But it could be intentional?"

Gregorio's voice lowered, "It could, yes. But, if someone meant someone harm, it would be easier to cut the brake line completely. Not just make holes or tears in it."

"But would that cause a different result?"

"Yes. If a brake line were cut, the brakes would fail much faster. The damage would be almost instant."

Maite took a deep breath, "I see." Then she forced a smile to her face. It took every ounce of her composure to say what she said next: "Most likely my Anna drove over something rough. I'm always telling that girl to be more careful."

Gregorio relaxed, "I told Santiago that the rough rocks up at the Kingsbury Grade, or even the rocks and sagebrush on their own ranch, could possibly puncture the brake lines."

"Did Achaval believe that?" Maite asked—more calmly than she thought possible.

"He really didn't. He got it into his head that someone sabotaged Xavier's truck."

"I'm sure he was just upset by the whole thing. And worried for his son," Maite reasoned. She didn't want Gregorio to dig further into this until she did some digging of her own.

"That's what Emelia said, too." Gregorio smiled, "You women are usually right."

Maite forced a chuckle, "I will remember that you said that! I wish I heard more men say the same."

Gregorio turned back to the truck, "I can get this fixed for you as soon as I can get a new line. But, with the war, and the Thanksgiving holiday, it might take me longer to get the part. It shouldn't be too expensive, though."

"I'm glad to hear that. Thank you for your help, Gregorio. By the way, we're having a Christmas dinner dance on December 19th. Be sure to bring Emelia and the boys."

"I'm sure they'd like that." He started walking to the back door of the boardinghouse. "We'll pick up the truck in the morning, and I should have this fixed by Tuesday or Wednesday."

Maite nodded, but her mind was elsewhere.

With her French-English dictionary at her side, Maite sat at her escritoire. She painstakingly wrote the following letter that she would put into the next morning's post:

Laramie Life Insurance
700 Weber Street
Stockton, California

Dear Monsieurs:

I am writing to inquire about any insurance policies in the name of my dead husband. His name was Pierre Elissetche. He was born on 11 février 1891. Can you send me information? Do you have any policies in the name of Maite Elissetche (12 septembre 1894) or Anna Elissetche (7 avril 1929)?

Thank you.

Maite Elissetche

The Sierra Hotel, Highway 395, Gardnerville, Nevada

Then she wrote this letter, in Basque:

M. Miguel Irigoyen

Highway 20, Rural Box 64

Yuba City, California

Miguel,

I hope you, Rosie, and the family are well and healthy. Anna and I send our pottak to you from Nevada. We hope we can see you soon—it's been so long. Pierre was very fond of you. He said that you were the fairest and best sheepman he had ever worked for. Your advice meant a lot to him.

I have a question: What was the average price per head for ardiak and the price per head for bildotsak between abendua 1939 and aprila 1940? I am looking into the paperwork from Pierre's estate. By the way, did Joanes Larralde ask you for this same information after Pierre died?

Thank you for your help.

Maite

After a brief interruption from Anna and shooing her off to help with the dinner preparations, Maite finished the letters and tucked them into their envelopes with quivering fingers. She took a deep calming breath, hoping her instincts were very wrong.

Tuesday, December 14, 1943

After Anna vanished into her room to study for her arithmetic test, Maite's mind was on the letters waiting for her in her bedroom. The responses to her letters had finally arrived. After waiting for weeks. Outwardly, she was calm, but her insides were a twist of nerves. She stuffed garlic into the lamb shanks for dinner later, nicked her finger with the paring knife. She could wait no longer. She had to know what the letters said. "I'll be back in a few minutes. I cut my finger a little. Can you finish prepping the shanks and the soup for a short while?"

Teresa, always so sweet, agreed, which Maite appreciated. What a nice girl she was. Wrapping her finger in a kitchen towel (even though it wasn't really bleeding), Maite quietly entered their apartment. She said a quick prayer when she saw that Anna had closed her accordion door. As silently as possible, Maite entered her room and closed the door—as slowly as her anxious nerves would allow. Sweeping up the envelopes, she tore open the letter from Miguel Irigoyen first—it would be much easier to read:

Dear Maite,

I am happy to hear from you. Rosie sends her love. I looked into my records, and from diciembre 1939 to abril 1940, the price per head was $7 to $7.50. Do you need help with something? I am glad to help you however I can.

Miguel
— Oh, Joanes never asked me anything about the ardiak and bildotsak prices.

Maite's heart was pounding loud enough to be heard in the kitchen. Joanes had only paid her Pierre's portion based on a value of four dollars a head—a value that Joanes said he had gotten from Miguel Irigoyen. This was just nearly half of what they were worth.

Joanes had lied to her. He had cheated her out of money that her husband had worked so hard for. After Pierre had trusted him. Angry tears flooded Maite's blue eyes. She wiped them away. Tucking the letter back into the envelope, Maite reached for the other piece of mail from Laramie Insurance in Stockton.

Dear Mrs. Elissetche:

We are pleased to offer our assistance. If we can meet your insurance needs in the future, we would be pleased to assist you. As you are his next of kin, we can confirm that a policy insuring your late husband, Pierre Elissetche (DOB: 2/11/1891), was taken out on September 15, 1939 by Mr. Jean Larralde. Upon your husband's passing, a disbursement check in the amount of $2,500 was made to Mr. Larralde on January 9, 1940. On his original application, Mr. Larralde indicated the reason for securing this policy was that Mr. Elissetche was his business partner.

Further, as you are the person insured, I can also confirm that a policy was also taken out in your name a few weeks ago—on October 15, 1943. This policy was also

*secured by Mr. Larralde. The death benefit would be in the amount of $2,500. On
his application, he indicated the reason for obtaining the policy was that you were
engaged to be married.*

*If you believe any of this information to be in error, please let us know promptly
and we will investigate accordingly.*

Cordially,

Mr. Charles Beckett, assistant manager

Laramie Insurance

Nausea rose in Maite's stomach. She took deep breaths to calm the rioting
emotions that pulled at her. She knew, without hesitation, that Joanes Larralde
had been behind the death of her husband. He planned for it, he profited from it,
and he lied to everyone about it.

And he planned to do the same thing to her. He wasn't going to win this time.
He would pay for his evil, and not just in the next world.

In this one.

Wednesday, December 15, 1943

Maite herded Victor Arrossa, snuffling and coughing, into Benat's car to drive him
up to the doctor in Carson City. It nearly took the work of a sheepdog to manage
it, because Victor kept finding reasons to avoid the trip:

I feel better now.

Ez, that's not blood in my flema.

I'm allergic to the medikua.

I will not pay someone five dollars to tell me I'm fine.

But Maite refused to take no for an answer. So what if she had to threaten the
old man by saying that if he didn't come with her to the doctor that she'd only
serve him overcooked eggs from now until the end of time? She wasn't above such
trickery if it resulted in Victor not dying of pneumonia.

Louise had offered to drive Victor, herself, but Maite refused, "It's fine. I need
to stop by the department store to pick up the Christmas gift I ordered for Anna."

The doctor diagnosed Victor with bronchitis and the beginnings of pneumonia. Over Victor's objections, the doctor gave him a shot of penicillin and
admonished him when he tried to light a cigarette in the examination room. Victor
grudgingly accepted the cough syrup and the penicillin tablets the doctor also gave

him, while pretending not to understand English when he further instructed him to go straight to the hospital if he wasn't improving in three days.

As they were leaving, Maite pulled aside the doctor and, using a combination of English, French, and Spanish, told him that she was having trouble sleeping. Then she asked if there was anything to help with that.

The doctor gave her a dozen low-dose capsules of pentobarbital and told her to use them sparingly. Maite wasn't sure what that word meant, but as she wasn't planning to take them, she didn't care.

The doctor's receptionist only charged Maite $1.10 for the pills. This was a relief since she didn't have much money—Joanes Larralde had seen to that.

Victor saw Maite pocket the medicine, but he didn't comment. He was too busy asking the nurse when he should take his penicillin—with his breakfast wine, his lunch wine, or his dinner wine?

"Mr. Arrossa, you're not supposed to have alcohol with this medication. Do you understand?"

Victor put a wrinkled hand to his ear, "*Nola? Ez dakit ingelesa.*"

Sunday, December 19, 1943

The dinner was going well. The guests were raving about the butternut squash soup and the oxtail stew with the mashed potatoes. After Maite checked on Anna—who was red-cheeked with fever—she sent Teresa and the other servers to take out serving dishes and tureens to the last tables in the dining room. While the kitchen was empty, Maite prepared a dinner tray for Teresa to take upstairs for Joanes. She was glad he wasn't going to show his face at the Christmas party—no one wanted him there, anyway. Least of all her.

From her pocket, Maite pulled out three capsules of the pentobarbital. Opening one of the capsules, she emptied the powder into the bowl of soup—mixing the golden liquid until it dissolved. Then, she folded the contents of the second capsule into the mashed potatoes. She poured oxtail stew over the top. Heart beating faster, Maite hurried to dump the last portion of pentobarbital into a small empty glass. Topping it off with red wine, she set the glass on the wooden tray in front of the soup bowl and dinner plate.

Maite rubbed her quivering hands against her apron. She took a deep breath, once again, and thought of Anna. Her dear daughter was living without a father because of this man. She loved Pierre, of course, but the thought of what had been taken from their child made her rage burn like a hot iron.

Joanes Larralde would not take more from them. He would not take anything more from Anna.

The door swung open; Teresa entered carrying two empty soup tureens. Her light brown hair was falling from her ribbon into her long, slender face. Maite went to the young woman, "Here, let me fix this for you, *neska*." Reaching up, she swept up Teresa's hair and tucked it tightly under the ribbon. Pulling one of the bobby pins she kept on the edge of her apron, Maite secured the hair, "Voila! How's it going out there?"

"Everyone loves the dinner! Marie Alpetche wants the recipe for the soup. She said it was the best she's ever had."

"Ba, there's no secret to it," Maite shrugged. "Sautéing vegetables in *xingarra* grease will make any soup delicious. That's a fact."

Teresa nodded to the dinner tray, "Are you finally going to have something to eat? You've been on your feet all day."

Maite's heart sped up, "Not yet. But soon. This is for Joanes." With fingers that were nearly trembling, Maite picked up the tray and handed it to the young woman, "Can you take this upstairs to him?"

Hesitation tightened the muscles in Teresa's long, slender arms—and her face darkened at the mention of the sheepman's face. Even though Maite's mind was preoccupied, she still noticed, "Something wrong, Teresa?"

Teresa shook her head as if the motion would wipe away what she had been thinking, "No, it's fine. Joanes is just . . . not the most pleasant man."

Maite held her breath, still holding the tray, "Many people feel that way. But do you have a particular reason of your own?" The way that Teresa's soft gaze couldn't meet Maite's in that moment felt very telling. "Teresa?" she persisted.

Again, not meeting her eye, Teresa deflected, "He makes me uncomfortable, that's all. It's nothing to worry on."

Maite's gut—which she vowed henceforth to never ignore—knew that it was something more. More than the young woman would ever admit. But she wouldn't pry any further. Feeling more resolved in her decision, Maite pressed the tray into Teresa's hands, "Here. I will hold open the doors for you. You can go up the back way."

With no choice left but to follow, Teresa trailed Maite as the woman opened the back door. Pintto immediately greeted them, sniffing their aprons and skirts as the scents of the dinner clung to the fabrics. Maite headed to the left and the staircase that led upstairs. At the top of the stairs, Maite opened the door to the end of the boarders' hallway. Joanes's room was the third door on the left. As Teresa passed by Maite into the hallway, the older woman said, "Hurry along, *neska*. I'll get some plates for us to eat. You need more meat on your bones. I don't want you to blow away in the *haizea*."

Determination and stubbornness ratcheted Maite's nerves as she descended the outer stairs. The plan was in motion. She was committed to the task now.

All she had to do now was wait.

About an hour later, while Teresa and the two server girls were busy cutting and passing out the dessert, Maite brewed a large pot of coffee for the dinner guests. She set the coffee urn on the counter in the dining room next to the stack of mugs. Maite glanced around to make sure everything was in order. Teresa was handling the dessert, and the American girl, Barbara, was trying to clear dirty dinner plates. She was in a tug of war with little Roberto Sarratea who was insisting on licking his plate clean before he let Barbara have it. The blonde teenager's face was flushed with irritation as she fought with the boy over control of the plate. Finally, his mother Emelia noticed the exchange, and with a cry of embarrassed admonishment, forced Roberto to stop being a "disgusting *zerria*."

Unnoticed, Maite retreated into the kitchen. She began to tidy up the pots and counters. A short while passed. Then, Maite heard the scraping of the dining room tables being pushed aside. A few moments later, Mrs. Sagouspe began playing the first jota of the evening. The young women would be distracted now.

It was time.

Before she could change her mind, Maite grabbed a pair of gardening gloves from the pantry and pulled them over her hands. Slipping out the back door, she retraced her steps upstairs. But, this time, she entered the hallway and stepped quietly to Larralde's room. Just as she was to reach the door, Victor emerged from the other end of the hallway—presumably from the toilet. Spotting her, Victor waved at Maite, wished her a "*gau on*," and then coughed up a giant *flema* into his red and white handkerchief before closing himself up in his room once again.

Exhaling shakily, Maite briefly considered turning back. But, no, she would press on. With all luck, Victor would think that this whole thing had been a *gripa* fever dream that happens when you ignore the nurse's instructions and take your medication with red wine, anyway.

Gloves covering her hands, Maite slipped into Larralde's room. Closing the door behind her, she turned to see Joanes lying face down on the floor near the foot of the bed, his cheek swollen from the impact the flesh made when he passed out and fell against the footboard of the bed. He was snoring loudly, saliva dripping from the corner of his mouth onto the wood floor.

The pills had worked. Just as she had planned. At the sight of Joanes Larralde lying there, Maite felt disgust and rage fill every corner of her heart. She stared at him for a few moments—as the realization of all this man had done paraded through her mind like a motion picture. Each scene worse than the last. Anna would never know the truth of this story. Not ever.

Anna. Her Anna. Smart, stubborn, and loving Anna.

The thought centered Maite. It made it easier to do what must be done.

Reaching into Joanes's pocket, she pulled out the pocketknife that he always kept there. He didn't stir or move—other than the heaving snores that rippled through his body. Opening the blade, Maite saw that it glistened at the edge—it had been recently sharpened, she could tell.

This would make it all the easier.

With the strength she had gained from years of work in a kitchen, Maite reached down. With her left hand on the side of his sweaty neck, she tucked her right hand, with the blade, beneath his chin. In one clean, strong movement, Maite slid the knife through his neck. Blood immediately spilled onto her hand, but she quickly pulled away. Joanes stirred slightly, but his snores turned to gurgles as the blood began to pool on the wood floor of the room.

Maite set the knife next to his body and stepped closer to the door. She took a few steadying breaths as she watched his blood leave his body. Maite expected to feel remorse, regret, fear—but she didn't feel much of anything. For a second, that scared her—she didn't feel anything at all. What did that say about her? The woman she was? She was a good woman . . . At least, she had always considered herself as such. But now?

Maite then proceeded to make the room look like Joanes had been attacked by an intruder. She tilted the lamp to the side, turned over the chair, mussed the bedding and mattress.

Turning away from Joanes Larralde, she steadied her shoulders. With her left gloved hand, she opened the door—keeping the bloodied right glove from touching anything. Stepping into the hallway, she closed the door behind her. Quickly pulling the gloves off her hands, Maite stuffed them into the pocket of her apron. But she then felt a prickle of awareness and unease overtake her.

She looked up. Two doors down, near the back door of the hallway, Antton and Mitchell Lauden stood, watching her. Antton was holding his accordion in his arms. The men were riveted by the pocket of her apron—as if they had seen her hide the bloody gloves inside of it. Alarm and worry battled over control of their faces, but Maite was momentarily stunned by the sight of the two men together.

Puzzle pieces from the last few years fell into place in her mind. Antton not seriously courting any women. Mitchell's frequent presence at the boardinghouse. Maite knew what it was that she saw. She knew that relationships between men happened—she was not a prudish or a stupid woman.

She stared at them.

They stared at her.

Each of them worried about what the other had seen. And what that meant.

Maite adored Antton—she had no reason, and nothing to gain, by mentioning this to anyone. Not a thing. So, with a nod, Maite reached up and drew her fingers across her lips, letting them know that she would repeat nothing about what she had seen.

The tension in their faces softened. And, with that, a mutual understanding was reached between them. With a nod, Mitchell turned away and exited through the back door—his cane clicking on the wooden landing outside. Pushing his accordion further onto his shoulders, Antton walked past her to the staircase leading to the bar downstairs.

A few moments later, Maite followed Mitchell out the back door. As she descended the stairs, she saw Mitchell climb into his car that was parked behind the boardinghouse. A few moments later, his headlights flashed as he drove away. Letting herself back into the kitchen, Maite was relieved to find it empty. Accordion music continued to drift through the wall from the dining room—no doubt the young women were enjoying the music.

There was a small wood heater in the corner of the kitchen that she used on cold mornings. Most of the time, the heat from the stoves and ovens were enough to heat the space. But early in the morning—on the days the frost tipped the sagebrush with icy glitter— Maite liked to light the iron pot-bellied stove to chase the chill away. Benat kept her stocked with firewood outside, so it was a nice comfort on those days. Maite threw the bloody gloves into the cold stove. On the next cold morning, the gloves would be destroyed.

The music calling her, Maite stepped into the dining room to watch the dancing. Her heartbeat slowed as she watched the guests laughing and having a good time.

They had no idea what she had just done.

Thirty minutes later, Domingo Echeveste climbed the front stairs to approach Larralde's room. He had a hunting knife in his hand. He knocked on the door, "Open up, you *bastardoa*." When there was no answer, Domingo pushed open the door to find Larralde lying on the floor in a pool of blood. Adrenaline began to pump as Domingo realized that the horrible man was actually dead. That he had been attacked by someone . . . who was not him?

Confusion and anger continued to swirl.

Larralde needed to pay for what he had done to him, though. And to his Catalina! Domingo found himself stomping to the dresser in the corner. Opening the top drawer, he saw a bunch of undershirts, underwear, and socks. Rummaging underneath it, he felt two small boxes. One contained a gold pocket watch and the other a diamond engagement ring. Before he could think any further, Domingo pocketed them and dashed out of the room. He quickly retrieved Catalina's sweater from his room and fled down the stairs and back into the dining room where the rest of the guests and boarders were laughing, drinking, and dancing. He calmed his breathing. He had to appear normal. Catalina was dancing with little Roberto Sarratea, who was trying to teach her the steps to the *Zazpi Jauziak*. Domingo raised a hand to Maite, "*Kafea*, please, Maite?"

"Of course. Cream and sugar? Or brandy?"

"All of it."

About an hour later, just before the bar was to close, after an evening of . . . well, entertainment . . . Tomas Hardoy stumbled back to the hotel. Stopping for a cup of coffee before heading up to his room, Tomas was still seething after his conversation with Larralde. All the high balls he drank at the casino probably didn't help his mood, either. Draining his cup, he nodded goodbye to Antton and excused himself. As he passed Larralde's room, his anger exploded again, and he reached up to pound on the door. His angry fist propelled the unlocked door open, revealing a scene of horror.

Larralde was dead, sprawled in a pool of blood. The room a mess, eerily lit by the lamp that had been knocked over. Tomas was incredulous. Someone had got to the bastard before him! This very night! A bubble of hysterical laughter threatened to escape. He swallowed it down. He whispered, "But, he still didn't pay that hospital bill! He died before paying it." He cast an eye around and spotted Larralde's wallet peeking out from the corner of the mattress. Stepping around the blood on the floor, Tomas dashed over, grabbed the worn leather wallet, and stuffed it in his pocket.

Closing Larralde's door behind him, Tomas walked quickly to his room, and shut himself inside. Breathing heavily, he tried to clear his mind that was cluttered by anger and alcohol. His instinct was to run. But he could not be the one to find the body. He could not leave until after the body was discovered.

Later that night, as Antton headed back to his room after the Christmas party, the bartender caught a whiff of something strange. A metallic, musty smell. A suspicious feeling rolled up his spine. Turning to Joanes's door, he pushed it open and saw blood—everywhere. He almost couldn't absorb the scene in front of him. Panic and nausea fought their way forward, and he battled them back. The cut on Larralde's neck was neat and perfect. Maite was skillful with a knife. She knew how to make trimming a rack of lamb into a work of art.

Antton backed away, pulling the door closed. He could not be the one to find the body. No, someone else would be the one to find it.

Pity them.

Someone was going to get into trouble for this crime. That was certain. But it couldn't be Maite. It just couldn't. She had a daughter to raise. Antton suspected his time in Nevada was coming to an end soon, anyway. As much as he loved Mitchell, he couldn't be with him forever. The senator had plans for his son— and it didn't include Antton. It was impossible. He knew how the world worked. Mitchell would have to marry Bridget Farquhar and forget he ever knew him. He couldn't stick around to watch it happen. It would tear him up inside.

Maybe it was time to take a trip Los Angeles. Or maybe New York.

Antton knew that it was time for a new life.

Friday, December 24, 1943

Christmas Eve dinner was long over, and everyone had gone to bed. Benat, Louise, and Teresa had just left. Only Antton remained in the bar, wiping down the counters and polishing glasses. His heart beat a little faster as he cast glances at the clock on the wall above the sink. Mitchell should be here soon. It was always a terrible combination of missing him, wondering when he'd see him again, and fear that it would be the last time they could be together. He soaked up each moment.

And then, the front door opened. Antton's heart leapt. But instead of seeing Mitchell, it was Benat returning. The older man stamped his feet on the rug by the door and blew on his hands to warm them up. Confusion pulled at Antton's brows, "Is everything alright?" It was very unusual for the hotel owner to be here this late.

"*Bai.*" Benat climbed with a groan onto a bar stool, "My bones are aching in this cold."

"Well, maybe you shouldn't run around close to midnight," Antton remarked dryly.

"I know. But I was hoping to talk to you in private. I told Louise I forgot my wallet here," Benat leaned forward onto the bar, his kind eyes intent and serious.

"What is it?" Alarm prickled his spine.

The older man glanced around, to make sure they were alone. His voice lowered, "We need to make sure everything is as it should be. About Joanes."

"How do you mean?" Antton was as cautious as when he picked up shattered glass from a champagne flute in the sink.

Benat was intent. "Larralde wasn't a good man. He did many bad things. But we have a chance to make sure everything turns out alright. Do you understand what I mean?"

Antton set down the rag, "What are you getting at, Cedarry?"

"We cannot let anyone go to jail for this. What was done, is done. And it cannot be undone." Benat pulled out a cigarette and lit it. The older man must have been very worried—he hadn't smoked in years. "But more lives should not be ruined because of this. Do you get what I am saying?"

"I—I think so." Antton thought of Maite. Of what he had seen that night. But, surely, Benat didn't know? He needed to find out first. "Maybe you should tell me what you are thinking?"

"On Tuesday morning, I found bloody gloves in the pot-bellied heating stove. I was going to have a cup of coffee and it was chilly. So, I started the fire. I came in early to get the cash from the dinner to take to the bank. Didn't have a chance to do it on Monday, because, well, it was crazy once Teresa found the body."

A cold sweat itched across Antton's shoulders. Benat knew. He did. "What did you do with the gloves?" Antton breathed shakily.

"*Oy yoy*, I burned them of course. I am not an *idiota*!" Benat chastised his bartender with an incredulous snort. "The *polizia* would have found them. I had no choice." The man paused for a moment, collecting his thoughts. "Maite had good reason to do what she did. I am sure of it."

His voice barely above a whisper, Antton admitted, "Joanes killed her husband and cheated her on the sale of his sheep. And that's not all he was planning to do. She told me so the other night. I swore never to tell a soul. But I trust you to keep a secret."

Benat waved him off, "Of course! Don't be silly. No one must know. Not ever." Then, the older man grew impatient, "Anyway, as I was saying. We have a chance to make things right."

"How?"

"I know you are friends with Mitchell Lauden. I know he is coming this evening to spend time with you." Benat said this in a matter-of-fact manner, as if he were telling someone the weather forecast.

The bottom fell out of Antton's stomach, "What do you mean?"

"I know everything that happens in my hotel," Benat shrugged. "But your friendship is not my business. Not really." The older man leaned forward,

"However, this may be helpful for us. Mitchell is a clever and reasonable man. I think he will help us."

"Help us do what?" Antton watched the words come out of his employer's mouth. It was like he had never seen the man before. It was the oddest conversation of his life.

And then the hotel owner surprised him once again with these final words:

"Joanes Larralde needs a will. We will make sure he has one. After all, even if he didn't pay his debts in life, he can do so in death."

And so . . . it was done.

Witness Interview
(Property of the Douglas County Sheriff)

Case No: 22-43
Date: Fri, 12/31/43
Time: 3:30pm
Witness: Victor Arrossa
Interviewing Officer: H. Williams

HW: Good afternoon. Mr. Arrossa, is that correct?

VA: You call me Victor.

HW: Thank you, Victor. May I speak with you for a few moments while you sit here on the front porch?

VA: Bai. I like to watch cars go on road. Every man hurries. Why they go so fast? Life is fast. Don't make it go faster.

HW: My life would be easier if more people thought the way you did.

VA: People think old men no understand.

HW: This is Anna's dog here with you, yes?

VA: Pintto likes to watch cars. He is too old to chase them now. I am too old, too. We understand each other.

HW: Victor, do you know what I want to talk to you about?

VA: You want to know who killed Joanes.

HW: Well, yes. Of course, I do.

VA: But does it matter who did it?

HW: I'm pretty sure that it does. It's my job to find out.

VA: I thought your job was to protect innocent people.

HW: It is. I do both things.

VA: It is not possible to do both things all the time.

HW: What do you mean by that?

VA: If solving your investigation hurts innocent people, is that the right thing to do?

HW: Punishing someone for a crime they have committed is important to maintain order. It's why we have laws.

VA: What if the man killed is not innocent?

HW: What are you saying, Victor?

VA: Joanes Larralde was a bad man. He does not need your justice.

HW: Mr. Arrossa, you need to tell me what you know.

VA: I am an old man. What could I know?

HW: Victor, please.

VA: Ba! You worry too much about the wrong things.

HW: Then help me worry about the right things.

VA: The right thing is to protect innocent people. Always.

HW: Are you talking about someone in particular? Someone I need to protect?

VA: Yes. And I think you know who that is.

HW: Are you talking about Anna?

VA: That girl cannot lose a mother and a father because of that man. You understand?

HW: I—I think so.

VA: Justice is done. Understand? We Euskualdunak have taken care of it.

HW: So, what do I do now?

VA: You are a good man. You will know what to do when it is time.

HW: Well, damn. This day has not gone how I thought it would.

VA: Gizon lusea, let me buy you a Picon. I think you need it.

**INTERVIEW REMOVED FROM RECORD, 1/3/44

Art by Maialen Petrissans

ACKNOWLEDGEMENTS

There are so many people that helped to make this novel possible. To my early readers and cheerleaders (you know who you are!), your feedback and encouragement meant the world to me—and were instrumental in bringing Anna and the people of the boardinghouse to life.

To Professor Annie Graver Garner, my editor-extraordinaire, your kindness and expertise allowed me to shape this tale into something that I didn't know it could be. I am in your debt.

To my Basque family (near and far), thanks for your patience with me while I worked on this novel. Especially when I asked you weird (and sometimes alarming) questions—and didn't offer any additional details. You helped me greatly and didn't even know it. Without you, the residents of the boardinghouse wouldn't have felt like such good, old friends.

To the staff of the Center for Basque Studies, I am grateful for your commitment to Basque stories and Basque storytellers. I'm beyond thrilled to have partnered with you in bringing this story to the world.

And, lastly, to my Aita—Jean-Baptiste Guéçamburu. Even though you probably thought the idea of me writing a novel about a Basque murder was odd, you answered every question I asked and trusted me to make sure that the villain was just as evil and *gaistoa* as the ones in the old Westerns you love so much.

Maite zaitut, Aita.